BLOODIED HANDS

BELLANDI CRIME SYNDICATE BOOK ONE

ADELAIDE FORREST

Copyright © 2021 by Adelaide Forrest

All rights reserved.

No part of this book may be reproduced in any form or by any electronic or mechanical means, including information storage and retrieval systems, without written permission from the author, except for the use of brief quotations in a book review.

Cover Design by Adelaide Forrest

❀ Created with Vellum

ABOUT THE AUTHOR

Adelaide lives in her tiny house with her husband and two rambunctious kids. When she's not chasing all three of them and her shepherd/husky mix around the house, she spends all her free time writing and adding to the hoard of plots stored on her bookshelf and hard-drive.

She always wanted to write, and did from the time she was ten and wrote her first full-length fantasy novel. The subject matter has changed over the years, but that passion for writing never went away. She has a degree in Psychology, and prior to having her kids she worked as a therapist using horses in her treatment strategy and working with adults and kids with disabilities.

Adelaide started her journey as a published author in September 2019 with her other pen name, Kenna Bardot, where she writes reverse harem. Having achieved her passion of becoming an author, she's expanding with the launch of Adelaide Forrest.

ABOUT BLOODIED HANDS

She was an innocent, caught in the wrong place at the wrong time.

Involved in a bank robbery that never should have happened in my city, Ivory found herself staring down the barrel of a gun. Only my protection prevented them from taking what has always been mine.

She should have stayed away. Instead, she charges back into my life like an Angel come to save me from my bleak existence. She has no place in my world where hardened criminals toy with the lives of the innocent. A better man would send her back to her quiet life.

Too bad I'm a Bellandi man through and through.

We always play to win, and what we win, we always keep.

Bloodied Hands is a full-length standalone novel with an HEA, but the series presents a better reading experience when following the suggested order.

This series contains dark elements, including over-the-top antiheroes who do as they please. Read at your own discretion.

SOUNDTRACK

"Dancing With Your Ghost" - No Resolve
"You Find Me" - The Sweeplings
"Stuff of Legends" - Daughtry
"Super Psycho Love" - Simon Curtis
"Even If It Hurts" - Sam Tinnesz
"Just Found Heaven" - Daughtry
"Sex & Stardust" - ZZ Ward
"Peace" - Alison Wonderland
"Notorious" - Adelitas Way
"As You Are" - Daughtry
"Secrets" - Written By Wolves
"Hurt" - Christian Reindl feat. Lloren
"I'm Dangerous" - The EverLove
"Guest Room" - Echos
"Ashes" - Braden Barrie

For every person who has ever heard the words
"Don't quit your day job."

PROLOGUE
IVORY

Twelve years ago.

I smiled up at Matteo, watching the way his eyes lit up with amusement as I giggled at him. He'd teased me, tormented me about the shyness I still felt when he touched me, although I'd given him my virginity a week prior. There was no way I could feel anything *but* shy, not with the way his stare had taken on a new brand of heat.

There hadn't been a repeat performance, even though I'd desperately wanted one. We didn't have a place to go, not without ruining my reputation, and Matteo maintained that I was too sweet for a backseat romp in his car.

I begged to differ, at least after what he'd shown me sex was like.

The humor in his eyes fled suddenly, disappearing to a cold mask I didn't enjoy seeing on his face when he stared over my shoulder. It wasn't unusual. That distant expression of his was what everyone else saw of Matteo Bellandi. When I turned his face back to mine and caught his eyes with my own, the smile slid from my face, slowly morphing to apprehension.

He stared down at me with the same cruel expression.

The one that he *never* used for me.

"We should talk, Ivory." Even his tone had gone cold. No life to it, his humor of only a moment ago a thing of the past.

I just didn't realize it would be the last time I felt like I mattered - like I was special.

Ivory.

Not his Angel.

But Ivory.

I flinched back, my hand leaving the smooth skin of his jaw as I stared up at him in confusion. I couldn't think of what I might have done to warrant such a change in behavior.

"What's wrong?" I whispered.

"Graduation is in a few days. It's time for us to go our separate ways." I would have sworn I knew Matteo - would have sworn I knew the boy I loved with every fiber of my being enough to recognize the tick in his jaw. The frustration eating at his face, even beneath the impenetrable coldness that he emanated.

I was wrong.

"Wh-what?" I stuttered, flinching when his arms released my waist and he stepped back to a more polite distance. I eyed the other students, hating that they were watching me have my heart ripped out. He blindsided me and judging by the whispers breaking out among the teens lingering on the front lawn of the school, I wasn't the only one.

"Come on, Ivory. You didn't really think I would go off to college in the fall with a High School girlfriend tying me down, did you?" He ran a hand through his hair, tossing a flirty smile over my shoulder at some unknown person behind me. He hadn't even finished dumping me, and he was already *flirting*.

"Why? Why did you-why did you fuck me if you were just going to dump me?" I hissed, steeling myself and trying to control the tears that threatened to make an appearance. No matter how shattered I felt, I couldn't let him see it.

"Have you looked in a mirror?" He smirked at me, as if taking my virginity and dumping me within a week was acceptable. "You're a hot piece of ass, baby. Getting in your pants was kind of the point of the entire year I spent getting you there. Now I've had it." He shrugged, and I winced.

I didn't know this boy.

I didn't know him at all.

"You don't mean that," I pleaded, my voice a hoarse whisper as I started to lose the battle with my own emotions. "You can't mean that," I repeated.

"Sweet, naïve Ivory. What world do you live in, so stuck up in that pretty little head of yours? The lion doesn't love the lamb, Ivory. Especially not just one of them when there's an entire field begging to be eaten." He shook his head at me, pressing a thumb to my quivering lips, the lips he claimed to love so much. "You weren't bad...for a virgin." A startled sob broke free. "See you around, Ivory. Hey, Shauna! Wait up!" he called, jogging around my frozen body.

Shauna.

The girl he'd been screwing before he started dating me. The one who had spent an entire year tormenting me that he'd finish with me soon enough, and he *always* went back to her.

I stood frozen, only snapping out of my trance when Sadie appeared at my side. "Hey, sweetie. Let's get you out of here, yeah?" she asked, and I think I nodded. Tears streamed down my face, but I couldn't understand why.

I wasn't sad.

I didn't feel *anything.*

Deep down, I knew that wasn't normal. I shouldn't be numb.

It was only high school, only my first love. There would be others, I tried to remind myself.

But even then, I knew no one would ever make me feel the way Matteo did.

I turned to leave, but Duke invaded my other side, ushering me off the lawn and *away* from the direction Matteo had gone. It didn't stop me from seeing him, his arm wrapped around Shauna with one hand tucked into the ass pocket of her jeans.

Still there was nothing but a vibration in my ears, as disbelief coursed through me.

I loved him.

And I'd been *nothing* all along. Nothing but another notch on his bedpost.

Sadie murmured to me, letting Duke tuck me into his side as they led me to his car in the parking lot. Sadie climbed into the back seat, leaving me to be the passenger. Duke drove with a hand resting on my knee, making circles with his thumb that should have been comforting.

It wasn't until we got to my house and they guided me to my bed that I broke down in sobs.

The bed he'd made love to me on.

Well, apparently the bed he'd fucked me on.

"Shh, it's okay sweetheart," Duke soothed, wrapping his arms around me and tucking me into his chest. "You're going to be just fine."

"I love him," I whined.

His body stilled, before he ran a hand through my hair. "I know, honey. I know you do. He's such an idiot." I vaguely knew of Sadie's sniffles behind me, where she ran a hand up and down my back supportively.

"I can never go back to school," I protested, realizing everyone had seen my very public humiliation.

"You will march your ass into that school tomorrow with your head held high and pretend you do not give the first fuck about him." I nodded in response, but we both knew it was bullshit. I wasn't Sadie. I wasn't strong enough to pretend something like that.

We lapsed into silence, my heart hardening with every tear that fell.

I would never be heartbroken again.

No man was worth *this*.

1
IVORY

With the tenderloin smeared in dijon mustard and wrapped in duxelle covered prosciutto cooling in the fridge, I set to laying out my puff pastry in preparation. I rolled it, needing that perfect quarter of an inch thickness so I wouldn't overcook my beef while I waited for the pastry to bake to golden perfection.

"You're insane, you know, that right?" Sadie asked.

"And why am I insane today, my darling?" I teased her, thanking the sweet baking gods that her sense of humor had never changed.

"Why are you making a Beef Wellington again? Your food isn't usually so pretentious, even with that fancy culinary degree of yours that didn't see much use." She raised her brows at me, as if daring me to contradict her.

I used my degree.

Just not in a restaurant or catering business.

"I'm doing a new series. Kind of a food bucket list, I guess. I'm torn between calling it *Food to Eat Before you Kick It or Famous Last Meals*. I had readers submit the best foods they've ever eaten and made my own recipes from what they submitted." I trimmed the edges of my pastry to what I knew I would need to wrap up my beef.

Contrary to what Duke might think, I cooked a recipe at least half a dozen times before it was ready for the blog. There was a reason that I was always happy to let him taste test, and by taste test I meant eat the entire thing once I had a feel for the flavor profile I'd created.

Eating the same thing over and over was exhausting.

No matter how amazing it tasted.

"Clever," Duke chuckled, always supportive of me and my passion. Though it wasn't surprising. Sadie was my kick ass and take names best friend who ran a boxing gym. Duke was a close second for the best friend status. The dreamer of our trio, he was a successful sculptor who had somehow defied the odds and made a real career for himself in an impossible industry.

In his head, if that was possible, well then so was my blog. And it had been, the whole thing grew faster than I could handle, and I found myself overwhelmed with trying to keep up with it. But whereas working in the restaurant and running a catering business had been purely exhausting, the blog was a good stress.

It distracted me from the fact that I wasn't getting any younger. Distracted me from the fact that I still hadn't fallen in love since my sophomore year of high school. I pulled the beef from the fridge, setting the plate down next to my puff pastry on my white marble counter. I'd bought the house just outside the city for a steal, knowing it was a dump. The affordable price left me with enough in my budget to fix it up slowly as I made money. Once I'd quit my job at the restaurant, money had been inconsistent and unreliable. Whether catering or with my blog, I could easily have a slow month anytime, so keeping my monthly expenses low was critical for me.

I paid cash for just about everything I did.

Slowly, my beloved house was coming together. I finished my kitchen and master bedroom, my sanctuaries in a house that was otherwise...shit.

It was otherwise shit.

But I loved my counters, and the natural lighting was perfection for photos for the blog. "It sounds interesting, I suppose," Sadie relented, and I smiled at her teasingly. It wasn't often that she relented her somewhat more assertive opinions. From Sadie, saying it was interesting meant the idea must have rocked.

I'd take it. Her lips pursed into a smile she tried to fight, giving away that she knew I saw right through her crap.

"When can I eat this thing?" Duke asked, eyes narrowed on where my hands oh so carefully lifted the beef and rested it in the center of my pastry. After a quick wash of my hands, I set to wrapping it up and sealing it tight. I brushed it, cutting the top to release air as it baked, and fought the urge to chuckle when Duke cleared his throat at me, still waiting for an answer.

Honestly, he should know better. I'd answer when I finished with my step.

"It has to bake for 40-45 minutes," I said after I'd placed the sheet in the oven and set the timer. He groaned, and I chuckled at him as I set to washing my fingerling purple potatoes in the sink opposite them. The task meant I couldn't see them, but after over a decade with them I knew exactly what they would do as soon as I turned around.

Make faces at me. Because we were mature like that.

I ignored it.

"Why purple potatoes?" Sadie asked when she finally realized she'd failed to get a reaction from me.

"They're a little denser and nuttier in flavor. Mostly, I just prefer them because they look so fucking pretty on the plate," I admitted. "For something as visual as the blog, and especially the more visual social media sites, that's super important."

"You keep cooking like this, and I'm liable to get fat." I snorted a laugh at her, pressing my face into the back of my forearm.

"Please," I laughed. For my 4'11" friend, who was so fit she could take out a full-grown boxer in minutes, getting fat was ridiculous. Stacked with lean muscles, even Duke was fit with forearms sculpted like a Greek God.

When I said he was a sculptor, I meant a mixed materials sculptor. He was just as likely to work with wood or metal as he was with clay. The man didn't discriminate, and some of those materials required some serious strength.

I'd tried to help him once.

Let's just say it hadn't gone well.

At all.

Now in his words I just sat there and looked pretty. I loved to watch him work but learned my lesson quickly and stayed out of his way.

As soon as I had the potatoes set to roast and popped them in my double oven, I moved on to setting up the place setting for the photos in my little breakfast nook. "Soooo...." I stilled. It was *never* a good sign when Sadie hesitated to speak her mind, and I knew exactly where she was going.

Where she was always going.

"There's this guy, he comes into the gym."

"Sadie," Duke warned on a growl. He was my fervent

defender. I didn't need to date, not when it always ended in disaster.

"She can't stay a marriage pit forever!" Sadie hissed. "Eventually, she will have to open herself up to considering getting there with one of these guys, but the only way that will happen is if she *dates,* Duke."

"I hate it when you call me that." I winced, setting a plate down on the table a little too loudly.

"It's true, Ive." Her voice gentled as I made my way back to the space behind the island where my two friends sat, staring at me as if we were walking a very dangerous line. "Ben wanted to introduce you to his parents, and you bolted. Chris *proposed,* and you never saw him again. They were both amazing guys. You're a marriage pit. Too afraid to let anyone in."

"Stop it, Sadie," Duke said, eyeing the way my hands clutched the island like I could break it.

"It's been over ten years." Sadie's voice gentled with sadness, and I could feel what I hated to hear in her voice more than anything. The *pity.*

Because we both knew I was broken.

Broken in a way that I would eventually have to accept that love just would not happen for me.

Never again.

"Maybe it's time to look at what's right in front of you," she whispered cryptically, and I felt my brow tense in confusion.

"I don't see you with a ring on your finger," Duke snapped, and I raised my eyes to them.

"Stop it, both of you," I reprimanded them. "If I go out with this guy from the gym will you lay off?"

Sadie's eyes lit with hope, and she nodded. "You gonna give him an actual chance?" There was skepticism in her loud, honey-toned voice. I hated knowing that I'd put it there after twelve years of failed romances and first dates that went nowhere.

"Yes," I agreed. "I'm tired of being alone. It's time I tried to find a decent man, a good man. Someone who can give me a content life, if not an overwhelming romance." I gave a bitter smile, ignoring the pained look on Duke's face. He'd always encouraged me to practice self-healing, to put myself and my mental health before a relationship. I didn't want to disappoint him, but it was time to accept that some things just couldn't be fixed.

I was one of them.

"How's the gym?" I asked, washing some extra mushrooms. I needed the change of conversation desperately, and I knew Duke well enough to know he was too busy worrying about me to be the one to grant it.

Sadie allowed it, thankfully. She knew she'd pushed as far as was intelligent for one day. She twiddled with her loose, wavy dark brown hair as she turned warm honey brown eyes my way. "It's great. You know I love it there and business is booming."

"I'm sure prancing around in your tight little workout clothes has nothing to do with that," I chuckled. She returned the humor, shrugging like she didn't have a care in the world.

"Nobody said I wasn't smart. Mom and Dad miss you though. They said to tell you to stop by for dinner soon."

I smiled. "How about they come here?" I grimaced. Sadie's mom was great at a lot of things.

Cooking was not one of them.

Duke snorted out a laugh, the tension of my agreement to date fading into memory as Sadie and I burst into giggles. "Yeah, let's do that instead."

2

MATTEO

I zipped up my slacks, turning away from the pouty expression on the freckle free face of Jessica, staring up at me from where she'd knelt to suck me off.

Or was it Jennifer?

I shook my head, realizing just how little her name mattered when I'd never see her again.

I saw none of them again.

"Thanks, babe," I said, standing up and making my way to my office door. "Let a bouncer know if you need a ride. They'll call you a cab on me if your friend headed home without you." I shoved the door open, looking back at where she still knelt on the floor, wide eyes turned my way in disbelief.

"I just swallowed your load," she protested, and even I had to admit that there was something so unappealing in the tone of her voice. If she hadn't had those thick lips and the sleek chestnut hair to go along with them, I never would have looked past it long enough to get her mouth on me. "You didn't even get me off, and you're kicking me out?"

"Not at all," I drawled, stepping away from the door and going around the side of my desk to sit in my ergonomic office chair that was closer to a throne in resemblance. I spun around, facing the two-way mirror and looking down on the club floor below me. "You're more than welcome to go back to the party. It looks like a good night."

She stood, slowly jutting out her ass in her slinky, sequined mini that barely covered said ass. "Or I could stay. The fun doesn't have to be over. I have other things to offer." Her hands rested on the opposite edge of my desk, and I eyed them in distaste. The sight of her hands on my desk was enough to send me over the edge, completely distracting me from what should have been a delectable display of cleavage.

I inwardly cursed my cousin Lino. I rarely came to *Indulgence*, too caught up in running the other side of the business. He was one of very few people I could trust with my legitimate businesses, and despite his more carefree manner, he was dedicated to earning the biggest profit and running a tight ship. "Sorry, didn't think you were so dumb you couldn't tell I was done with you. I don't do seconds. I came, I'm done. That's all you'll get from me." I turned back to the paperwork resting on my desk, touching the touchpad on my laptop to bring up the digital file I needed to review.

She gasped, huffing her indignation at me when I didn't even bother to look away from my work. Her heels stomped against the hardwood floor as she stormed out of the office. "Shut the door!" I called after her, not even surprised in the slightest when she didn't listen.

"Women, am I right?" Lino said, leaning against the door frame and grinning at me.

"Oh, thank fuck, can I go home now?" I stood, grabbing

my jacket off the back of the chair and shoving my arms in. "I can't handle the music here, not anymore."

"You're getting old, Matteo," Donatello announced, stepping into the room with Scar and my Uncle Gabriele following behind them with a smile.

"You're one to talk, old man." He grinned at me, remaining silent when it became obvious my Uncle had something to say.

"Got a new potential madam who wants to meet with you. High class, and I hear good things about her girls," he said.

"She here?" I asked, buttoning up my suit jacket.

"VIP section. Says she insists on meeting with you if you're planning to buy her out and add the girls to your roster." With a nod, we all left my office and Lino locked it behind him. Since we didn't talk business in public, unless we used it as an intimidation tactic, we walked in silence. I'd be damned if I lost money for someone running his mouth needlessly.

VIP was halfway up to my office, with the main floor visible for the VIPs to survey like they were in charge. They got to play at having power, while Lino and I ruled over it all with an iron thumb. The woman who sat in the VIP section stood immediately when we strolled down the steps. The middle-aged woman had wrapped her body up in a white pencil skirt and elegant black blouse. She'd styled her blond hair into a perfect updo, showing that she was the epitome of class, despite what was a rather questionable profession.

Criminal, if we were being honest.

She was in good company.

Two younger, equally high-class women flanked her, and I knew from a glance at them they were two samples of the product she offered in her stable. The brunette looked vaguely familiar, and I knew it was possible I'd had her before. But my tendency toward brunettes with big lips meant they blended together.

Except for the only one that mattered.

The other, a stunning African American woman, smiled at me demurely.

Like there was any fooling the man who was looking to buy the rights to her pussy. None of us were innocent, and a coy smile couldn't have fooled the devil in that scenario.

"They're pretty," I said, gesturing for the women to take their seats. The brunette stayed standing, but the other two sat gracefully. I took my seat across from them, not even glancing away when my Uncle and Lino sat on either side of me. "How do I know they're any good?"

"Would you like to sample the merchandise?" the madam asked, giving me a humorous smile. "If these two aren't to your liking, I can assure you I have a wide variety. We could arrange an appointment." I considered it momentarily but decided that professionals weren't likely to have what I was looking for.

No one did.

I turned a glance Lino's way, silently asking if he wanted to give either of them a go. He shook his head, surprising me. Lino was normally much less particular about his bed partners than I was, so a freebie with a professional was right up his alley. I knew whatever had happened with Samara that he'd needed me to cover for him, it must have been big. He'd been in love with her for as long as I could remember. His best friend. The daughter of his father's housekeeper. I knew better than to mention her with Uncle Gabriele around. The women we protected were not on the tolerated list of discussion topics, not when Gabriele would threaten them if we so much as hinted at exploring something real with them. The brunette climbed into my lap, perching on my knee as if she belonged there.

I fought the urge to bristle. I didn't enjoy being touched, outside of what was necessary to get off. Cuddling was not my style, and for that reason I never had sex with a woman in a bed of any kind. The last bed I'd had sex in had been in High School, and if I had anything to do with it that would be the last time.

The only time I'd ever made love.

"You don't have to pay me," the brunette whispered. "Like last time. You were so good; I'll give it to you for free again." I turned a cold glare her way, not reacting when she flinched back and nearly fell off my lap.

"I don't do seconds," I hissed, and she nodded meekly, returning to take the seat next to her employer. "I'll send a few of my guys over to your stables tomorrow. They'll pay; I don't like men who expect freebies from the girls they run. If they're impressed, then we can meet again to discuss the possibility of expanding my existing operations."

"Yes, Mr. Bellandi. Thank you for your time." The woman was smart, I gave her that. She stood, extending a hand for me to shake and then the three of them were off.

I stood, nodding to Lino with a look that communicated that we *would* have a conversation about Samara the next day. "I've arranged a date for you with Luca Morelli's daughter, Elena. You're taking her to dinner tomorrow," my Uncle ordered.

"No, I'm not." There was no inflection in my voice, nothing to betray my annoyance at his constant interference with my love life.

"She's a good match, beautiful, and she knows exactly what we expect of her because her father's in the life. It's time you choose an appropriate match to continue your family line. You need a successor," he argued, blocking my path when I moved to leave.

"No, I don't. Lino can take over if something happens to me. We've had this discussion before, and I will not marry someone I don't care for just to appease your insecurities about the future of this family. I couldn't have the one I wanted, so now I just won't have anyone at all." With my monotone rant over, I shoved past my Uncle and made my way down the steps to the main club floor. After navigating gyrating bodies, only of the ones too wasted to realize they were standing in the path of a predator, I made my way out the side door and was grateful to find Donatello already waiting. How the man was always exactly where I needed him, I'd never know, but I wouldn't take it for granted either. We slid into my Aston Martin, and I drove through the streets of Chicago on the way back to my manor outside the city.

3

IVORY

My lungs heaved as I pushed, telling myself just a bit farther. I'd taken my regular route, pushing my speed faster than my usual jog. Something in me had woken up that morning needing to run, needing that feeling of exhaustion that could only come from a too-strenuous workout. I could have hit the gym instead; I was positive Sadie would love the opportunity to beat my ass into fighting shape.

Normally I might have taken her up on it, but the bucket list series for my food blog, *A Dash of Sass,* had propelled the blog from paying the bills to insanity what seemed like overnight. I didn't have time for a run, but damn if I'd give it up. I needed the blankness that came with a hard run, nothing but the ache in my legs and not enough air in my lungs.

I passed the park on my left, hooking a right onto 111th Street and passing Sadie's gym. Finally giving in, I slowed to a stop, catching my breath with my hands on my knees to rest. After a brief pause, I picked up a walk, pulling my phone out and turning off the music in favor of pressing it to my ear and dialing my mom when I saw she'd called me.

"Hello," her familiar, airy voice answered.

"Hey, it's me," I wheezed.

There was a brief pause, "are you running again?"

"Oh, for the love of God, mom. We've been through this," I argued with a chuckle as I passed another jogger I recognized from my daily runs. He smiled at me, and I returned it. I didn't know the guy's name, but I could tell you at exactly what time in the morning he hit the corner of 111th & South Trumbull. He was cute, all lean and tall with a mop of blond hair on his head and a kind smile.

I'd long since stopped caring how much of a fright I must look when he saw me every day, already two miles into my run by the time we crossed paths. "I just don't think it's safe for a young woman to be out running alone like that. Dad and I can get you a treadmill if it's about the money. We have some saved up."

"Ugh, no," I groaned. "It's not the money. I hate running in one place. It takes the fun out of it."

"Fine. Just be careful, please," she pleaded, and I resisted my chuckle in the face of her genuine concern. As an only child, my parents worried far too much about my safety.

They also worried far too much about my lack of a husband and family.

Saying they wanted to be grandparents would be an understatement.

"You're coming to dinner tonight, right?" she asked, and I shook my head at her with a huff of laughter. It was Sunday. They usually came over to my place mid-week, but Sundays had always—and would forever—be my mother's territory. She wouldn't even give it up to her "fancy chef daughter."

"Yep, I'll see you tonight, okay? I'm about to go into the bank."

"Okay, sweetheart. Love you."

"Love you too, bye." I hung up, feeling appreciation for my meddling mother and father. Even when they were sticking their noses into my love life—which they no longer did too often after setting me up on too many failed dates with their friends' sons—they meant well. They meant the best.

They'd just been head over heels in love for too long to consider the possibility of love not being meant for me. I didn't have a soulmate.

That didn't mean I had to be alone.

I walked into the bank with my phone in my hand, emitting a long, low groan when I only made it a few feet inside.

People crowded the interior, to the point I could barely see the front of the line from my place at the back.

Didn't anybody work normal business hours anymore? I'd thought having an unusual profession would work to my advantage, but so many people mid-morning was just one more sign of the way the workforce in Chicago was changing. I took my place in line behind a middle-aged woman, who gave me a sympathetic smile, undoubtedly having had the same reaction when she walked in only a few moments prior.

I pulled out my phone and stared down the screen as I scanned through all my unaddressed social media notifications. I couldn't keep up with it all anymore. The blog had officially gotten away from me with its success, and while the money was fantastic, I needed to consider hiring a social media manager to take that element off my hands.

I didn't bother looking back when the door opened

behind me. With the crowd already in there, it stood to reason that the door was revolving.

"Nobody move!" a male voice yelled from the doorway. A woman screamed, and I turned back to find three men standing just inside the door, black ski masks covering their heads and AK-47's in hand. My phone dropped to the floor in shock as one man used a gun to hit the security guard in the face where he stood frozen. I jolted in place from the sound of my phone hitting the floor, bending down to snatch it up. Even in that moment, I appreciated my expensive, protective case. Usually it was water damage or food that the case saved my phone from, but I supposed bank floors worked too.

Two of the men moved to the tellers with bags, while the other stood guarding the door. "Everybody in the corner!" he yelled, and the crowd scurried over quickly.

I couldn't say what possessed me to do it, but as everyone else attempted to hide behind each other and be as small as possible, I threw my shoulders back and stood tall. An elderly woman shuffled her way over, fidgeting with her walker in her hurry to comply with the orders of the bank robber watching us pointedly. I took her arm, giving it a reassuring pat as we left the walker in favor of getting her into the corner.

"Thank you, dear," she said with a shaky sigh, patting my arm when I'd maneuvered her into the corner. I nodded, shoving my phone into my jacket pocket finally and making my way over to grab her walker. After just a few seconds of standing without it, it was clear that the woman needed it for stability.

"Get back in the fucking corner," the man at the door warned, deep brown eyes peeking out from the holes in his ski mask as he glared at me.

"She needs the walker. That's all," I placated, holding my hands out in front of me to show I wasn't a threat. Though admittedly, if a guy with a really big gun was concerned about me then we had definitely entered backward land.

"She'll live." He pointed his gun at me, and I flinched and ignored the whimper a woman behind me released at the prospect of the gun being turned on the hostages.

"Fine. Be a douchebag. I mean, you are robbing a bank obviously, but it takes a special brand of asshole to leave an elderly woman without her walker," I mumbled, unsure what exactly had come over me. The others behind me were afraid, and so was I. But I was also just *pissed*. There was no way I would die without ever being loved, especially not shot full of holes in a fucking bank robbery.

Though, if I didn't shut my mouth that might happen regardless of how I felt about it.

Instead of firing the gun, I watched as the man's chest shook with laughter. He lowered the gun and tipped his head at me. "By all means, go ahead. I wouldn't want to add asshole to my rap sheet, sweet thing," he drawled, and I bristled.

I had a feeling I'd fucked up.

Regardless, my feet carried me the extra distance until I wrapped my hands around the walker. A hand landed on the other side when I moved to lift it, and with a nervous swallow I turned my face up to glare at the robber staring down at me with amusement dancing in his eyes.

When our eyes connected, his eyes narrowed, and the amusement fled. It was rather comical to watch whatever was passing through his mind as the thoughts were so very visible on his face even when I could hardly see it. "Ivory?" he asked. I froze at the sound of my name on his lips.

"Do-do I know you?" I stuttered in shock.

"No. No, of course not," he said, stepping back a few steps and backing his way toward the door. "Time to go! Now!" he yelled to his friends.

Why I couldn't just let him leave, I'll never know, but my curiosity had me pressing forward, somehow convinced he wouldn't hurt me after whatever he'd realized. "How do you know my name?" He backed away so quickly that he nearly tripped over his own feet, his eyes wide with fear.

"Tell him we didn't know. Never would have done this if we'd known you were here. Never. Make sure he knows we didn't touch you, yeah?" His buddies' eyes widened as they looked at me, seemingly as lost as I was. They fled out the door regardless, hopping into a van waiting at the curb.

"But I don't understand. Tell who?"

"Bellandi. Tell Bellandi it's all good." He hustled out the door without another glance back leaving me with only one question.

Matteo.

How the hell did a bank robber know my high school boyfriend?

4

IVORY

The next few hours passed by in a blur of police interviews and news cameras shoved into my face as I tried to escape the insanity of the scene that followed the robbery. To say the police wanted to know my connection to Matteo Bellandi had been putting it lightly, and they were disbelieving and disappointed to find that I hadn't had one in *twelve fucking years*. My heart stuttered in my chest. I'd never thought to see Matteo again, and honestly after what he'd done to me, that was for the best. I couldn't say how I'd react.

Would I still love him? Would he still take my breath away? Would I hate him? What if I didn't care about him either way? Then what excuse did I have to hide behind when I just couldn't fall in love with someone?

I realized with a start that I was nervous. And it seemed far worse than the typical nerves that went along with seeing an ex and wanting to prove you were better off without them. It was more than wanting to avoid shrinking back into that weak, pathetic, *broken* girl he'd made me into.

Even after twelve years, I was still in love with the ghost

of a man who had never existed. I was still in love with the lie Matteo had shown me, and what happened after I saw the real Matteo would always haunt me.

Always.

I pulled my gently used Toyota Yaris up to the house in Barrington Hills where I knew Matteo's family lived back in high school, feeling beyond awkward. I'd never been to the estate when we dated, Matteo preferred to keep me separate from his family life that he'd explained as "complicated." He'd been to my house. He'd spent time with my parents, but he'd never allowed me the same courtesy.

That should have been my first sign that something was wrong with our relationship.

Even never having been there, it was common knowledge where Matteo lived. His family's wealth was legendary, so much so that some people speculated that their business practices were shady, but most attributed that to jealousy. There was no family as synonymous with success as the Bellandi's.

I'd known going to the estate was my best bet as soon as I realized my curiosity couldn't let me forget the incident in the bank without finding out why there was *any* connection between Matteo and I. I wanted him out of my life, scrubbed completely from any trace of him. Call it a near death experience, but I was determined to move on once and for all.

And to do that, I needed answers.

Massive wrought-iron gates sat blocking the driveway, making me release a sigh of frustration. I *so* did not belong on that estate.

A security guard at the gate stopped me, and I rolled down my window with a smile. "Can I help you, ma'am?" he asked, giving me a once over that stated he found me unimpressive.

Ouch.

I wasn't wearing Versace or anything, but I had dressed and done my makeup to prepare for facing the man who broke my heart all those years ago. Like any sane woman would do. "I'm looking for Matteo Bellandi," I smiled.

"Baby, whoever you are he doesn't do seconds."

"I—what?" I asked, throwing the car into park once I realized that getting inside would not be as simple as I'd hoped.

"You know. He never does the same woman twice. No matter how good she sucks cock, so stop thinking you're different." He shook his head, looking at me like he couldn't believe I had the audacity to turn up on Matteo's doorstep.

"I'm not—"

"Turn the car around and be on your way."

"You don't understand—"

"Really? Because you look exactly like all the other bitches he brings around."

Okay, double ouch.

That one got a physical wince. From what I'd seen in school, he appreciated variety. So I didn't exactly know what *that* was about, but I wasn't touching it.

Nope. No way.

"Look Mister, I'm not looking for another round. I just need to speak to him. Urgently. Just," I sighed, pinching the bridge of my nose as he turned to walk away. "Tell him Ivory Torres is trying to get in touch with him," I called, shaking my head and wondering if answers were worth this shit.

"What the fuck did you just say?" he whispered, snapping to a stop and turning back to me.

"That I don't want another round?" I asked, flinching when his steps prowled toward me. His hand touched the roof of my car, his upper body leaning down to put his face level with the window as his wide brown eyes met mine.

"Your name. What did you say your name was?" His voice raised a bit, not to the point of yelling, but enough that I knew he meant serious business.

"Ivory Torres?" My voice was barely a whisper, and I felt a piece of me shrivel when, yet another strange man recognized my name in connection with Matteo.

What the fuck had I gotten myself into coming here?

"The Ivory?"

"Umm, well I suppose so. It's not exactly a common name, is it?" I grimaced with an uncomfortable chuckle.

He turned his back on me without another word, going to the guard booth and picking up his cell. I ran a hand through my hair aggressively, feigning casualness as I did my best to eavesdrop.

Because you're damn right I fucking eavesdropped. I was surprised I didn't stick my head out the damn window.

"Yeah, boss. Ivory Torres is here for you." A pause of silence while the man on the other end of the phone spoke. "You got it." He ended the call with a touch of his finger to the screen and hit the button to open the gates. They creaked open slowly, acting every bit as heavy as they looked. I ran my hand through my hair again, biting the corner of the inside of my lip and losing some of the nerve that fueled me to drive there. "Go on through, drive right up in front of the house at the circle and someone will show you where to go."

"I—okay." My hands went to the steering wheel as my eyes fixated on that gate. Even when it opened fully, I didn't shift my car to drive.

"I'm sorry, Miss Torres. Meant no disrespect to you. You

won't get any going forward." I turned wide eyes his way finally.

Because there was zero chance, I'd be seeing him *again*.

Fuck that.

"I—okay," I repeated, putting my car in drive and going through the gate in a daze.

I was in trouble.

I was in so much trouble. My Uncle would kill me, if he ever found out I was here. My father would kill me too. What the fuck had I been thinking driving up to the house of someone who had criminal connections like I was invincible?

Fuck.

I thought about turning around and escaping the way I'd come, but the gate closed behind me and running away now that Matteo knew I was there felt humiliating. I drove my car up the rest of the driveway, feeling my eyes bug out when the house itself came into sight. It was massive, in a way that was unnecessary—ridiculous even. An intriguing mixture of white stone and grey brick, I felt minuscule in my tiny car. Pulling up in front of the house where the guard at the gate had directed me, I found an older gentleman standing on the stone steps with a bright smile on his face. I shifted into park slowly, taking a deep breath and releasing it on a sigh as I turned off the ignition. Grabbing my purse out of the passenger seat, I opened my door and unfolded myself as gracefully as I could manage. The last thing I needed to do was flash someone my goodies at Matteo's house. I was getting the distinct feeling that was *not* the kind of man I was looking to attract.

"Miss Torres, I presume?" a man greeted as I shut the door and stared in shock at the house. "My name is

Donatello. I manage Mr. Bellandi's home. If you'll follow me, he's asked that I see you to his office."

I nodded wordlessly, letting him lead me in the huge dark wood doors and into the sprawling mansion. I'd obviously known he was wealthy, but I'd never imagined this. I knew I was stalling. But I couldn't stop my eyes from darting around the foyer in awe. I'd never seen wealth like this before, let alone stepped inside a home of that caliber. The floors were tiled in Mediterranean tile; the walls painted off white with huge archways connecting the rooms in the place of doors.

"Best not to keep him waiting," he said with a polite smile.

I nodded, picking up my pace as I followed him. A curving staircase led upstairs, but we bypassed that in favor of stepping around it to a narrower archway that led into a hall. "Matteo still lives here?" I asked. I couldn't see that. We were a decade out of high school. The man nodded. "I never got the impression he got along with his father," I added, deciding there was no harm in exposing how little I truly knew about the man of the house.

"His father passed some time ago. The estate is much more practical for security reasons than the Penthouse in the city where he lived prior, and so he moved back here after his death." He didn't seem hesitant to reveal Matteo's personal information to me, and I had to wonder if that was common. Surely, a man of Matteo's stature would be interested in confidentiality.

I agreed, thinking back to the gate and the walls surrounding the property. I had a feeling it was nearly as secure as the White House. We stopped in front of two impressive, heavy wood doors. With a smile back at me, he tapped his fingers against it twice. I drew in a shuddering breath, hating the audible way it displayed my fear of what might wait for me behind those doors. Once again, I questioned if I was making a mistake. Perhaps I was better off not knowing, not seeing, not feeling again.

Because the truth was, I had felt little of anything since he'd broken me.

"Enter," a deep, masculine voice returned, following Donatello's knock. My heart stalled, having thought never to hear that voice again. It had changed, deepened, become more commanding as if there was almost no trace of the boy, I'd loved remaining. And yet somehow, my soul recognized it on some deep level that nearly brought tears to my eyes.

After all the time that had passed, just the sound of his voice through a closed door was enough to bring me to my knees.

Donatello opened both doors with a flourish, waving me forward with his hand and a bow of his head. I took a deep, steadying breath before I managed to will my feet to move into the room.

My eyes darted around the opulent space, reflecting on the way the decor in that house made me feel cheap in my forest green button up and short white petal skirt with silver rivulets all over it. I felt out of place and realized I'd never belonged in Matteo's world.

No wonder he dumped my ass.

At least my heels made me feel classy, looking stunning and strappy all wrapped around my ankles in forest green suede against the dark hardwood floor. "Ivory." There was a smile in his voice, and I turned to the left where the room curved to find him staring at me from behind his desk, pen still in hand. Though his head tilted down to look at the paper he'd been writing on, his eyes fixated on me with startling intensity.

The breath whooshed out of me, confronted with that impossibly handsome face. In high school, he'd been all about clean edges, the blond-haired All-American boy next door with the stunning blue eyes and boy muscles packed onto his frame however he could. A decade later his hair was darker, browner than blond, and it only made those piercing azure eyes of his seem brighter. His once clean-cut face was covered in some cross between stubble and a very short, well-groomed beard. He'd bulked up, his lean frame a thing of the past with no issues packing on muscle now that he'd aged, that much was visible even covered by the designer suit he wore. He was everything he'd been in high school, intimidating and unattainable, but now he was just *more.* The pen fell to the paper in front of him with a clatter that drew me from my stare, and I shook myself a bit. "Ivory," he whispered again, standing with a smile and walking around the desk to approach me. His lips found my cheek in greeting, and I winced when the contact sent a shiver through me. "You're as beautiful as I always knew you would be."

I flushed, staring up into his intense gaze. He stood too close, far too close, and I shifted back a step pointedly. "Thank you," I murmured awkwardly. Years ago, there'd been obvious affection in the way he looked at me, humor always in his eyes when they landed on me. That was absent, *gone*, only an almost dark, unsettling intensity remaining. "You look good too," I returned. The smirk he gave me communicated that he was arrogant enough to know just how much of an understatement that was.

Lie of the century.

His smirk melted into a grin. "What are you doing here?"

His words were harsh, but his tone was gentle, almost mystified, and laced with his own disbelief.

I understood it very well. Standing in front of him after all those years of pain was a surreal experience, I had no desire to repeat. I wanted to get it over with and be on my way.

"I was at the Byline Bank in McKinley Park this morning when three armed men wearing ski masks came in to rob it," I said in answer, deciding to just be blunt with the situation. I was growing increasingly suspicious of whatever might have brought criminals to identify me in connection with Matteo.

He stilled, his body freezing in a way that felt unnatural. He didn't so much as twitch aside from the movement necessary to form his next words. "Did they touch you?" His voice was carefully controlled.

"No. As soon as one of them got a good look at me, he begged me to tell you they didn't know I was there. That they couldn't have known I'd be there, and to tell you they didn't touch me."

"Ivory—" His face gentled, movement returning to his body suddenly. He leaned further into my space, and I backed up another step. I would not allow him to cross that line, not after everything he'd done. All I could do was get my answers, say my peace, and move on with my life finally.

"Why would bank robbers know my name? And why would they panic because of you?" My arms crossed over my chest, and my teeth sank into that spot at the corner of my mouth that had practically become a chew toy under all the stress of the day.

"You're under my protection. You have been since high school." His voice hardened slightly as his gaze traveled down to my crossed arms. He didn't appear to appreciate the posture, or the attitude behind it, but kept his mouth shut about it.

"Right," I grumbled. "Well, let me make something very, very clear then. I do not want your protection." The remaining gentle look disappeared in favor of hard, cruelly handsome lines. "Remove it, and I will go on living my life like you do not exist just as I have done for twelve fucking years."

"Be very careful," he grumbled under his breath. His nostrils flared at me, what had once been a relaxed posture tensing as he stood taller.

"I want nothing to do with you or whatever the hell it is you're involved in where criminals are afraid of you. You let me live my life without interference, and if I get gunned down in the street then so fucking be it," I hissed, glaring up at him. The muscle in his jaw ticked, his glare turning positively glacial. "It will be better than being a part of whatever this is," I mumbled, turning on my heel to leave.

The doors I'd entered the room through had closed, courtesy of Donatello no doubt. I'd been too wrapped up in the enigma of a man behind me to notice.

It wouldn't happen again. I swore it on my soul, I would never see Matteo again.

He wasn't worth it.

I barely had my hand wrapped around the handle before Matteo's palms pressed against the wood beside my head, and he leaned into me—caging me in.

Fuck.

I'd forgotten what it was like to have a man make me feel short. At 5'7" I wasn't the tallest woman, but I was no slouch. It took a large man to make me feel tiny. Matteo's 6'5" was effective.

"You've been very foolish coming here," he murmured, near my ear. His breath tickled the flesh, sending a shiver racing through me. "I let you go twelve years ago, and it was the most difficult thing I've ever done. Did you really think I would do it twice?" I ignored my confusion at his words. Like he'd walked away for any reason other than wanting to fuck around.

"There's a difference," I gasped as his mouth trailed over the side of my neck in the whisper of a caress. Barely there, so subtle that with anyone else I might have wondered if it was a figment of my imagination. But I knew Matteo's lips, knew his mouth, knew his scent.

"What's that?" The humor in his voice even sounded arrogant. He knew how affected I was by his touch, and I stilled my body and willed it to shut the hell up.

"I wanted you then," I hissed. "I don't anymore."

"Ah, my Angel, you expect me to believe you have not missed my touch? That you are not already wet for me?"

Why did that voice of his have to be so deep, so *fucking sexy*? I wanted to turn around and rip out his vocal cords, just so I couldn't torment myself with the prospect of him using it to seduce other women who looked like me.

"Fuck you, Matteo." I grumbled, yanking my head away from his wandering lips.

"You should be careful, Angel. I'm a dangerous man now. I do not tolerate disrespect." He stepped away from me, as if the sound of that nickname in his voice wasn't enough to bring the threat of tears to my eyes. As if the teasing torment of his breath on my neck had been nothing but a game. "I have business to tend to tonight," he said as he straightened his suit like he was a gentleman and not a deviant who'd just violated my space. "I'll pick you up at seven tomorrow for dinner."

"That will never happen." I laughed, turning to look at him over my shoulder only briefly. He had to be kidding me.

"*Cara mia,* you will be ready and waiting, or I will feast on you instead."

I gasped. "Go to hell, Matteo."

"I've lived in Hell for twelve years, Angel mine. It is time for me to feel the sun again." With that, he moved to sit in the chair behind his desk.

"What does that even mean?" I asked, and he tilted his head to look at me thoughtfully. "You don't even know where I live," I pointed out, turning the sterling silver knob on the door and pulling it open.

"Ivory," his voice called out, and I paused in my steps to go over the threshold. "I mean it, Angel. You will be ready for dinner at seven."

"Or what?" I whispered, raising my chin and turning to face him. "I won't have sex with you. I won't ever make that mistake again."

"We will see about that," he smirked, picking up his pen once more. "You're too naïve to know when you're playing a very dangerous game. I am not a man you say no to."

Donatello appeared in the doorway, eyeing the tension between us. "Miss Torres, may I be of some assistance?" he offered, seeming to want to dissipate the anger pulsing through the room. My heart thudded in my chest. I couldn't say what it was about Matteo's threat, but I knew he meant to make good on it. However, that would happen.

"No, thank you," I snarled, feeling badly for the older man as I turned and stormed toward the door. "I'll show myself out."

"Ivory!" Matteo called behind me, but I kept walking. I didn't stop, even when I heard Donatello's steps following me.

"Miss Torres," he pleaded, but I ignored him as I fumbled through my purse to dig out my keys. I had a moment of panic where I thought the gate wouldn't open when I got to it, but as soon as I put my car in drive it started to open. Whether it was Donatello or Matteo who ordered the guard to let me out, I didn't care at that moment.

I was too concerned with the fact that if he'd wanted to keep me there, *he could have.*

There was one thing I was sure of; Matteo was even more dangerous to me than he'd been twelve years ago.

And there was no way in Hell I would ever see him again.

Over my dead body.

5

MATTEO

I turned my glare Donatello's way. A lesser man would have cowered under the weight of it, although it wasn't actually aimed at him. Not intentionally.

That right was reserved for the angel who'd just fled like I wouldn't follow her into the pearly gates themselves to drag her back with me. "Send Scar to follow her home and get me everything she's been up to for the last twelve years." My older friend nodded, turning and striding out the doors with his cell to his ear - already calling Scar no doubt. "Don? I want him on her 24/7 but tell him to be discreet for now."

He didn't speak, just nodded his understanding as he made his way out the front door. Scar was already waiting at the curb, one of the BMW's being pulled up by another one of my guys.

Satisfied that he would catch up with her, I turned back to stride through the halls of my too-empty house, all while the knowledge that it wouldn't be so empty for too much longer settled in me. I'd have Ivory there regularly soon.

There was no other option. She'd settle into her new reality, eventually.

She didn't have a choice, since I wouldn't let her go again.

Seeing her again had been like a punch to the gut. She'd been beautiful, even in my decade old memories, but somehow, she was even more stunning standing in front of me, all grown up with no remaining trace of the youth she'd been at sixteen. All that sleek chestnut hair that I knew shone auburn when the light hit the strands just right hung down to her narrow little waist in layers, bisecting her where her lithe body tapered out to the hips that seemed to defy the odds. The Portuguese side of her heritage somehow packed all the right curves onto her slight frame, like her body just couldn't decide if it wanted to be slim or curvy. Her mother's French influence had given her the beautiful ivory skin that was her namesake, that generous dusting of freckles across her nose and cheekbones only drawing attention to her sea-green eyes.

Any of the little details that comprised Ivory would have been enough to make her memorable, but it was the thick, lush lips that had haunted my life for over ten years. Whether she wore them relaxed or pillowed, spread into a blinding smile, or wrapped around my cock while she drove me wild with her innocence, I could never get the image of them out of my head.

By the time Donatello returned to my office, I'd sat down in my chair and started tapping my pen against the desk idly in my impatience. It wasn't characteristic of me; distractions weren't something I allowed in my life.

It was too dangerous when one wrong move was the difference between life and death, not just for me but for the people who counted on me.

Donatello took a seat on the other side of the desk, quirking an eyebrow up at me. He'd never actually met

Ivory, couldn't have had the opportunity when I'd refused to bring her around my family for her own safety.

But he knew of her—had seen her. Even then, he'd been one of the two confidants who knew just how obsessed I'd been with my angel.

"How long will you be entertaining Miss Torres this time around?" His amusement faded for something close to disappointment. He knew as well as I had that I'd broken her when I ended things the way I did. Back then, I had to rely on he and Lino to make sure she was coping.

Healing.

Moving on.

All the things I'd never been able to do.

I knew that he'd be disappointed in me if I forced her to experience that all over again just for a few quick fucks. I stared back at him in response, and that disappointment faded and replaced with a pleased grin. "Right."

"I'll be needing an appointment on Jeweler's Row. I want something custom and quick." I picked up my pen, finishing the paperwork on my desk with a quick flourish of my signature before handing it off to Donatello to send out with a messenger.

"I'll make the arrangements." His eyes crinkled in the corners with his bright smile, and I shook my head even as my own lips tipped up slightly.

"Nothing but the best," I reiterated, and he nodded in a wordless representation that it didn't need to be said. He stood to leave me to my work, undoubtedly having plenty of his own to do now that he needed to run twelve years' worth of data on Ivory and find me the best jeweler in Chicago who could work on my tight schedule.

"I'm proud of you, son," he said, his voice cracking with the emotional weight of the bond that held tight between us. My father hadn't been a loving man, had tolerated *no one* loving me. That hadn't been enough to stop Donatello from showing me rare moments of affection when I earned them.

Lino saved me from having to respond when he shoved the door open and burst into the room. He was literally the only person who got away with it, but even being who he was my hand twitched toward the pistol in the top drawer of my desk. "Heard you saw Ivory?" he asked, plopping his ass down into the seat that Donatello vacated.

I pinched the bridge of my nose between two fingers and released a sigh. "For fuck's sake, she just left fifteen minutes ago."

"What can I say? Your guard has a big mouth. He was all excited that he'd finally laid eyes on *the* Ivory Torres. Nervous wreck about it too, worried she's going to demand his head or some shit." He leaned forward in his chair, stripping off his own suit jacket and making himself comfortable.

Shit. He was in for the long haul.

"Why would he be worried about that? Did he touch her?" Even I wasn't immune to the menace in my voice, something I rarely noticed. It happened too frequently to give a shit, but when Ivory was threatened, well, *that* was a different story.

"Nah, just told her she looked like every other bimbo you bang. Before he realized who she was, anyway."

My fists clenched beneath the desk, and I swallowed loudly. "He said what?"

"Shit, man. I thought you'd closed that door a long time ago," Lino whispered, seeming to finally alert himself to the dark energy pulsing around me.

"She came back to me. That's my sign she's mine, so I'm taking her." I shrugged, turning my attention to where

Donatello watched our exchange with a mixture of horror and amusement. "Who's at the gate today?"

"Christian," he answered hesitantly.

"Right, tell Ryker to make it very clear to Christian exactly what happens when someone runs his mouth to my woman. I want him alive, but I want him to know what the consequences are for calling her a whore."

"Woah, I think you're overreacting—" Lino objected, and I turned my glare his way. "How could he have known, Matteo? You spent twelve years looking for her twin to warm your bed."

"Does it look like I give a fuck?" I hissed, turning back to the spreadsheet waiting for me on my computer. I needed to run through the numbers from the last shipment, and I needed Lino to update me on the latest numbers from the businesses, and I needed it done before I went to inspect the cleanliness of the new brothel my men had sampled.

I might run escort, but I only ran the best of the best. Women who made six figures a year and would be free to retire young and live a good life if they were smart.

For the first time since I'd taken over, a voice questioned me.

Because Ivory wouldn't like it. When she found out that was.

But she'd deal with it.

She didn't have a choice.

6

IVORY

The deep breath I took before I opened the front door wasn't nearly enough to prepare me for the shit storm I was about to walk into. I knew that.

But there was nothing else to be done for it.

My father flung the door open with a sudden jerk, grasping me around the back of the neck and pulling me into his arms with a shudder. "Christ. Jesus fucking Christ almighty," he mumbled into the top of my head.

"Daddy, I'm fine," I protested in a mumble against his chest. The press of his shirt against my face muffled my voice, nearly suffocating me. "Well, at least death by hugging is better than being shot," I joked, and I heard my mother's gasp from somewhere further in the house.

How she'd heard me, I'd never know. The woman had eyes and ears everywhere.

"Ivory Leonora!" she cried, and even without being able to see her I knew she pressed her hand to her chest in outrage. She was nothing if not dramatic.

"It's true," I announced, giving my father a shove until his arms fell away. Even at 59, the man was fitter than most 40-

year-old men because of his own inability to sit still. The number of times I'd heard him say, "idle time is wasted time," during my youth would make most of his Air Force buddies cringe.

My mother's arms closed around me as soon as I could breathe in peace, and I sighed. I couldn't blame them for their concern. Seeing your daughter on the news as police ushered her out of a bank following an armed robbery wasn't something most parents had to experience.

I'd called them back before going to Matteo's house, making sure they knew I was okay once I'd realized I'd been on the news. Still, the whole thing seemed to be far more traumatic for them than it was for me, and I'd been the one staring down the barrel of a gun.

"My baby," she cried, tears soaking my shoulder where she'd rested her face. I was taller than my mom, even when I didn't wear heels. Having gone straight to their house for dinner after seeing Matteo, I hadn't changed out of my impress-the-ex outfit.

Though I regretted dressing to impress.

Like a lot.

I shrugged off the anxiety plaguing me. I'd figure out how to deal with Matteo's threat in the morning, because there was no way to ponder it with my father staring at me.

Where my mom saw everything that happened, my father saw every thought inside my head.

Safe to say, I hadn't gotten away with anything as a teenager. Well, except for the one time I'd had Matteo in my bed in high school. After that experience, I'd gone the straight and narrow for a few years until I graduated. After that, well, that had been a different story.

My father cleared his throat. "All right Alice, you've coddled her enough. Let the girl in the house."

"Me? You suffocated her!" Mom protested, though her arms relented and released me finally. With a groan, I walked off into the house, leaving them in their own entryway to bicker as usual. They had a special love, the love people dreamed of finding. That didn't mean that they weren't as sarcastic with each other as possible before they got all kissy and gross.

I did *not* need to be around for that part.

Mom's fried chicken sat on the granite counter, waiting for her to move it to the huge oak table in the dining room. I grabbed it and moved it over, with the sounds of their arguments fading into the background when the humorous jabs at one another started to ease into affection. By the time they made their way into the kitchen, I was pulling the collard greens out of the pot and putting them in one of mom's serving bowls. "Oh honey, you didn't need to do that. I would have used the white bowl," she said, coming up and taking the macaroni and cheese out of the oven.

"Of course," I snorted. "If I'd used the white bowl, you'd have wanted the orange one. Anything to be the opposite of what I pick, contrary woman."

She huffed at me and started to object. "I am not—"

"Woman, you're the most contrary person on the planet," Dad announced, pulling out his seat at the head of the table. "Who the hell cares what bowl the food's in? You going to start taking pictures of it too?"

"Honestly, Martim. These things matter." I took my seat to Daddy's right, serving myself and listening to him gossip about which flight attendant was hooking up with his co-pilot. Apparently, it was quite the scandal—what with the woman being 26 and the pilot in his 50s. Normally, I put on a good show of listening to him sound like a teenage girl, but that day—given everything that had happened—my head just wasn't interested in his idle gossip. I poked at my food, barely eating and contemplating what I would do about Matteo the next day despite my resolution to forget him for the time being.

"Okay, what gives?" Daddy asked.

"What do you mean?" I mumbled, snapping out of my trance and forcing a bite of fried chicken into my mouth.

"You seemed fine about the robbery, my little warrior," he teased, reaching over and pinching my cheeks. I stuck my tongue out at him. "So why are you so in your head now?"

I sighed, dropping the chicken to my plate and biting the corner of my mouth while I contemplated what story I could tell my parents about Matteo. There was no way I'd ever admit I'd gone there, especially because a criminal had known him. "I talked to Matteo," I said vaguely.

My mother stilled, and I glanced at my father to watch his brow furrow. I was under no illusion that he didn't know what Matteo I meant, so I knew his next question was his attempt to give me time to rethink the course of our conversation. "Matteo who?"

"You know, Matteo Bellandi. From high school." I shrugged, as if discussing the boy who'd made me cry myself to sleep for weeks could ever be a casual occurrence.

"And where did you see him?" Mom asked, she forked some greens into her mouth, chewing as if she found them distasteful, but there was no doubting the fact that it was Matteo she found disgusting.

"I didn't," I lied. "See him, I mean. He saw me on the news and reached out to see if I was all right or if there was anything he could do. That's all." My eyes glanced at mom's curtains on the big picture window behind her, seeing that the rods needed dusting. "If you need me to come over and help with the housework, I can do that. I know you have trouble reaching some high places." I changed the subject deftly, knowing mom would bristle at the insinuation that she couldn't clean her damn house herself.

She started to do just that, but Dad's deadly serious voice interrupted her. "I do not think so, young lady. You are not changing the conversation like it doesn't matter that piece of shit somehow got your phone number. You're getting a new one. End of story." He stabbed a piece of macaroni and cheese, shoving it into his mouth angrily.

"What good would that do? With the assets the Bellandi's have access to, he could just find that number if he wanted it," I pointed out. Whether Matteo had my number yet was irrelevant. I'd known for twelve years that he could find me if he'd wanted.

He just hadn't wanted to.

"Ivory—"

"Besides, do you realize what a hassle it would be to change my number? I run my business through it." I shrugged, ignoring his pointed glare.

I sent mom a pleading look, that she took with a sigh and directed my father's attention elsewhere with the promise of further gossip about work. I tuned in better, feeling his eyes on me too attentively for my taste several times throughout dinner.

But we survived without mentioning Matteo again, and when I went home after dinner that night, I was even more determined to make sure I never had to tell them anything about him again.

It was better that way for everyone.

Especially me.

***

My white dress with big tropical coral flowers floated around me with the breeze, and I thanked the heavy cardigan I wore for keeping it down. As a rule, floaty skirts were dangerous in the windy city, but that never stopped me.

Sadie said I had an aversion to pants. I couldn't argue against it. I wore them only when it was necessary to fight off the cold, which was why I wore a dress despite the chill to the Spring air.

I hurried into the restaurant, not even surprised when I found Duke and his family already sitting and waiting for me. I'd changed my clothes last minute after spilling my pet leopard gecko Smaug's water bowl all over myself like a complete idiot, and me running late following some random catastrophe wasn't as rare as it should have been.

Duke turned to face the door, his down-turned blue eyes meeting mine as he shook his head and a smile played at his mouth. I shrugged with a grin of my own, hurrying over and taking the empty seat next to him. Leaning in, I placed a kiss on his cheek and smiled at his mom and brother.

His mother returned the smile, her eyes warming as she looked at the two of us. She'd made no secret of hoping the two of us would end up together one day, and I knew she analyzed every move we made around one another to notice any subtle difference. If we'd ever crossed that line, she'd know before we told her. That much was obvious, since the woman missed nothing where her sons were concerned.

"Hey, Gendry," I murmured.

"What? No kiss for me?" Duke's older brother chuckled, and I narrowed my eyes at him in a glare.

"Why don't you kiss my a—"

"Okay! So good to see you, Ivory, my dear. Should we remember we are in a restaurant and have a nice brunch, without the lot of you bickering like you're still children?" Amelia cut me off. When she turned her face back to the menu in her hands, I stuck my tongue out at Gendry. "I saw that," she drawled, her lips quirking up even though her eyes never left her menu.

Creepy.

"How do you do that?" Duke mused, opening the menu that sat on the table in front of me. I ignored the hint, not even glancing at the menu. Asshole just had to make fun of me every Monday when we met for brunch.

"It's a mom thing. You'll understand one day, Ivory," she said pointedly, and I snorted water back into my glass. Because I was a lady like that.

"I think I'm missing a certain requirement for having children," I chuckled. The waiter saved from whatever response she might have when he came over.

"Can I get you something to drink, miss?" he asked, and I gave him a smile that was probably a little too happy. I needed a drink for the way the conversation was about to turn. As much as I loved Amelia, I just couldn't sometimes.

"A mimosa, please." Duke chuckled, his face hitting my shoulder. I knew I was practically begging the waiter to bring me my drink tout suite, and there was no way anyone missed the tone.

"Are we ready to order brunch?" the waiter asked, totally barely cracking even a bit of humor.

Oh, he was good.

"Nope, just the mimosa for now!" I announced, flicking Duke in the forehead until he reared back with a flinch.

"That hurt!" he protested, rubbing at the spot with a crease in his brow.

"I'll have the nutella french toast with a side of bacon," Gendry said, handing his menu to the waiter. I turned my glower his way. "She'll have the crab benedict, hollandaise on the side." Not only had he thrown me under the bus by ordering *his* food, but the bastard had ordered mine.

It wasn't even like I could protest that he'd ordered wrong, because he hadn't. It was the same thing I got every week. I handed my menu to the waiter, shrinking back in my chair to pout while Amelia and Duke ordered their food. "I'll be right out with that mimosa, ma'am," the waiter announced before he turned to flee the table.

"How did I go from a miss to a ma'am? Did I age ten years in the last five minutes?" I teased, desperate to deflect Amelia away from the pointed way she looked at me.

"You two aren't getting any younger. When are you going to give me grandbabies?" I sighed, leaning forward to bang my head on the table. The woman had a very, very thick skull for this determination that Duke and I were meant to be an item.

"Shouldn't you be pressuring Gendry?" Duke asked. "He's older."

"And he also has never brought a girl home. I can't exactly pressure him when he's determined to remain eternally single, can I?" Amelia steeped her hands, and as soon as the waiter dropped my mimosa in front of me, I took a long swig.

"I've never brought a woman home either, mom," Duke laughed. Amelia raised a brow, turning her attention my way. "Ivory doesn't count. You know we aren't dating."

And we never would. I'd been friends with Duke since second grade. There was no way we would ever go there. "I don't understand you two," Amelia shook her head, sipping at her water in a polite way that made my gulp of mimosa seem vulgar. "I wonder who the kids will look like."

Oh, for fuck's sake.

It would be one of those days.

"I have a date," I interrupted. "Tonight." It didn't matter that I had no intentions of going on said date, but it was enough to deflate Amelia to sighing.

Duke stilled beside me. "Sadie set that up fast."

"Not him. Different date," I answered vaguely.

"Where did you meet this one?" Amelia asked with pursed lips. A look passed between her and Duke, and I ignored it. Neither one of them were fond of my failure of a dating life, for very different reasons. Duke worried I'd get involved with the wrong man and get hurt. Amelia hated everyone who wasn't her son.

"I've known him for a long time," I evaded. They both let the subject drop, and Gendry was nice enough to steer the conversation toward work and the tension melted away.

As much as I hated Amelia's insistence to make something out of nothing, Duke's family was as close to me as my own.

They were my family too, and when his hand rested on my thigh and he took my hand in his, I knew they always would be.

No matter what a colossal fuck up he might think I was when he found out about Matteo.

7

MATTEO

I flipped back and forth through the pages. The folder Donatello had handed me felt obscenely light, and I knew there was no way in Hell he'd included everything there was to know about Ivory for twelve fucking years. I'd wanted to give the man the benefit of the doubt, since he so rarely did anything less than a thorough job. A quick scan confirmed there was something missing. A mishap with the printer no doubt.

I shoved the papers back in the file folder, standing from my desk chair and going in search of the man. There was a matter of hours before I would pick Ivory up for our date, and I needed all the information I could get.

God knew I would need it.

The sound of Donatello's voice reached me, his voice a loud hum as he puttered around in the kitchen with fixing lunch for my guys on duty. I tossed the folder on the island counter, not angrily, but impatient as I ever was. "Where's the rest?" I asked, slipping my hands into my pockets. He turned from the stove, quirking his lips at me and shaking his head like he couldn't quite believe it himself.

"That's all of it."

"It can't be. She's an adrenaline junkie, and you expect me to believe that she's spent the last twelve years cooking and moving from one failed career to another until she finally settled on a blog? Ivory's way too social to be content with a career like that. She'd never survive not being surrounded by people nonstop, not unless something happened." I shook my head, picking a kalamata olive out of one of Donatello's little bowls that he kept pre-measured ingredients in. The man was meticulous.

"I looked at everything," he admitted, rolling out the dough for what appeared to be his Mediterranean flatbread. "There was nothing there, Matteo. From what I can see, that adrenaline junkie you remember disappeared without a trace at eighteen."

"What happened at eighteen?" I reached for another olive, shaking out my hand when Donatello smacked me away with the rolling pin. I narrowed my eyes on him, and he grinned back at me. The old man knew he was one of three people who could get away with something like that and live to tell the tale.

"No idea." He shrugged, setting down the rolling pin in favor of combining his toppings in a small bowl. "Before that, as you saw in the folder there were some parties. She snuck into a club at least once and got caught. Went out joyriding with a college guy who had a motorcycle when she was a junior, normal teenage stuff." My fists clenched at the reminder she'd been with other men. Even if there was no evidence to suggest she'd been sexually involved with the biker, I knew from looking through her file there'd been others.

I had no right to be pissed. No right to be jealous since I'd been the one to walk away from her.

That didn't make me feel any less murderous.

"She wouldn't have just stopped."

Donatello twisted his lips up into a grimace. "Did you consider the fact that maybe she was only an adrenaline junkie because of you? You encouraged that part of her, without that influence she might have settled into an easy life. It would explain why she went through so many career changes before she found a successful one."

"And not being social now?" I pinged my eyebrows up, watching him coat the dough in olive oil with a silicone brush like it was an art canvas.

"Well, for what it's worth, that seems like it may have changed immediately after you left her. She remained close to Ms. Hicks and Mr. Bradley, but her friendships with others dwindled by the time the next school year started. Given what my granddaughter says about school, I suspect that once you dumped her, she lost her popularity and the bulk of her friends. She was never the it-girl by her own merit, but because of your interest in her. Once you moved on—"

"So did the rest of the school. Fuck," I groaned. I always seemed to underestimate just how cruel women were to one another.

"I imagine being betrayed by you, and subsequently by most of the people she considered her friends, would be enough to make her hesitant to put herself out there again. Perhaps less trusting of strangers." Donatello sprinkled the topping mixture and feta cheese on the flatbread before shoving it in the oven.

I sighed, knowing his theory probably had merit. Ivory had never taken rejection well, and she'd always been too trusting. While part of me wanted to be pleased that she'd learned that valuable lesson, I hated that they had ostracized her because of me. I'd never wanted to hurt her, let alone cause other people to hurt her too. "You realize it's ridiculous that you cook a fucking flatbread for my security, right?"

He froze. "Do they not like my flatbread?"

I shook my head with a smile. "They like it, Don, but they're killing machines. You'll give them a complex with that shit."

He sighed in disappointment. "I dislike it when you curse."

"Of all my sins, cursing is the big concern?" I chuckled.

He rolled his eyes, shooing me out of his kitchen. I didn't have the heart to point out that once I'd moved Ivory in with me, it would become her territory. "It is the most unnecessary."

"Did you get me a jeweler yet?" I teased, even as I backed out of his space. I'd let him enjoy it while it lasted.

"She'll be here noon tomorrow."

I grinned at him, and I knew it was the one I wore when I'd conquered something impossible. "Perfect."

8

IVORY

It was normal for Duke to walk me home after brunch. The restaurant wasn't far; it was midday, and I walked just about everywhere if I could. That didn't stop him from thinking I needed an escort. Since his house wasn't far from mine, he'd taken to hitching a ride to the restaurant with his brother so he could escort me home.

He'd tried walking me there in the beginning, but you know, he got sick of asking if I was ready yet. I got sick of him asking if I was ready yet. It was better for both of us he wasn't there to nag me in the morning.

I hated waking up.

The silence between us wasn't typical, and I knew he could tell that I wasn't telling him everything that needed to be said about my date. Duke knew me as well as anyone. So, on the way home, I called Sadie. I needed her advice on what to do about Matteo, so she might as well save me the trouble of explaining twice. She'd been putting in a ton of extra hours at the gym since her dad had handed over the reins but was fine to skip out. It wasn't like she did training or worked the front unless someone was out, so she had more freedom to set her own hours.

Her empty car was in my driveway by the time we made it there. Not surprising since she and Duke were both prone to using their keys nearly as often as I used mine. Flashing a quick, awkward smile for Duke, I led the way up the steps to my little cottage of a house. The door opened, since Sadie never locked the damn door.

Sadie had her ass planted on one of my bar stools at the island, as she flipped through the notes, I made for the next few recipes I'd be sharing on the blog. "I want to eat this one," she said, stabbing a finger into the page for my swiss chocolate mousse cake. It wasn't uncommon that she and Duke would call dibs on specific recipes, as if there wasn't always plenty of food for both, anyway.

"It will go straight to your ass," Duke smirked, ducking when Sadie hurled the binder at him.

"Hey!" I protested, scurrying to pick it up and shoving loose pages back in - praying to all that was holy that they weren't mixed up. I did not have time for that shit.

"You! What was so important, Miss Cryptic Phone Call?" She spun on the stool, jabbing that finger in my direction.

I chewed on the corner of my mouth, casting a glance at Duke out of the side of my vision. His jaw tensed, that strong, angular bone structure of his highlighted in the light flooding in my windows. "Why don't we sit?" I sighed, making my way over to the couch. Sadie hopped off the stool, plopping into her favorite armchair dramatically.

"Will there be yelling?" she asked, eyeing Duke where he stood too still. I knew he'd be pacing back and forth any second.

I nodded. "Safe bet."

"Oh, for fuck's sake, Ivory. What did you do?" I paused

before answering, considering my words carefully. Perhaps there was a way to get through the coming storm *without* mentioning Matteo's name. Duke dropped his head to his chest, mumbling under his breath. "Why? Just why?" I knew he wasn't talking to me; his mumbles were always directed to himself.

I ignored them.

"I uh, just need advice. Best way to get out of a date."

"Just text him and say you changed your mind," Sadie answered, scowling at me like I'd lost my marbles. I'd canceled plenty of dates in the past.

"Well, I don't have his number, actually," I pointed out, wiggling my toes in my heels. The polish on one of my toes was chipped, and I immediately scowled at it.

"Please tell me you're kidding me," Duke hissed, and the telltale sound of his shoes thudding over my hardwood floors announced the pacing had begun. "Why exactly are you going on a date with a guy if you don't even have his number?"

"Well, I mean—" I paused with a sigh. There wasn't much to be done for avoiding his frustration. "I didn't *exactly* agree to go on the date at all." I drew out the first words of the statement, rushing the rest out in a mumble in a pathetic hope it could somehow be misinterpreted.

No such luck.

He froze, and Sadie turned wide eyes his way. As irritating as his pacing might have been, we both knew it was terrible when he was still. "Excuse me?" That voice was a deadly whisper, and while my friend was volatile and emotional, quiet was something he rarely ever achieved. When he was silent, it was just bad.

"Honey—" Sadie tried to soothe him, sensing the shit show hovering just under the surface.

"Why is there a date in the first place if you didn't agree to it, Ivory?" he asked.

"He told me we were going out. Said he'd pick me up at seven," I whispered.

His eyes closed, and his voice remained a whisper for the next words. "You told him where you live?"

"No! Don't be ridiculous," I protested.

"Then what is the problem?" Sadie asked. "He can't exactly pick you up if he doesn't know where you live." Her voice melted into a laugh, but Duke's face didn't change. He knew I wasn't quite so dramatic that I would risk his anger for no reason.

I winced, twisting my lips into what I knew was a very unattractive grimace. "I'm not so sure that's true in this case."

"What does that mean?" Duke's voice dropped further, and he crossed his arms over his chest as he strode over to stand in front of me.

I tilted my face up to look at him fully, giving him my best innocent expression to placate him. "I—well, he's probably capable of finding out where I live pretty easily," I admitted.

"Who?" Duke's voice trembled, and I knew he had a very good idea.

"Duke—" I started.

"Who is the fucking date with, Ivory?" he warned.

"Matteo," I whispered against my better judgment. Duke's body went taut, and he stared down at me in disbelief before storming through my living room and out my back door to the yard.

Okay, that seemed dramatic.

"Honey, where did you see Matteo?" Sadie's voice asked softly, and I didn't miss the way she stared after Duke. Like his pissy fit was more important than getting me out of the stupid date I didn't want.

"The robbers at the bank, they recognized me somehow. Begged me to tell Matteo that they didn't hurt me. I wanted answers so I—"

She cut me off with a gasp. "Oh no, please tell me you didn't!" she shrieked, drawing Duke back into the house. His shirt sleeves were rolled up, his normally neat blond hair all messy.

"Didn't what?" he asked, slowly. "What did you do, Ive?"

I steeled my shoulders. I didn't care if it had been stupid in hindsight, I wouldn't be treated as if I was a child incapable of making responsible decisions because I'd made *one* mistake. "I went to talk to him. I wanted to know why they would recognize me."

"Jesus Christ," Duke hissed. "What were you fucking thinking?!"

"I thought that I had a right to know!" I yelled back.

"You also had a right to just be grateful that they didn't shoot you in the face and leave it at that. If someone is connected to criminals, you do *not* go to their house and make demands!"

I stood, storming my way into the kitchen and grabbing a cutting board out of it.

I needed to cut something.

I figured a vegetable was probably better than Duke's pretty face.

"Well, I did. It's done," I sighed, pulling a cucumber from my fridge and tossing a container of Duke's favorite homemade hummus onto the island.

"Okay, okay," Sadie stood, giving Duke a wary glance as she stepped up and leaned onto the counter. "Don't get dressed. Put on some sweatpants, throw your hair into a knot on your head, and look a mess. Matteo Bellandi does not take a woman on a date when she looks more prepared for a movie night at home."

"Okay, okay that works. I can do that," I sighed in relief. I grabbed the peeler from the island drawer, making quick work of the cucumber. I knew she was right. Matteo probably took his dates to high-class restaurants and made them think they had a future before dumping them on their ass when he was done with them.

"Pack a bag," Duke interrupted, taking a furious bite out of a cucumber as soon as I sliced it. "You're staying with me for a few days."

"I can't do that. I have to work. I have photos to take tomorrow. Your kitchen isn't my favorite for that," I argued, shaking my head and discounting it immediately. There was no way I would be forced out of my home.

"Then I'll bring you back and hang out with you while you work tomorrow." Once he'd made quick work of the cucumber, he put the cover back on the container of the hummus and shoved it in the fridge. I widened my eyes at the counter, before turning them his way when he snatched the knife out of my hand and brought it and the cutting board to the sink to wash.

Since when did he wash my dishes?

I shook my head, turning and leaning back on the island. "You only have one bed."

"We'll make it work," he shrugged, acting far too casual considering his outburst before.

I did not like the sound of *that*.

He shoved the cutting board and knife in the strainer, turning to Sadie. "You want to pack for her?" Sadie stifled a laugh, because even she knew this was uncharacteristic behavior for Duke. He wasn't pushy. He wasn't an asshole.

His hand hit the railing of the stairs, and his foot was on the first step when I called out to him. "I'm not going, Duke."

His eyes hardened as he turned his glare to me. "You are."

"No. I'm not letting him chase me out of my house just because he said he'd pick me up for a date." I omitted the other stuff he'd said about making a dinner out of me if I wasn't ready. That definitely wouldn't help the scenario at the moment. "Look, if he shows up. If anything escalates, you're close. I know to call you. Odds are, he won't even turn up. I can't imagine I'm worth the effort of tracking down my address. It's not like he's lacking for company." I knew I was placating Duke, but I hated the protectiveness he constantly showed over me with men. Like he was determined that *every* man who was interested in me was a douchebag, just because Matteo had been. He sighed, dropping his head to stare at the stairs.

"Fine," he grunted. He turned, striding out the front door without another word.

"Well, that could have gone better," Sadie said.

I nodded.

"Yep."

***

How was it I didn't own a single pair of bummy sweatpants?

Sadie would stage an intervention if she found out.

The only yoga pants I owned were leggings and hugged my legs and butt way too much for me to face Matteo in. In all fairness though, I hated pants. When I was at home, I lived in skirts, dresses, or pajama shorts. I eventually tracked down a pair of pajama pants my mom had given me in one of her tirades about being dressed appropriately for a home invasion. Because wearing pants instead of booty shorts would protect me if someone decided he wanted to rape me. That said, I did like the fabric, big watercolor flowers on a black background with a wide, grey waistband and they were loose and comfy.

For pants.

I'd shoved an old, loose grey tee over my head, kind of hating the way it hung off one shoulder. But it was the baggiest shirt I owned, so it would do. My trusty slippers were stuck on my feet, and I was far too unsettled to relax. Smaug had taken up residence on my shoulder, just hanging out and enjoying the ride while I paced in a mimic of Duke's earlier movements.

My phone chimed with a text, and I unlocked the screen to see a message from Duke asking if Matteo had shown. A glance at the clock confirmed it wasn't even seven yet. Typing out a quick response, I did my best to keep my snark out of it.

"I know, I know," I said to Smaug as I walked to the kitchen and grabbed a bottled water out of the fridge. I chugged the contents, feeling thirsty.

Who was I kidding? My mouth was the Sahara.

"I'm being ridiculous. There's no way he'll show." I shoved my hair into a bun on top of my head just to be safe, careful not to dislodge Smaug. He glared at me although I'd taken care. "Don't look at me like that, Mister," I scolded him.

I jumped at the sound of the doorbell, glancing at the clock on my stove with wide eyes. Smaug's little claws dug into my skin through the t-shirt, and he looked at me—an echoing panic in his adorable little face.

Seven on the dot.

"Coincidence, right?" I asked, swallowing and making my way to the door. A glance through the peephole confirmed it was, in fact, Matteo Bellandi standing on my step and looking as breathtaking in a black suit as he had the day before. If I hadn't known better, I'd have sworn Smaug shrugged his shoulders at me. I backed away from the door, wondering if there was any way to hide the fact that I was home.

I could just *not* answer the door, right?

"Open the door, Angel," his hard voice demanded, an unmistakable edge to his tone.

"I don't think I will," I shouted through the door, clapping a hand over my mouth as soon as the words left me.

So much for that.

"Ivory, we can do this the easy way or the hard way. It's your choice." Something thudded against the door, and I peeked out to see him leaning against the frame on one hand, his face just above the peephole.

"What's the hard way?" I whispered, and I fully thought he wouldn't answer.

"I pick the lock," he didn't hesitate to say, and I blanched.

"You wouldn't dare! That's breaking and entering!" I backed away from the door, realizing it might not matter that much to him if bank robbers feared him.

Fuck. I totally should have gone to Duke's.

I hated being wrong.

I really, really hated it.

"I'll call the police!" I shouted, nabbing my phone off the island of the kitchen and hurrying back to the door. The sound of metal scraping on metal sounded through the door, and I flung it open on a gasp. Two odd little metal sticks stuck out of the deadbolt, and I barely had time to turn amazed eyes Matteo's way before he backed me into the house. Slamming the door shut behind him, he advanced until my ass hit the console table next to the foot of the stairs where I kept my keys and such. He ripped the phone out of my hand, glancing at the screen where Duke's text was open and tossed it onto the table behind me. I swallowed when he put his hands on the wall next to my head, caging me in.

"If you think the cops are dumb enough to get between me and my woman, think again. There isn't anybody in this world who will save you from me." I stared up at him, wincing as Smaug's claws continued to dig into me.

Safe to say, he wasn't a fan.

Matteo let his arms drop from the wall, his eyes giving me a once over, and he pinched the bridge of his nose between his fingers and sighed as his eyes caught on Smaug. "Ivory, the fuck is that?" The exasperation in his voice was a little too like Duke's every time I brought Smaug to his house.

"He's a gecko, and his name is Smaug," I objected, reaching up with one hand and holding it out for the lizard. He gladly abandoned his favorite perch, wiggling his way into my hand. I ran my thumb over the back of his head to soothe him, before turning and walking away from Matteo in favor of setting Smaug in his tank where he'd be safe from whatever storm was brewing. As soon as I had the lid on, Matteo spoke.

"Good. Now go get dressed. Our reservation is for eight."

I turned to him, my reflection shining off the stainless steel of my fridge in the kitchen. "Are you insane?"

He shrugged, seeming to genuinely consider the answer. "It's possible."

"Get out," I scoffed, shaking my head and moving around him to get to the front door. I swung it open quickly, gesturing him out the door. When he just raised a brow at me and didn't move, I sighed to keep myself from stomping my foot.

"I made reservations at *Vecchio,*" he said pointedly. I knew in that moment he'd done his research on me. The only time a man would rub reservations at the hottest new restaurant in town in a woman's face was if he knew she was a food-addict.

I eyed him suspiciously. "They're booked six months out," I argued, crossing my arms over my chest. "Did you blow off some other girl to harass me into going with you?"

He chuckled. "No, sweetheart. It is safe to say that I do not take women to dinner."

"Oh well, keep with that tradition then, yeah?"

"I know you want to go. I can see the gears turning in that pretty head of yours." His voice lightened to genuine amusement as he watched me struggle to ignore that temptation. *Everyone* talked about that place, but it was impossible to get in.

"Unless you're willing to let me take someone else there and use your reservation? I'll pass," I hissed, and the amusement fled those harsh features.

"You go to dinner with another man, and we will have a very, *very* serious problem, *Cara mia*." I flinched back at the menace in his tone and felt my brow furrow as I stared at him. There really was no trace of the boy I'd loved in the man in front of me.

And something about that drained all the fight right out of me. I fought back tears, unwilling to let him see just how much he still affected me. "Please, just leave," I begged.

He was indifferent to my deflation, or he just didn't care. He stepped forward, crowding into my space and shoved the door closed again. "Go get dressed," he whispered, and I thought I might have caught a moment of regret in his blue eyes as he looked down at me more gently.

I shook my head, chewing on my lip and suddenly finding my floor fascinating.

I needed to mop.

"I don't want to scare you," he whispered, his fingers catching under my chin and lifting until I met his intent gaze. "But you will go to dinner with me. Now, you can either change, or you can go in pajamas. Your choice."

I glared at him, jerking my face out of his grip. "Go to Hell."

He sighed, biting out a "fine." The next thing I knew his hands were on my waist, and he lifted me off my feet. My stomach hit his shoulder, and I breathed out a sudden oof.

"What are you doing?" I hissed, squirming on my perch as he turned for the door. "Matteo, I'm not even wearing shoes!" He shrugged, jostling me as he pried the door open. I couldn't believe he'd hauled me over his shoulder like I was nothing, the fucking Neanderthal. "Okay!" I relented. "Put me down, and I'll change!" He closed the door, and I could feel the smug grin on his face even before I saw it.

"Ten minutes." I widened my eyes at him, turning and fleeing up the stairs to my room to hunt down something that would be appropriate for Vecchio without looking like I'd put in effort. I didn't even have time for effort.

Because I had ten fucking minutes.

※※※

It ended up being a good thing I didn't have time. Matteo couldn't wonder if I'd gotten ready for him or if I'd tried to look my best.

He already knew I hadn't.

I'd grabbed the first little black dress I found in my closet, and it was really a gamble which one I'd throw over my head.

I might have had a slight addiction to them.

I'd only had time to swipe on quick eyeliner and mascara, thanking the eye makeup gods that for once they both cooperated. A red lip tint followed, and I tore my hair from its bun to fall loose around my shoulders. A change of underwear and bra, and I shoved the dress on over my head and slipped my feet into my favorite strappy yellow heels for a pop of color. I couldn't ever go all black with my clothes.

I didn't stop to think about my dress until I started walking down the stairs, using the railing to secure myself when my legs felt like they'd collapse beneath me. But the moment Matteo looked up from the phone where he'd been typing vigorously, I could feel the way his eyes trailed up every inch of my bare legs.

I glanced down at my chest, feeling my breathing constrict when I realized I wore *that* dress. The one every woman had in her closet - the one that existed purely for the purpose of seducing a man. A sweetheart neckline, with everything above it disguised with a delicate and feminine lace. The dress was sleeveless with an asymmetrical hem lined in a wide band of lace. One side? Appropriate length, but the ruched and shorter side was the shortest thing I owned. The lace on that side was wider, offering some level of modesty that wouldn't have been there otherwise, but the color of my skin was unmistakable as it peeked through. It wasn't scandalous, and was entirely appropriate for Vecchio, but I shouldn't have worn it for Matteo.

I never would have chosen it if I'd had time to think. I swallowed as his blue eyes met mine, seeming impossibly dark suddenly, like two sapphires glittering at me dangerously. "You're breathtaking," he murmured, holding out a hand for me as I approached the last step. I took it with an exhale, trying to forget the way my skin had heated when he stared at it. Like a man dying of thirst, who'd seen water for the first time in days. Like he couldn't believe I was real, nothing but a mirage.

I shrugged it off, knowing it meant nothing.

Nothing ever meant anything to Matteo Bellandi.

"Should we go?" I asked, and Matteo nodded. I hurried over to my coat closet, nabbing my black bolero jacket and shrugging it on. I glanced at my purse, knowing it was too big to bring to dinner with me. I tore a clutch off the top shelf of my closet and tossed in my phone and debit card quickly. When I went to the door, Matteo snatched the keys out of my hand and guided me out the front door as he turned off all my indoor lights. I hit the switch for the outside light, watching in fascination as he locked my door for me and checked the door twice to be sure it was shut tight.

"You need a security system," he nodded gruffly, pocketing my house keys. He took my hand, tugging me toward the dark grey car in my driveway. I didn't stop walking but gasped at the sight of it. Because even though I knew nothing about cars, I knew it was sexy as hell.

"What is that?" I whispered, and he glanced back at me with an arrogant smirk. He knew damn well how sexy that car was.

"It's an Aston Martin," he said, and I rolled my eyes.

Of course, it was.

I did not understand what that meant, aside from it being another indicator of how far apart we were in terms of the worlds we lived in. "Do you want to drive?" he asked, and I gave him a wide-eyed look.

"No, thank you," I whispered. He opened the passenger door, helping me navigate my way inside gracefully.

The door shut with a thud, and I buckled myself in. Everything I remembered about Matteo showed the ride itself might be a terrifying experience. The driver's side door opened, and he dropped into the seat with a smooth glide that looked entirely at home in the luxury car. He grinned at me when he closed the door. "I have to say I'm surprised. I'd have thought you'd have jumped at the chance to take her for a spin."

I nearly flinched, assaulted with memories of driving his Mustang in high school and pushing every limit he set for me. Instead, I steeled my features into a cool mask and shrugged. "You know nothing about me anymore."

He winced visibly, shifting the car into reverse and backing out of my tiny little driveway. It was comically short compared to the curving road you took to get to his estate. When he put the car in drive, I let the purr of the engine relax me into a semi-comfortable state. I could do this. I could get through dinner and then send Matteo on his way after making it clear I wasn't interested in being one of his good-time girls.

No problem.

Staring out the window, I didn't see when he reached for me. But I felt it when his hand skimmed my thigh, grabbing my hand in his and holding it while he drove. His skin rested on my bare flesh, and I felt goosebumps rise from the contact. I tried to free my hand from his grip, but he held steady, not even releasing me when he shifted gears—instead taking my hand captive with his to do it. "Let go," I ordered.

"Nope, I don't think I will," he said, keeping his eyes on the road and not even bothering to glance my way.

"This isn't a date," I hissed.

"Of course, it is," he laughed. "I'm taking you to the nicest restaurant in the city. You look beautiful. I've been inside you. It's a date, Ivory."

"Twelve years ago doesn't count, Matteo. Plenty of men have been inside me now," I lied. Obviously there had been more than just him, but my numbers were still embarrassingly low for my age. At least when I wanted to toss them in his smug face.

"*Never* talk to me about the other men you've been with," he ordered in his deadly voice. "I will not be held responsible for what I'll do to them if I'm forced to think about it."

"You really are insane. Did you think I'd become a born-again virgin after you dumped me?" I chuckled, shaking my head. His grip on my hand tightened, not crushing but *vibrating* with fury. Somehow, he kept himself from hurting me.

"Angel—"

"Not an angel, Matteo. Not anymore. You ruined me, remember?" I hissed, shifting my legs away from our hands when he tried to rest them there again.

"I didn't ruin you," he growled. "I made you mine. In a way that no one else will ever be able to do." He dropped my hand, having no place to rest them comfortably. I tucked it under my thighs, not willing to risk him grabbing it again.

"And then promptly threw me away. Congratulations," I laughed. "You must really value your belongings." He was silent for a moment, and I could feel the tension radiating off him. When he pulled into the parking lot of the restaurant and drove straight up to the valet, I was shocked when he hopped out of the car so quickly.

"Do not open that door," he ordered the valet who'd moved to assist me out with a pointed finger in warning.

The glare he gave the valet was enough to make the poor boy look like he might pee himself. Tossing his keys at the other one, he slammed the door and strode around the car on quick, efficient steps and pulled open my door himself. I took the hand he offered, pivoting my legs out until I could let him lift me up and out of the car. My hands smoothed my dress down just to be safe as I turned a polite smile to the boys watching us from the hood of the car. Their gazes were too intense, too shocked.

"You've been here before." I winced at the accusation in my voice. I didn't own Matteo. I had no right to be jealous, even as the thought of him bringing another woman to the nicest restaurant in town to wine and dine her slid through my veins like something insidious. He put a hand at the small of my back and guided me up the front steps. Even though the restaurant was technically outside the city, the crowd still lingered out the door. The natural stone building was stunning, like something out of a movie as he led me in the front door. That traitorous hand of his never left my back, somehow feeling far too intimate despite the dress that separated us.

"Mr. Bellandi," the hostess said with a blinding smile. "It's so good to see you again." She ignored me completely in favor of turning hazel eyes up at him with a flutter of her lashes. "Will you be needing a seat at the bar tonight?" I didn't bother to control my eye roll. Women could be such bitches. "Or I could probably squeeze you into Kendra's section, if you'd prefer—"

"I have a reservation for two," Matteo cut her off, glancing down at the podium meaningfully.

"Oh. How nice of you to take your—" she paused dramatically "—sister to dinner?" I snorted. Full on fucking snorted in the entryway of the nicest restaurant I'd ever been in.

You couldn't take me anywhere, I swear.

The hostess finally hardened her gaze into a glare she narrowed on me. Matteo's voice dropped low as he whispered to her. "My woman. Now, apologize." I swallowed uncomfortably, glancing at the pissed off man next to me.

"I—I'm very sorry, miss," the hostess stuttered, turning frightened eyes my way to avoid Matteo's wrath.

I shrugged, suddenly feeling sympathetic enough to let her off the hook. "It's fine, really. I'll be done with him tonight, so feel free to make plans with him after he takes me home." I smiled at her, and she blanched back at me. Matteo's growl was unmistakable, as was the way the hostess flinched back.

"Alex, take their coats," the hostess called, and a boy came from the coatroom. Matteo's stiff fingers helped me out of mine, and he handed them to the boy with venom written all over his features.

"Do not even attempt to make plans with me later," Matteo said before the hostess could get a word in edge wise. "Ivory here doesn't seem to realize the seriousness of our relationship just yet, but I assure you, I'll be remedying that."

The hostess nodded, grabbing two menus and strutting off toward what I could only assume would be our table. Matteo's hand pressed into my back a little more forcefully, like the frayed edges of his control were slipping in the face of my sass.

Still, he pulled out my chair like a gentleman, and I was about to slide into it with a polite thank you when a man's voice caught both of our attentions. Matteo went ramrod still, the only motion he made was to grasp me around the waist as he pulled me into his side forcefully.

"Matteo!" The man made his way towards us, only sparing a glance for me before he turned his dancing brown eyes back to Matteo. I'd been dismissed after only a glance, but for once I couldn't say I minded. Even in that moment where our eyes had connected, something about the way the dark brown of them glinted gave me the creeps. The way Matteo kept me plastered to his side only confirmed that he was *not* someone I wanted fixating on me.

"Adrian." Matteo's voice was flat, no emotion to him when he answered. They shook hands, postures tense.

"I'm glad I ran into you. I wondered if we could discuss—"

"Not tonight," Matteo said sharply, his arm tightening around me until I had no choice but to turn my body in to face his. Feeling awkward, I raised a hand to rest on his chest. The motion had the unintended benefit of soothing something raw inside Matteo, and even though his body only relaxed a fraction, I felt it in every inch of my body that was plastered to his.

"Understood." Adrian turned dark, dancing eyes to me. Suddenly, he seemed to find me *very* interesting, and his eyes passed over me from head to toe. "And who might this be?"

"Ivory," I answered, forcing my lips to curl into a tentative but polite smile.

Adrian held out a hand, and I placed mine in it when I realized I had no reason not to, nothing that could be perceived as anything other than an insult, anyway. Raising it to his lips, he pressed a kiss to the back of it. "You are a rare beauty, Ivory." Matteo growled, whether at the words or the sight of Adrian's lips on my skin I would never know, and Adrian turned wide eyes up to him with a smirk.

"Oh, I see. It's like that, is it?" Matteo didn't answer, but Adrian dropped my hand, regardless in the face of Matteo's eerie silence. Adrian's smile was no less intimidating as he looked down at me again. "It was lovely to meet you. I'll let you two enjoy your evening." He turned, striding back to what I had to presume was his own table. I sat finally, letting Matteo push my chair in for me.

"What was that?" I whispered as he took his own seat across from me.

"Adrian is a business rival," he answered shortly, opening his own menu. I didn't continue my questioning immediately, as the waiter came and took our drink order. Matteo ordered a bottle of wine, that I had to assume was insanely expensive. I ignored it, letting him act in his high-handed way.

It was one dinner; I reminded myself.

Eat some delicious food and then get out.

"Do you know what you would like?" Matteo asked after the waiter left.

I widened my eyes at him dramatically. "Are we really not going to talk about whatever that was?"

Matteo sighed, setting his menu on the table and turning his attention to me finally. "It was business, and you *Cara mia*, are not part of my business. I would like it to stay that way."

"Because I'm so naïve I couldn't possibly understand your business?" I hissed.

"No, because it is much safer for you if you're not involved. I may be many things, but I will always do whatever it takes to keep you safe."

The waiter came back, saving me from having to

respond to the ridiculous lie of that statement. The polite smile he turned down at me was polite, all clean-cut charm. "What can I get for you, Miss?"

"The spring risotto," I said with a smile.

"An excellent choice." The man gave me a bright smile, before turning to Matteo. "And for you, Sir?"

"The bistecca fiorentina." Matteo's voice was short and curt, and I looked up to see him glaring daggers at the waiter. "She's not on the menu, so don't look at her like she's a piece of meat."

I gasped. "Matteo!"

"I apologize," the waiter whispered backing away from our table. "I didn't intend—"

"Go," Matteo snapped.

"What is wrong with you?" I hissed at him as soon as the waiter left. I could feel eyes on me from all around the dining room, and my cheeks heated with the realization that his moment failed to go unnoticed. Matteo nodded to someone over my shoulder, and I turned to find another Italian man nodding back at him. "Who is *that?*"

"My security," Matteo grunted.

"That poor waiter didn't deserve—"

Matteo held out a hand, silencing me with his domineering bullshit. "He wanted to fuck you."

"Maybe I should let him," I taunted, standing from the table.

"Sit down," he ordered, but I ignored the command I heard in that too-sexy-for-his-own-good voice.

"I'm going to the powder room." I shook my head as I walked and followed the sign to the back hall of the restaurant. Miraculously, there was no one in the bathroom, and I vented to myself as I went about my business. "Fucking ridiculous man. Like I needed a man to chase off someone because he *looked* at me. What kind of caveman bullshit is that?" I came out of the stall, surprised to find a woman standing at the sink when she hadn't been before. She smiled at me, kindly not commenting on my tirade that she must have overheard. I'd just finished washing my hands and accepted the hand towel from the attendant, when the door opened, and Adrian appeared in the mirror behind me.

"Get out," he said to her. She slid her eyes to me, before seeming to decide better and fleeing the bathroom.

I swallowed, turning around to face the man who'd strolled right into the ladies' room like he belonged there. "Any chance you haven't realized this is the women's bathroom?" I whispered, and he threw his head back and laughed. It was a shame there was something so *off* about him, because if it hadn't been for that, he'd have been attractive. Not Matteo-level sexy, but handsome in his own right. Deep golden skin and dark hair, he was the epitome of tall, dark, and handsome. Even as he stepped closer to me, getting right in my business until I leaned back on the counter with both hands. He drew up one hand, letting his fingers trail over my cheekbone gently, and he watched the contact intently. "So exquisite. I can see what drew him to you."

I swallowed again, jerking my head away from his hand as much as I dared. "Matteo won't be pleased to know you touched me," I whispered. A few hours ago, I'd have said it was an exaggeration, but after seeing the way he reacted to men even looking at me, I couldn't be so sure.

"I imagine not, no," Adrian grinned. "That's part of the fun, you see? Though I imagine we'll have plenty of fun in our own right. I had to be sure you knew that I am interested and willing to risk the wrath of Bellandi should it mean you are the reward."

"That's flattering," I huffed. "But I'm afraid I'm not interested."

"Ah, sweetheart. It's adorable that you think—"

He broke off when the door flung open, Matteo's enraged energy filling the bathroom as he rushed in. The man he'd referred to as his security followed behind him, looking exasperated but pissed off too. "Take your hands off my woman," Matteo snarled. "Or I'll remove them for you."

Adrian stepped back, raising his hands as if he was innocent. "We were only talking, Bellandi," Adrian placated with a shit-eating grin.

"She does not exist for you. Get that through your fucking skull." Adrian smirked back at him, and Matteo's face turned positively feral. "This is not something you want to test me on, Ricci." Adrian didn't utter another word as he strode to the door, but he paused long enough to wink at me just before he left. Matteo cursed, balling his hands into fists. "Scar's on her. Round the clock," he ordered the security man. He nodded, turning and striding out of the bathroom, seeming content to go about his duty as Matteo ordered. "Are you okay?" Matteo turned to me, his hands cupping my cheeks. Momentarily distracted by how good they felt—especially compared to the icky way my skin crawled when Adrian touched me—it took me too many precious seconds to draw away. I needed him to not touch me. Needed to never remember what it felt like when his hands were on me.

"I'm fine," I nodded, taking a deep breath to compose myself. It hadn't been bad. He'd barely touched me. It was nothing like the last time.

I'd be fine.

Matteo studied me, sighing at whatever he saw on my face. Taking my hand, he guided me back to the table. We settled in, and our food followed within minutes. I did my best to steady my shaking hands, drawing a fortifying breath into my lungs. The glass of wine on the table proved too tempting to ignore, and it took everything in me to not spill it all over my dress. "Did he touch you, Angel?" Matteo's low rumble should have been frightening, but for whatever reason in that moment he wasn't the monster who haunted my nightmares. He showed me a glimpse of the boy I loved, the fake boy who had never existed, letting the terrifying enigma of a man drift away.

"Nothing too serious." I gave him my best effort at a reassuring smile. He hadn't touched me in any way that should have been traumatizing but given my history—given the way I reacted to the touch of men I didn't know—it was too much.

Being with Matteo already had my body strung tight, lingering on the edge of some cliff that I just knew I could never let myself fall over. To do so would be to fall to my heartbreak again. "You're shaken."

"It's not every day that pushy ass men seem to fixate on me." I twisted my lips into a saccharine smile, almost hoping that he would take the bait and stop with the sympathetic, almost caring act.

We both knew it was a lie when all was said and done.

"You can tell me, you know. Whatever it is that—"

"Can we not? Please? Whatever it is, is none of your business." He stared at me like he might argue, before finally tilting his head down in a nod.

"Very well, *Cara mia*. Tell me about your blog."

I sighed, not even pretending to hide my distaste that he would have done such thorough research on me. "What's there to say? It's a blog. I post recipes and photos of my food; people try them and love them. I make money through advertising mostly, but also some affiliate programs and stuff like that. You know, I use so and so brand of spatula and get a kickback from it."

"Seems like a smart way to make more money. Is a food blog common?"

I tilted my head in thought. "They aren't uncommon, by any means. You can find them all over the internet, but not everyone makes a full-time income from them. It all depends on how determined you are and if having it be your job is something, you're even interested in to be honest." The waiter brought out caprese salad, not even once glancing in my direction.

I felt a growl threaten in my own chest, because it wasn't enough that Matteo acted like a wild animal, but apparently, I needed to as well. I picked up my fork and ignored Matteo's self-satisfied grin that he turned on the waiter. There was something so feral in it, I couldn't blame the poor guy when he scurried off in a hurry.

"Are you always so territorial over all your dates?" I asked, stabbing a piece of tomato and shoving it into my mouth without preamble. The light drizzle of balsamic over it burst on my tongue pleasantly.

"I don't date," he answered with an eyebrow raised. "I don't even bring women out in public, so it would be hard to be territorial. Aside from you, I can't think of a single woman that I would object to seeing her take another man to bed as soon as I finished with her." My mouth was only inches from my wine glass, but thankfully I hadn't taken that sip just yet.

I had a feeling I'd have spit it all over the table.

And my food. That would have been unforgivable.

"Well that's, um, interesting," I faltered. How did one respond to that kind of confession?

He chuckled at my discomfort, taking a sip of his own wine. Watching his throat work while he swallowed the liquid shouldn't have been an aphrodisiac. It appeared, that literally everything about Matteo screamed sex. It was most unfortunate. "I don't have any use for women in my life. I don't particularly enjoy conversing with them, and I most definitely don't enjoy the way they view me as a meal ticket."

"You just enjoy fucking them and then tossing them aside? I guess some things never change." I hissed the words, watching as Matteo's jaw clenched in fury.

"What I did to you is nothing like what I did to all the women who have filled the void in your absence. I know it will be difficult for you to believe, but I did what I had to do at the time. One day, perhaps you'll understand. But do not compare yourself to others. You're nothing like them."

I swallowed, running my tongue over my teeth after I set my fork down, having finished my caprese salad. "And how am I any different? Just because I was a virgin?"

"You're different because you mean something to me, because you meant everything to me." The waiter collected our plates, and I fixed my gaze on the glass of wine in front of me.

"If that were true—"

Matteo cut me off, grasping my hand in his. "Not tonight, Angel. Soon, but not tonight."

I nodded, drawing my hand back to my side of the table. Matteo allowed it, seeming no more interested in having a physical altercation than I was. It was unfortunate enough that the tenseness to our conversation wasn't missed by the people dining closest to us. "Donatello told me your father passed," I said to break the silence that started to spread. "I'm sorry."

"Don't be," he chuckled. "The world is better for my father being gone."

I swallowed, because that didn't bear good things for the kind of man Matteo had become, given that I knew even as a child he was groomed to take over his father's businesses. The Bellandi Corporation had been passed down through generations from what anyone could tell. "I'm kind of surprised you never ended up married to Shauna." I laughed, and a twisted sort of humor filled Matteo's face.

"What in the fuck would make you think I'd marry Shauna? She wasn't particularly the most pleasant to spend time with." He was right, even people who Shauna didn't torment knew she was catty and cruel—just as likely to stab you in the back as she was to smile to your face.

"She used to tell everyone you were engaged. That your families had arranged for the two of you to be married like we live in the dark ages. Uniting two proper Italian families," I cringed with a scoff.

Matteo swallowed, "Ah. Well that was true enough before you, but I refused and given Shauna's propensity for sleeping around it wasn't difficult to navigate my way out of it. Old Italian families like mine, things like that matter. There are unfortunately certain expectations for our women, and if those aren't met than negotiations become difficult." I stared at him, not completely comprehending. "Last I spoke to her father; she'd moved to New York to try and start fresh. I've no idea how that worked for her."

The waiter delivered our dinners, and I dug into my risotto with a slow, savoring bite. The creamy flavor practically melted on my tongue; the hint of cheese delectable. My eyes drifted closed on a moan. When they opened, it was to Matteo's darkened blue gaze on my face. I cleared my throat awkwardly, taking a sip of my wine to dispel some of the tension I felt. "The whole Italian thing is that important to your family? It just seems so...dated? People intermarry all the time."

"Not in families like mine. My father was unorthodox, taking my mother for a wife. I guess they felt like they needed to make up for that by ensuring I settled down with a good Italian woman." I cut through my stalk of asparagus, popping the bite into my mouth. It hurt to have it confirmed that he would always be destined for an Italian woman, because no matter what happened or didn't happen between us, Italian I was not.

"Your mother wasn't Italian?" I asked to dispel the awkwardness of what his confession did to me. I knew we wouldn't ever really be together, obviously I knew better than to have expectations or even hopes where Matteo was concerned, but to hear it so blatantly spelled out struck something in me down. I shoved it away. I could feel the hurt later, but in front of Matteo, I was determined to make him believe me unaffected.

I didn't want him.

Couldn't want him.

He shook his head, slicing a bite off his steak. He held out his fork, offering me a bite of the meat in the same way he always had back then. Ever the foodie, I always needed to try everything at the table. At least if I'd never had it. I shook my head, the smile on my face horrified. He leaned across the small, intimate table for two, and the forkful hovered just in front of my mouth. Knowing it would be a bigger scene than I felt like causing to continue to deny him, I had no choice but to open my mouth and accept the beef in. Matteo slid the fork inside, eyes fixated on the motion as my lips sealed around it and plucked it off the fork. I hummed my approval as the intense flavor coated my tongue, and I chewed.

After a moment's delay, he sat back in his chair and resumed eating. "My mother is Norwegian," he admitted. "She and my father had a fling when she was in the city for college. Brief, sex motivated. She got pregnant with me, so they had no choice but to get married really. Given my family's conservative values, there was no way to avoid it even with her heritage." That explained how Matteo had lighter hair than Lino, and I imagined the rest of his Italian family. "They hated each other. Spent most of my childhood fighting, until my mother decided she just didn't care. As soon as my father died, my mother left town and never looked back."

"She left you?" I whispered.

"We were never close, and she felt trapped in her marriage with my father. So once she was free, there was nothing keeping her here."

"Except for her son," I hissed as I finished my last bite of risotto.

"Not all women are meant to be mothers, my Angel. Neither of my parents were suited to the role. Thankfully, their hatred of one another kept them from repeating the mistake. Would you like dessert?"

I forced a smile for his sake, trying to rein in my hatred for him in the wake of his confessions. No wonder love was so foreign to Matteo. He'd never been loved in his life, never even seen it. I felt sorry for him, because I knew that no matter how much it had hurt, the love I'd experienced had been a bright light in my life. "No. As much as it pains me to admit, I couldn't eat another bite."

He laughed, requesting the check from the waiter and

turning the conversation to inquiries about Sadie and Duke even though I knew he didn't care what they were up to. He'd hardly tolerated either of them in high school when they were a necessary evil to being with me. Sadie was too nosy, too in my face and bubbly and demanding for Matteo's tastes, and Duke was a man. Even then, Matteo had always been possessive to the point of excess.

While we waited for the check, the stares he gave me were disquieting in intensity, as if something was coming and he was trying to get a read on my reaction.

I just hoped the thing that was coming was him dropping me off at home and never looking back.

It didn't seem likely.

※※※

We'd ridden back to my house in silence. Matteo's body vibrated with tension, whatever affected him so much at the end of our dinner still visibly pulsing through him. He didn't try to hold my hand in the car, but that could have also been because I sat on it. When he pulled into the driveway, I held out a hand for my keys. "Thank you for dinner," I said politely. "It was nice to catch up."

It was as clear a dismissal as I could manage without being outright suicidal with the man who looked ready to snap at any moment. He glanced at my hand with disgust in his eyes, shoving his car door open and stepping out.

As soon as he slammed it shut, I winced.

"Poop," I whispered to myself, watching as he prowled around the car. I hadn't paid enough attention to realize he'd shut the ignition off, but I figured that probably didn't bode well for me. Likely meant he didn't mean to just see me to my door. "Double poop scoops."

My door opened quickly, and I unbuckled myself and let him guide me out like the gentleman he liked to pretend to be. His hand took up residence at my back, guiding me up the steps to my house as the car door closed with a thud behind me.

My breathing was erratic, and I fought to control the rising panic.

He couldn't seriously think I would sleep with him.

Could he?

He dug my keys out of his pocket, and I let out a sigh of relief when his eyes met mine. They were more relaxed than I'd seen him all night, more at ease with whatever was going on in his head. I reached out to take them from him with a smile, my breath freezing in my lungs when he turned away and used them to unlock my door himself. When he pushed the door open lightly, he gestured me inside. Pausing in the threshold, I turned to say goodnight in one last bid to keep him outside my house. Outside my sanctuary where he didn't belong.

His eyes were soft when my gaze met his, soft and dark and full of the promise of all the things I believed the last time I'd let him have all of me. "Goodnight, Matteo," I whispered, putting a hand on the door and standing my ground.

"Aren't you going to let me in, *Cara mia*?" he asked, and his voice vibrated with something dark. Something dangerous. Something I didn't understand in the slightest but knew well enough to fear.

"No," I whispered, stepping back and slamming the door in his face. I gasped when his foot blocked it from closing and backed up as he prowled inside. He didn't turn to face it as he closed it gently behind him, stepping closer to me slowly. "Don't you dare touch me," I hissed, taking another step back. That *fucking* console table jabbed into my ass, and

I stumbled, glancing to the side and looking for a different escape route.

"Are you afraid of me, my Angel?" he asked as his body pressed tightly into mine. I whimpered, even through his suit I could feel every ridge of muscle packed onto his frame. He was a stranger to me; his body was nothing like the one I'd known once upon a time. "Because you should be."

"What do you want?" I whispered, hating how weak my voice sounded as I spoke.

"I'll never hurt you. Surely you know that." His voice cracked and his hand slid underneath the curtain of my hair to cup my face in his hand as he ran his thumb over my cheekbone. It was the same one Adrian had stroked, and I could practically feel him erasing the other man's touch with his own as possession glittered in his eyes. "I should walk away. Leave you to your life."

I swallowed, not having the guts to agree with him. As prepared for it as I was, as much as I knew it was the smartest outcome for me, the thought of watching him walk away from me like I didn't matter for a second time was devastating. His forehead hit mine, blue eyes staring into my soul from so close that I felt like he saw every crack—every hole I'd worked so hard to cover up over the years. No matter what a train wreck I knew whatever this thing with Matteo would be, I still couldn't look away. "I won't. This time around, I can keep you safe. I have to believe that," he whispered, but I got the distinct impression he was trying to convince himself of it more than me. "I'm not letting you go, Ivory. Do you understand what I'm saying?"

"No," I whispered honestly. Because I had a feeling that I really, truly, had absolutely no concept of whatever was happening. No control over it, not an ounce of real understanding.

"You will soon enough," he murmured, tilting his face until his lips pressed against mine softly and silenced my protest. Nothing but a light, teasing touch of his lips to mine, his gaze captivated mine even as heat flared through me from the smallest touch. He pulled away with a groan, his eyes closing and disconnecting me from that blue-eyed stare that threatened to steal away my sanity. His other hand came up to bury in my hair, tilting my face the way he wanted me. When I gasped, the pressure of his hand at my scalp and the sensation of him controlling me so thoroughly too much for me to handle, his lips crashed against mine.

There was no gentleness in that kiss, no trace of the man who'd softly memorized the feel of my lips on his from a moment ago.

All that remained was a dominating force. His hand where he cupped my cheek forced my mouth to open for him, and his tongue darted inside to tease mine. I whimpered, hoping the sound would alert him to the fact that he was taking too much, pushing too hard too soon.

Scaring me.

I was totally and completely trapped, surrounded by him. That was not something that I could handle. Not with him. Not with anyone.

My whimper seemed to fuel him on, his hand leaving my face to drift down my body in a slow, smooth caress that lit my nerve endings on fire. I'd thought they'd died a long time ago, but they flared to life with the subtlest touch from Matteo, even while I fought to maintain my sanity.

It was Matteo.

Not a stranger.

While I convinced myself of the fact that I was safe

enough and would walk away from whatever happened, Matteo groaned into my mouth. I realized at some point I'd started kissing him back. He pulled back enough to nibble at my bottom lip, and I moaned although I'd hated myself as soon as the sound left me. His hand slid around from my waist to my back, tugging me tighter to his body and then he slid it down and over my ass. My hips wiggled against him shamefully, and he squeezed the mound. Then he hoisted me up with one arm under my butt, setting me on the console table that I wasn't sure could support my weight.

His lips fused to mine again, expert strokes of his tongue against mine as he shoved my thighs apart and inserted his hips between them. With all of him pressed against me, it was impossible to miss the bulge in his pants as he ground it against me. His hands ran over the bare skin of my thighs as he shoved the dress up my legs and hooked his fingers into the waistband of my thong. When he moved to tug it down, I jerked back from him. My head smacked against the wall, but I didn't care as concern crossed his features. I shoved him away with two hands at his chest.

"Get off me," I protested, and his hands left my legs. His expression was torn as he stared at me, and I could see him trying to work out the kinks of how to get what he wanted. "You need to leave. Now." He stepped back just enough that I could hop off the table and shove my dress back down my thighs. "This isn't happening."

He sighed, running a hand through his hair before he nodded. "You're right. It's too soon." I knew my face must have morphed into one of shock. "I lost control. I miss you, Angel," he pressed one last soft kiss to the corner of my mouth, before turning and striding for the door. "I'll see you in the morning."

He opened the door, closing it behind him and was

gone. I hurried over to lock it, breathing a sigh of relief when there was something separating us. My back hit the door when I spun around and panted in a miniature panic attack.

Because what in the fuck was wrong with me?

9

IVORY

I woke up slowly, feeling so warm. Usually, I woke up cold. For years, I'd tossed and turned so much during the night that I would either wake up being suffocated by my blanket or freezing and the blanket on the floor. There was a definite weight pressing into me, but it was a comfortable one rather than the strangulation of being tangled in a comforter.

A sigh of contentment reached my ears, and I was still half-asleep enough that I had to consider if I'd been the one to make it. Snapping my eyes open suddenly, I panicked and tried to squirm out from whatever, *whoever,* laid on top of me.

In my bed.

When I'd most *definitely* gone to bed alone, after getting reacquainted with a certain battery-operated friend in my nightstand drawer.

"Angel, Angel," Matteo soothed me, holding me underneath him tighter as I struggled. I calmed minutely, freezing in place when I realized that my ass was rubbing against his groin, *his very hard* groin, in my inability to get out from under him. "Shh," he purred, taking my chin in his hand and turning my head back at an uncomfortable angle so he could see me. His lips came down on mine, soft and soothing even as my panic renewed.

"What are you doing in my bed?" I hissed, jerking away from his hold, and finally squirming out from under him. Judging from the position, he'd been lying on his stomach and covering my left side with his body, his leg cocked over both of mine.

"I don't like to wake up without you." He shrugged, watching me as I tugged the comforter up to cover my breasts. I wasn't naked, thankfully, but the tank and shorts I slept in with nothing underneath left absolutely nothing to the imagination.

"So you broke into my house and crawled into bed with me while I was sleeping?!"

He smirked at me, the fucking bastard. "Well, I couldn't very well climb in while you were awake, now could I?"

"You—I," I stumbled, lost for words. There was no remorse on his face, absolutely nothing to show he felt guilty for invading my privacy and doing god only knows what to my body while I slept. "You had no right."

"I have every right," he said, shocking me so much that my mouth snapped closed. "You're mine. You should get used to spending the nights together, Angel." My eyes drifted down to his chest, realizing he was shirtless for the first time once my panic had abated a bit. As much as he'd terrified me, as much as I wanted to hurt him for violating my bed, I didn't fear Matteo. I couldn't muster up any fear that he might hurt me physically, no matter how stupid that might have been. He'd always made me feel safe, like being within his arms was the *only* place in the world where nothing could hurt me.

My eyes didn't know where to settle as they darted around. His shoulders were broad, sculpted with biceps that must have been as thick as my thigh. His pecs were perfectly formed, and even sitting the muscles of an impossibly defined eight pack stood out and tempted me to lick every ridge. The tattoo on his chest caught my eye, a quote I recognized from Aristotle referencing the night following the light of day. When my eyes darted back up to his face, I knew he hadn't missed my reaction to seeing him. He stood from the bed, revealing thick thighs corded in muscle. Only a pair of black boxer briefs covered him, and they barely contained the *fucking anaconda* of an erection I remembered all too well. I swallowed with nerves as he leaned over me in the bed.

His face gentled, and he cupped my jaw and stared down at me in that intense way of his. "This is happening, Angel." His lips touched mine briefly, and then he turned and swaggered his way into my en suite bathroom.

I sat there, disoriented and freaking out for a minute. When the shower started up, I was up and fleeing my bedroom in case he decided he wanted company. I didn't dare change my clothes for fear of the creep appearing the moment I was naked, so I snagged my huge, baggy sweater that I curled up in when I read. Shoving my arms in, I fled down the stairs, only coming to a halt when I found two men sitting and drinking coffee at the island. I stumbled back a step, preparing to flee out the front door when they spun and saw me standing there.

"Miss Torres," one said, setting his mug down. "Is everything all right?" I stared at him, slight relief crashing through me when I realized he was the man Matteo had said was his security the night before. He stood, approaching me like I was a wounded animal. "Has something happened to Mr. Bellandi?" he asked, and I shook my head frantically.

"In the shower," I mumbled, not acknowledging his other question. What kind of question was that, anyway? How could things be all right with three men I didn't know in my home? I glanced down at my mostly bare legs, feeling suddenly exposed, but neither man's gaze ever drifted away from my face. "What are you doing in my house?"

The man tilted his head, a small smile crossing over his features as he shook his head. "I go where Matteo goes, ma'am. We weren't introduced last night. I'm Simon, Matteo's head of security."

"Okay, so you're his security. Ignoring the fact that you both *broke into my house,*" I paused to roll my eyes, ignoring the chuckle from both men. "Then who is he?" I gestured to the other man who sat at the island, dutifully drinking his coffee.

"That's Paolo. We call him Scar," Simon said with a polite smile. "He goes where you go." I blinked, stepping back from both men in favor of getting to my front door.

I was in way over my head.

I snatched my keys off the console, striding for the front door with another shake of my head. "Miss Torres?" Simon called, and something in his voice made me turn back to glance at him the moment my hand hit the doorknob. "It won't do you any good."

"What?" I whispered.

"Running. It won't matter. He'll never stop. Do yourself a favor, and just settle into your new life instead of fighting it, yeah?" My blood chilled at his words, and panic flooded my veins.

"Ah, you're scaring my Angel I see," Matteo said from the top of the stairs. His legs made quick work of hurrying down them to meet me at the foot of the stairs. Touching his lips to my cheek briefly, he kissed me goodbye like a husband leaving for work. As if our relationship was normal, and he hadn't broken into my home while I slept. I turned to face him, and I knew he could see the apprehension in my face. "Don't worry, Simon and I are leaving. I have business to see to." I breathed out a sigh of relief. "Try not to give Scar too much shit, okay?"

"You can't be serious!" I protested. "I'm not letting you put some babysitter on me."

"Bodyguard," Matteo corrected in a deep voice that left no room for argument. "Scar, why don't you take up position outside for the time being? I don't think Ivory is ready to have a house guest just now."

"Yes, boss," Scar grunted, chugging the rest of his coffee and sliding past me to get to the front door quickly.

"Is he just going to stand out there all day?"

"He'll do perimeter checks periodically. Aside from that he has the SUV." I hesitated, feeling horrible that the man would have to just sit out there, but steeled myself against the feeling. I wouldn't let an intruder remain in my home just because it was less comfortable outside.

"See you later, Angel," Matteo said, pressing a quick kiss to my unmoving lips and then he and Simon were gone without another word. Matteo's Aston Martin and what I presumed was Simon's SUV backed out of the driveway, and Scar's voice reached me from the remaining SUV when he rolled the window down.

"Go back inside, Miss Torres," he said, his voice void of

any form of inflection. I nodded, stepping back into my house. I went for my phone.

I needed Sadie.

※※※

Sadie sat at my island again, her customary place. Having had the two unfamiliar asses perched in the seats that my two best friends had claimed so long ago sent another pang of discomfort through me. She was far too quiet, though it was probably to be expected. She hadn't gotten the full story yet, only as far as the fact that I had in fact gone on the date.

She didn't know that I'd woken up to Matteo mostly naked in my bed.

Or that he'd invited two strangers into my home, because he had no boundaries when it came to me or my privacy.

I nabbed the onion from my drawer, setting it down on the cutting board a little too forcefully. "What are you making now?" Sadie asked, and I didn't miss the suspicion in her voice.

"Spring risotto," I said. "The recipe was fantastic, and I want to see if I can replicate it while it's still fresh, you know?"

My front door opened, and Duke's face filled my vision when he crowded into my space quickly. He took my face in his hands, his eyes boring into mine, and then they darted to glance all over my face as if he'd be able to see trauma. "I told you. I'm fine," I hissed.

"You also told me you wouldn't go on the date," he accused, and I winced.

"I didn't have much choice." My voice was a weak whisper. I so didn't want Duke to be present for the conversation I needed to have with Sadie. He would lose his mind.

"What does that mean? And what's with the beefcake screening your visitors? Christ, Ivory," he turned, plopping into his customary bar stool.

"He's her security, apparently," Sadie said, sipping her green smoothie through her straw.

"What the fuck? Why do you need security?"

"That's a really good question," Sadie concurred, and I knew I would not get out of admitting the entire story. Not now that I'd started.

"Can we just talk about this later?" I asked Sadie pointedly as I finished chopping my onion.

"Nope, not happening, Ive." Duke crossed his arms over his chest. I fished my pan out, slipping butter in and hanging my head once the heat was on.

"There was a slight incident at the restaurant," I admitted. "One of Matteo's business rivals became interested in me, cornered me in the bathroom. Matteo seems to think he's dangerous, so for the time being I'm stuck with Scar."

"Shit," Sadie muttered, and I watched as Duke's eyes flared. He stood from the stool, striding around the island to turn off the heat on my stove.

"Pack your shit, Ive."

"Duke-" I protested. We'd been here before.

"No, I let you try it your way. Do you see how well that worked out?" He pointed outside, where I could practically feel Scar watching our interactions through the mirror.

"I can't."

"Do not tell me you're getting sucked into his web again!" Sadie jumped up, hands on her hips. "Do you remember what happened last time? You were so happy with him, and fell so hard, and he *crushed* you!"

"I'm not!" I ran my hands over my face. "I just, I don't think it will matter if I'm here or at your house. You don't know the full story yet." I knew my grimace was visible and watched as Duke's face morphed in anger.

"What, Ivory?" Sadie's voice gentled, seeming to realize I was balancing delicately on the edge of sanity.

"He was here this morning when I woke up," I whispered.

"The goon? I figured he turned up at some point, since he's outside now," Duke said, and I turned wide eyes his way.

"No. Not Scar, I mean him too." I sighed, even I knew I was doing a shit job of explaining a shitty situation. "Matteo."

"What did he want? Introduce Scar?" Sadie asked, and I knew she was as confused as Duke looked.

"Matteo was in bed with me when I woke up," I spat out.

"You slept with him?" Sadie hissed, looking at me like I'd lost my mind.

"No! I went to bed alone," I explained. "He—I think he picked the locks. Crawled into bed with me while I was sleeping. Scar and Matteo's security guy were down here when I tried to leave. They told me it would be pointless to run. That he would never stop," I gasped, feeling the weight of their stares on me.

"Holy shit," Sadie whispered and her brow furrowed.

"Duke?" I asked, watching as his face hardened to a point I'd never seen before.

"He was in your bed with you? After he broke in?" I nodded, feeling tears pool in my eyes when he turned and strode out of my house without another word.

"Duke!" I yelled, chasing after him.

Sadie grabbed my arm, stopping me from following him

out the door. "Let him go. He needs to cool off, think things through. You know how protective he is of you."

I nodded, feeling like I'd fucked up again.

I shouldn't have told them.

"What are you going to do?" she asked.

"I don't know, Sadie. This time I really don't know."

10

MATTEO

I couldn't wait to get back to Ivory, but the life I lived stopped for no one. Taking a day off to spend with my angel just wasn't possible, especially not with Adrian sniffing around her like a rabid dog. Donatello poked his head in my office while Lino and I were going over some upgrades to one of the apartment buildings I owned within the city. "Paolo called. Mr. Bradley has left Miss Torres' home. In a fit, evidently."

I smirked. "I can't imagine he's pleased to know I'm back in her life."

Lino outright laughed. "Safe bet there. Wonder if he ever tapped that," he mused, and I leveled him with a glare. A lesser man would have cowered, but my beloved cousin only laughed in the face of what was a very real danger to his life. "When do I get to see her again? Is she still as hot as she was in high school?"

Donatello stepped between us, likely saving Lino from very serious pain. "She will be my wife. You will not speak of her in that way again."

Lino's eyes widened, and he barked out a laugh. "Holy

shit. Didn't realize you were *quite* that serious about it, man. I just enjoy pushing your buttons."

"I think I'd like to break your pretty fucking face," I growled.

"I would advise saving that anger for people who want to harm Ivory," Donatello inserted, distracting me from turning Lino's face into a bag of meat. "With Ricci's interest, a message needs to be sent about what happens to people who cross the line with her. It's your best chance of keeping her safe if you truly intend to install her at your side permanently."

I picked up the paperweight from my desk, the one fairly personal touch I allowed in a room that saw crime daily. The sea green globe reminded me of Ivory's eyes and had become a fixture in my life soon after I'd walked away from her. "Well, Ryker got a lock on the guys who robbed the bank. He's waiting for you if you'd like to convey a message," Lino said with a smug look. The bastard had been sitting on that information, withholding it from me the entire time he sat in my office, and we discussed apartment building renovations like I gave a shit about the specifics.

"Call him. Now. Tell him to grab them and meet me at the warehouse," I ordered, already striding out of the office. I grabbed my phone out of my pocket, dialing Ivory's number. I'd programmed mine into her phone when I'd snuck into her bedroom the night before, so her voice was predictably guarded when she answered.

"Of course, you went through my phone. Leaving no stone unturned when it comes to invading my privacy, huh?" I smiled, loving even that bit of fight and sass she had that hadn't been there before. I'd loved her innocent, but the slightly harder woman she'd become would be better prepared to live a life at my side.

"I'm taking you out tonight. I'll be at your place at six." She started to protest, but it fell on deaf ears when I hung up the phone with a grin.

My little angel was about to be mine again, in every sense of the word.

And she had no idea.

***

It was a struggle to wipe the smile off my face when I made it to the warehouse. The warehouse was located inside my territory, a necessary evil when you wanted to be sure no innocent bystanders heard victims scream. Riverdale was one of the worst areas of Chicago, and it was a very rare occasion that someone was foolhardy enough to play the good Samaritan in that area. Regardless, the abandoned building wasn't welcoming in the slightest, but the locked room that had once served as a freezer was fantastic for ensuring nobody ever stumbled across someone I needed to keep around for a while.

I should have been surprised to see Ryker's van parked in the back.

I wasn't.

As soon as the man found them, I had little doubt he'd set things in motion to get them here. He was efficient, his obsessive tendencies required nothing less. But there was nothing he hated more than an innocent woman getting wrapped up in a dangerous situation that she had nothing to do with. Even if I hadn't demanded blood because they'd put a gun in my woman's face, Ryker would have.

He had strange values, considering he was my most violent enforcer and nothing fazed the man. I'd seen him do some fucked up shit and never blink. But he didn't do women or kids.

Said that was the one thing his woman could never forgive. Not that he had a woman, or at least, not one who was aware he'd claimed her, since she was already married to another man.

I shook my head, because obsessive didn't cover it.

The man was a stalker.

I knocked on the steel, exterior door, and Ryker opened it up quickly. "Took you long enough," he grunted, turning and striding away. I turned the deadbolt, locking out any trespassers.

"I was on my way when Lino called," I snorted, and he leveled me with a dark grin.

"I may have already had them in my van." He shrugged his nonchalance, but it was fake. His steel-blue eyes glittered with excitement.

There was a reason the man was my best enforcer. Violence simmered in his blood, an unending rage that never seemed to quiet. I'd never asked where it came from. Even I didn't dare. Ryker was not the man you asked questions about himself. He was loyal, friendly with me and my other guys, but his life started when he joined up. He didn't have a past, was a ghost before he came to me.

That was something I understood.

So we didn't push. People who did ended up dead.

"How many?" I asked. I hadn't been able to ask Ivory exactly how many men had thought to rob the bank. I'd been flooded with too many emotions after over a decade of feeling nothing—suddenly overwhelmed by rage and fear and relief and real lust.

"Four. From what I can tell, three were inside and one

was the getaway driver. He never even laid eyes on your girl. Should we let him live?"

I hummed. "We'll see how I feel in the moment." Ryker smirked, and I knew he was relishing the fact that for once, I would enjoy the violence I took part in. Too often I was just a cold spectator, rarely getting involved myself unless I needed to send a very serious message.

Not this time. Not when it came to my Angel.

When he opened the door to the freezer, I let my face slide into that cold mask that the rest of the world knew. "Mr. Bellandi!" One man started in as soon as I filled the room with my presence. Ryker stepped off to the side, leaning against his table where he kept his tools. His ass hit it, and he grabbed one of his picks that he normally used to insert under fingernails. The crazy fuck set to cleaning out under his own nails with it, and if I'd been in any situation where I could have, I'd have laughed my ass off at the horrified look one of the more bloodied men shot his way. "We didn't touch her. I swear!" the man blubbered on.

"Yeah? Tell me how it went down," I challenged, crossing my arms over my chest and staring down the four men strapped down to wooden chairs that Ryker would throw in the incinerator after he finished up. I listened to the most bloodied man rattle on through his story, admitting that he'd pointed his gun at Ivory, but realized who she was as soon as he got close enough. Every muscle I had tensed, picturing what her terror must have looked like as she stared down the barrel of a gun for wanting to help an old lady. I could imagine the slime ball in front of me probably had filthy thoughts while he stared at her. Knowing the way Ivory seemed to draw people into her orbit, had there been need of a hostage, they'd have taken her.

My Angel.

Visions of her broken and bleeding body flashed in front of my eyes, and I reached behind my back to grab the handgun I'd tucked in there before leaving the estate. As soon as I held it in front of me, flicking off the safety, the man began to tremble. "Please, please no." I stepped forward, pressing the gun against his forehead. The stench of urine struck me, his pants wet as terror undoubtedly took over.

"You scared my woman. Can you imagine how she must have felt now?" My voice sounded colder than normal, even for me.

"Yes! Yes, she must have been terrified," he blubbered.

"And yet, she didn't piss herself. One Hell of a woman, if you ask me," Ryker chimed in from the sidelines, watching with interest.

I smirked at him, silently confirming everything he suspected of Ivory. He'd meet her for himself soon enough, and it filled me with pride to know that my friends, my men, would lay down their lives to keep her safe. I'd come a long way from the scrawny little boy who'd had to leave her for her own good.

I'd burn the world down if it meant she was safe.

I pulled the gun away from his face, watching as it morphed with relief. I fired a shot into his thigh, relishing in the way he screamed out his pain. Blood welled from the wound, turning his jeans an even darker hue. "You shot him!" One other protested. "You fucking shot him." I nodded to Ryker, who set down his tool and joined me as I shoved the gun back into my pants after hitching the safety on. Stripping off my suit jacket, I tossed it over the back of one of the spare chairs we kept in the corner. I undid my cufflinks, rolling up my shirt sleeves. Couldn't get them bloody before my date.

My fist connected with the nose of the man who seemed to think a gunshot wound to the thigh was the end of the world. The sound of a nose crunching beside me meant Ryker had taken to giving the men a stern reminder of exactly who I was.

Who Ivory was by association.

"I'm feeling generous," I announced. "You get to live." I struck again, hitting the soft flesh of the man's belly. He groaned his pain, and I glanced out the side of my eye to see the man I'd shot panting so hard he steadily approached unconsciousness. "The only reason you're not dead is because you brought her back to me. I'm feeling thankful for that."

"Yes, Sir," the smartest one grunted, taking Ryker's next punch like a pro. We set to giving them a reminder they would never forget.

No one touched Ivory. No one looked at her wrong.

Or they'd end up dead.

Or beaten to shit at the very least.

11

IVORY

My phone rang on the counter, and I jumped so hard I nearly sliced my finger off while chopping chives. That stupid man had me afraid of my shadow.

I wiped my hands off quickly, swiping the screen to connect the call even though I was really, really tempted to ignore it. "Hello?"

"Hey, Angel," Matteo's gruff voice said over the line. "I'm on my way to you."

I sighed, rubbing my temple in frustration. "I'm working. I can't go out tonight."

"I have a feeling you'll be trying that excuse often. What are you making?" I shoved down the twinge of excitement at the prospect of Matteo eating my food. I loved feeding people, to where I preferred cooking for dates and boyfriends rather than having sex with them. At least I knew I was good at cooking.

"Prime rib," I said hesitantly, glancing at the oven and roast that would be ready to pull out within a few minutes.

"What a coincidence," he said, and I could hear the

smirk in his voice. "I love prime rib, and I can't imagine you'll eat it all yourself."

"I was planning on bringing some to Duke. His muse has been insane lately, and he forgets to eat if I don't feed him," I responded, wincing when Matteo's snort sounded over the phone.

"I'll just bet he does," he said mysteriously. "I'll be there in fifteen."

"Matteo!" I called out, hissing out an annoyed breath when he hung up on me again. I glanced over at my camera sitting on the dining room table, asking myself why I'd bothered with putting off cooking until so late that my pictures would suck.

Oh, right. I'd wanted the excuse to not go out with Matteo.

The timer went off, and I grabbed my oven mitts to pull the prime rib out of the oven. The wire rack over the pan served as an effective cooling rack, and I transferred it to set over a cutting board so I could use the drippings to make my au jus.

With that finished, I snapped my photos of all the completed components before I sliced into the prime rib and prepped up three plates. One I popped into the fridge for Duke, knowing I'd shoot him a text that it was waiting for him if he got hungry. I'd just finished wrapping up Duke's plate when my front door opened, and I spun around quickly.

"I locked that for a reason," I pointed out, staring at Matteo's stunning face as he stripped off his suit jacket while he prowled toward me. He tossed his jacket, so it landed on one of the stools at the island, stepping into my space until his torso pressed into my chest. I gritted my teeth, staring at the spot where his white dress shirt was open at the top. Even all wrapped up in a fine suit and with the potential to be a gentleman, Matteo somehow managed a small rebellion from the norm that hinted at just how ungentlemanly he could be. The lightest dusting of hair peeked out from the bottom of the opening in his shirt, yet another reminder that the boy was gone. Replaced by a beast of a man who was nothing but bad for me. His hand reached out, running a thumb over my bottom lip as he tilted my face up to his. Soft, coaxing lips touched mine, and I had to fixate on remaining still. I wouldn't make the same mistake I'd made the night before, wouldn't kiss the devil in front of me.

He pulled back, an evil knowing in his eyes as he stared down at me. He knew exactly what game I was playing, that my lack of reception to his kiss had nothing to do with being unaffected and everything to do with trying to prevent myself from falling under his spell. "I told you, you need an alarm system." He took my hand, guiding me over to the breakfast nook where I'd set the plates and put out a bottle of Cabernet Sauvignon. I knew it wouldn't be up to Matteo's standards, but I wouldn't have bothered if I'd been able to stomach not having wine with prime rib. I didn't want him to read into it, but Cabernet was just perfect. He put me in a seat, somehow knowing it was the seat I always sat in, with my back to the windows so I could see my kitchen—my inspiration. He took his own seat, pouring the wine into our glasses without commenting on the wine itself.

"Would an alarm system keep you out?" I asked after the silence grew too large for my tastes.

"What do you think?" He grinned, a flash of teeth that spoke to just how animalistic the man was.

I sighed, rolling my eyes to the ceiling. "Then what

exactly is the point in having one? If it doesn't keep intruders out of my home?"

"I'm not an intruder, Angel. Soon enough, you'll welcome me into your home and bed. We both know these little games will be futile." He picked up his fork and knife, slicing through the prime rib that melted like butter in his hands.

I couldn't blame it.

Popping the meat into his mouth, he paused, chewing thoughtfully before emitting a deep moan of satisfaction that made me press my thighs together. "That's fucking incredible."

I shrugged, picking up my glass and sipping at my wine. "It's just prime rib."

And it was. Just great prime rib.

"You're gifted. Truly." Matteo's voice was astonished, as if he was seeing something about me for the first time. It suddenly felt too intimate, which was ridiculous. My cooking was far from a secret. Thousands of people read my blog every day, but something about Matteo had always seen beneath the surface to every facet of my being.

"Why are you doing this? Forcing your way into my life? Surely, there must be other women who could satisfy whatever need it is you think I'll meet—"

His fork dropped to the plate, and he stared at me until I fell silent under the force of that glare. "I am doing this," he paused, heaving a deep sigh. "Because you are mine. It's as simple as that."

"I haven't been yours for a long time, Teo," I protested, wincing at the way the name I'd once called him felt as it left my lips.

"You've always been mine, *Cara mia*. Even when we couldn't be together." He said it like it was so obvious. But the reality was he had spent over a decade fucking other women and leaving me to be with other men. That was not the man I wanted to belong to.

"I'm not interested in whatever weird kind of relationship you think it is we have. An open relationship? Something where you come back whenever you feel like it? Neither of those scenarios appeal to me, Matteo. I'm sure there are plenty of women content with what you're offering, and there's nothing wrong with that if it works for you. But I'm not that girl." I gave him a sad smile, setting down my silverware. I was finished—eating, playing his games, all of it. "I believe you know where the door is." He took another bite of his prime rib, defying me and my wishes to the last. When he'd finished his plate, he stood, watching me as I finished cleaning up my kitchen. It was an obsessive thing, always needing to clean the space down after every use. He glanced at my sage off-shoulder maxi dress, and his eyes tracked down to take in the nude heeled boots on my feet.

"You're comfortable in those?" he asked, and I furrowed my brow in confusion.

"Yes, though I'll take them off as soon as you leave." He knelt at my feet in front of me, shoving my dress up enough to inspect the shoes. I nearly lost my balance when he took one foot in his hands, twisting it gently to inspect the heel.

"They'll do. Let's go." Scooping up his jacket, he shrugged it back onto his shoulders but left the front unbuttoned. Like a crazy, elegant rebel.

"I'm not going anywhere," I protested. He seemed to consider his options and then nodded as if he was conceding defeat. With a heaving sigh of relief, I flinched when he stood directly in front of me and his hands grasped my hips in his hands. After he truly settled there, he lifted and heaved me up onto his shoulder. I grunted, smacking his back in struggles that went ignored as he turned and walked toward my entryway. He turned off the lights as he went, grabbing my keys off my console table and making for the door. "Matteo!" I shrieked. "Put me down!" Stepping out on to the front porch, he didn't seem to care that we must have been attracting attention from my neighbors—that they would likely call the police to report an abduction. "I need my phone at least. My purse." He swatted me on the ass with a resounding thump. It wasn't painful in the slightest, not through the combined fabric of my underwear and my dress, but the principle of it was shocking, regardless.

"Don't need them," he grunted, sealing my door shut with my own keys. When he turned and strode for the Aston Martin, I increased my struggles.

"Stop! Let me go! The neighbors will call the police, you know."

Matteo chuckled, turning me around so suddenly I felt dizzy. "You calling the cops?" he asked, and I had to wonder which neighbor he was harassing.

"No, Sir. Wouldn't dream of it, Mr. Bellandi. I didn't see nothing," my friendly, older neighbor Mike said, and his front door closed with a thud.

Traitor.

I imagined him retreating inside it, leaving me to the mercy of a man that he feared himself.

"Matteo, please," I begged as he pried open the passenger door.

"Get in the fucking car, Ivory," he ordered, setting me to my feet next to it. I nodded my submission, sensing something different playing beneath the surface of Matteo's sanity in that moment. Something had put him over the edge, and I suspected that it was me.

The only real question was what would he do about it?

I sat and pivoted my legs into the car, flinching when the door slammed closed. I had the brains to realize opening that door would likely be a very poor decision, so I sat with my hands in my lap. Matteo was in the driver's seat only a moment later, reaching across the center compartment to lean into my space and buckle me in himself. With a purr the engine started, and he pulled out of my driveway too fast for my liking. I gripped the seat next to my legs, trying to control my panic. "Matteo—"

"If you *ever* let another man *touch* you, I'll kill him," he snarled, his voice so menacing I froze in horror. That voice left little doubt to the fact that he meant every word, summoned straight from the pits of Hell. "We are not in an open relationship. No one touches you. No one touches me. It is you and I from here on out. Am I understood?"

I nodded, staring at my legs as he spoke.

"The words, Ivory. I need the words."

"Yes, Matteo. I understand," I whispered, fighting the urge to cry. I wouldn't let him know how much he'd frightened me. I may not have been the strongest of women, may not have been perfect, but I would be damned if I showed him my weakness. I'd survived him once, and I would do it again, but the second time around I would prove I could do it without letting my heart get involved in whatever twisted games he wanted to play.

He fell silent, driving us through the city, as I tried to reinforce my resolve.

Because I couldn't let him break me.

Not a second time.

I don't know where I expected a man like Matteo to take me on a date. Somewhere exclusive. Somewhere classy.

I never would have guessed he'd bring me to Millennium Park. We pulled up onto the side of the road, and Matteo was out quickly and approaching the three men standing on the curb and waiting for us. I recognized Simon and Scar immediately, but the other man beside them was a stranger to me. Matteo tossed the stranger his keys, and I couldn't hear the words that the two of them exchanged from my place inside the vehicle. Matteo strode over to my door, tugging it open with a smooth elegance that spoke to his proper upbringing. He gave me his hand and pulled me free from the car with less patience.

I officially ranked lower than the car in that moment. He guided me down the sidewalk and into the park with his hand at the small of my back. The Aston started up behind us, the strange man whisking it away to park it somewhere safely no doubt. As we made our way in silence, Matteo's expression was steely every time I glanced at him out of the corner of my eye. Shivering in the cold, I tried to discreetly cross my arms over my chest and rub some warmth into my mostly bare arms.

"Here, Miss Torres," Scar said from behind us. He shrugged out of his suit jacket, holding it out for me. My lips tipped in a sheepish smile, turning and reaching out a hand to take it.

"No," Matteo said from my side, shaking his head at Scar, who nodded and slid his arms back into the sleeves. Matteo stripped out of his own, draping it over my shoulders until I was suddenly cocooned in his scent—enveloped in the warmth from his body. I shuddered as his hands rubbed up and down my arms now covered in his jacket, releasing a sigh when his lips hit the top of my head. I could only hope that the cruel, dangerous Matteo had vacated his body in favor of the version of him I could handle.

Somewhat.

We resumed walking, picking up a brisk pace after Matteo glanced at his watch. A huge crowd had already formed, but Matteo and his guys made quick work of maneuvering us through it to get to the center near the back where the more relaxed listeners sat in lawn chairs compared to the ones who waited next to the stage. I was grateful for the width of the heel on my boots, and I realized with a start that was what Matteo had inspected back at my house. He'd been checking my ability to walk on grass. It was an oddly considerate, intimate, thing for him to have considered, particularly coming from the man who claimed he didn't even take women to dinner.

He guided me to a huge blanket on the ground, where another man in a suit stood guard. Matteo sat on the blanket, looking altogether unreal. Wearing an expensive Italian suit, handsome beyond belief, he emitted raw power even sitting on a blanket in the park. I sat down next to him, curling my legs to the side. Matteo's security moved behind us, remaining standing, and I tried to ignore them. They gave us enough distance that I knew they wouldn't be eavesdropping or anything of the sort, but it still somehow felt intrusive. Like their presence was just different from the hundreds of people around us.

I was distracted from the awkwardness when a song I recognized well started from the stage. The artist's voice rang loud and clear, and the listeners silenced immediately as my favorite indie musician played one of his first hits. I swallowed back my growing apprehension that Matteo seemed to know so much about me, because there was absolutely no chance that it was a coincidence. We sat in silence, listening to the artist sing about a woman who needed someone to lean on, about a woman who had gone through life alone for too long. I could feel Matteo's eyes on the side of my face, but I refused to look at him. He sighed, repositioning my body until I fell onto my back. My head landed on his thigh, and his fingers took to stroking my hair. Tilting my head away from him, I looked toward the stage. We were far away enough that I couldn't see much beyond the more avid fans who stood close to the stage, but it was better than acknowledging Matteo. His attentiveness in combination with the lyrics of the artist's songs was too much, it made the situation feel like a critical moment in my life.

A crossroad.

My heart pumped in my chest, despite what should have been nothing but calming. "You can trust me," he whispered. I huffed a laugh, resuming my determination to ignore him after the minor slip up. "I know things didn't end well before. There are things you don't know. Things you *can't* know just yet. I did what I had to do for your sake, Ivory, but leaving you was the hardest thing I've ever done. It broke something inside me, and if you haven't figured it out yet, that boy you loved no longer exists."

"I'll bet. You sure looked broken when you went off to fuck Shauna," I hissed.

He winced, looking ashamed for the first time I think I'd ever seen. Even in high school, Matteo had been unapologetic for his behavior, taking what he wanted when he wanted it. The boy who never heard the word no, the boy who had the world waiting in the palm of his hand if he so much as said the words. "I needed you to hate me," he whispered brokenly, and my head turned to face him and meet his eyes.

"You succeeded," I whispered back. "I've never hated anyone as much as I hate you."

His hand cupped my cheek as he stared down at me, a thumb trailing over the freckles on my cheek he'd once found so fascinating. "I'll fix it. I promise."

"No one can fix this, Teo," I murmured, hating how pathetic my voice sounded.

How broken.

"Just watch me," he challenged. I shook my head, returning to silence to listen to the music for the rest of the concert. I let it seep into my bones, remind me of what it felt like to be alone. I'd lived alone for so long, the prospect of not having to be for once appealed in a way I never expected.

I was so lonely that even a man I hated seemed like a decent option to cuddle me while I slept. To hold me still while I battled in my dreams. I determined that as soon as Matteo left me, and I knew he would eventually, I would stop looking for perfect.

Perfect didn't exist.

All that mattered was that I found someone who loved me.

Someone who held me.

Someone who knew me, because he asked me questions.

Safe. Content. That was what I needed.

Not a stalker who broke into my home and knew things about me that he shouldn't have known.

✻✻✻

My eyes were droopy, taking me back to the days of my childhood where I could not be a passenger in a car at night and stay awake. It just didn't happen. "Where are we going?" I asked, staring out the window as Matteo turned in the opposite direction of my house.

"Home," he answered evasively, his hand clenching the steering wheel tighter as he shifted gears and merged into traffic on I-90.

"My house is in the opposite direction, Matteo. Take me home," I protested, glancing over at the side of his face where his features glittered like the hardest granite. My eyes snapped wide open as unease became very real.

"My bed is bigger."

"I didn't invite you to join me in mine," I hissed, shaking my head in disbelief. I wanted to call for help, wanted to call Duke or Sadie to come pick me up.

But I didn't have my phone.

"I don't even have my purse, or my phone Matteo. I need those things. Please take me home," I begged. He grunted, pressing a button on the steering wheel.

"Boss?" Simon's voice came over the speaker.

"After we're safely in the estate, I need you or Scar to go to Ivory's. Get her phone off the kitchen counter and her purse. Bring them to the house." He glanced over at me, his eyes glittering in the light coming off the dashboard given how dark it was outside. "And a change of clothes for her to wear home tomorrow."

"Anything else?"

"That's all." The line disconnected, and I stared at him in disbelief.

"You can't just tell me I'm staying the night! I have the right to say no." My face twisted when he turned hardened eyes to me.

"We're done with these games. It's time for you to accept that I am not going anywhere, Angel." His voice softened, as if realizing just how much he was asking of me. "I want to move forward with the rest of our lives."

"And you just don't give a shit about what I want? That's promising for our future," I spat, and watched as his jaw clenched. I shut up, feeling like I'd done nothing but test Matteo's limits all night. He was angry with me, frustrated, and I truly didn't know the man well enough to know if that was just bad or if it was terrible for me.

The boy I'd loved never would have hurt me, but he was gone. A lie that had never really existed, one that Matteo admitted was gone forever.

I didn't speak until we pulled up to the gates of the Estate, the guard nodding to Matteo wordlessly before he opened it. Matteo drove in, and when I turned back to see the gates closing a feeling of hopelessness settled inside me. There'd be no escaping his fortress unless he wanted me to. We both knew that. "Matteo," I whispered.

"Quiet, Angel," his voice was low, a barely there whisper that increased my anxiety. Men like Matteo didn't need to yell to be terrifying. They could convey their dissatisfaction without a word, by just existing. He pulled the car to a stop quickly, hopping out and pulling me from my seat.

Donatello stepped out the front door. "Mr. Bellandi. Ms.Torres. Welcome home."

I resisted the urge to point out that it wasn't my home. That it never would be, and Matteo spared me from having to respond when he answered. "We're not to be disturbed. When Simon or Scar return with her things, put them in my office please."

"Certainly," Donatello nodded, watching with wide eyes as Matteo took my hand and pulled me into the house. We traipsed over the tile floors, and he pulled me up the winding stairs. I had to fight not to trip, my dress too long and my boots not prepared for the speed with which Matteo took the stairs. He didn't let me take in the landing at the top of the stairs, just turned down one of two hallways and led me all the way to the end.

The master bedroom was a very different style than the rest of the house. Modern, clean lines done in a combination of dark grey and tan, I had to wonder what prompted the difference between that room and the rest of the house.

"I never bothered remodeling the rest of the house," he answered my silent question. "But this room I did as soon as I moved back in after my father died."

"It's lovely." I shifted awkwardly, doing my best not to glance at the massive platform bed on the back wall.

"Get ready for bed." He jerked his head to a door to the bathroom behind me. I took it as my reprieve, retreating into the space and locking the door behind me. It was a continuation from the bedroom, white and grey marble with tan elements through the space. A huge deep soak tub, and a massive shower made for orgies dominated the space, but a massive two sink vanity caught my eye. I stepped in front of the mirror, trying not to think about how many women Matteo had caught in his web in that bathroom. I washed the makeup off my face, attempting to calm my raging heart and convince my eyeballs to remain in my skull, given they looked wide enough they might bolt at any moment.

I could do it. I had slept in a bed with Matteo the night before, unknowingly, but I'd survived. The next morning he'd take me home, and I'd get the fuck out of dodge. It was only one night. I stripped off my socks and shoes, stacking them in the corner.

A brand-new toothbrush in its packaging sat on the counter, and I used it all while wanting to keep my bad breath to spite him. When I went back to the bedroom, after hyperventilating for a few moments, Matteo stood next to the bed. His back was to me, and he stared out the window sipping a scotch. His suit was draped over one of the armchairs in the room, all his beautiful olive skin on display and only his ass covered by his skintight boxer briefs.

He turned, setting his tumbler on a coaster on the little table in the seating area. I took a step back as he prowled toward me, flinching when he only reached out a hand to clasp a strand of my hair. "You expect me to believe you sleep in your dress?"

"I don't have any clothes." I swallowed.

"That's because you won't be needing them until morning," he murmured, pressing his lips to mine briefly. "Take off your dress."

"No. I don't want this, Teo. I don't want you—"

"Ah, *Cara mia*, you always were a terrible liar," he chuckled.

"I'm not lying! This isn't—" I broke off, gasping when he leaned forward and pressed his lips behind my ear. His breath tortured my skin, making me shudder. "You're bad for me."

"Yes," he agreed. "But you're mine, regardless." His hands grasped the fabric of my dress, bunching it until it was a mound around my hips.

"Teo, stop," I whispered but the vehemence, the fear had gone. Nothing remained but anticipation. Because no one had ever made me feel the way Matteo had the night, he took my virginity.

No one had ever worshiped me the way he had.

"Tell me you aren't wet for me," he whispered, teasing my neck with the slightest scrape of his teeth against my weak spot. Even after all these years, he remembered exactly where to touch, where to kiss, where to bite to drive me wild. Even though I'd only had him inside me once, that didn't mean we hadn't done everything else over that year we spent together. "Come on, Angel. Lie to me again."

I didn't speak, didn't think I could put the words together to tell him I wasn't. And he was right, it would have been a lie, anyway. When his fingers brushed against me, I was ashamed of how shockingly wet the gusset of my panties was as it pressed into my skin. Matteo groaned, the sound vibrating against my neck until he pulled back to press his forehead to mine as those skilled fingers toyed with me through the thin barrier of my underwear. "It means nothing," I whispered, closing my eyes to shut out the intimacy of his stare.

"You want me to believe that any of the other assholes you've let touch you ever got you this wet when they've barely touched you? Your body knows me, just like mine knows you," he whispered, removing his hand in favor of pressing his torso to mine so I could feel the steel length of his erection.

"It means nothing," I repeated on a sigh.

"It means everything, Angel," he said, voice soft, nearly reverent as he tugged the dress up and over my head. I wanted to fight him, wanted to keep my arms firmly pressed to my side, but nothing worked. My body had always been putty in his hands.

Nothing had changed.

Big calloused hands stroked down my sides, a tremble in them as they graced over my hips and grabbed my ass. He lifted me, staring up at me with eyes full of emotion I suspected reflected in mine.

My eyes burned with the threat of tears. Because even with all we'd changed—even after he'd hurt me—after twelve years of just existing, Matteo was the only thing that could make me feel.

I loved him. Exactly as he was, no matter what he might have done or become. Matteo would always be the one who owned my heart, and that was exactly why I needed to stop. I needed to get his hands off of me. But somehow, as he carried me to his massive bed, my legs wound around his waist with a mind of their own. As conflicted as my mind might have been, my body had no such qualms as it quivered at the slightest stroke of his thumb against me.

He dropped me to the bed, and I bounced on my back only once before Matteo was sliding between my spread legs and leaning over me. His lips found mine, coaxing me to open for him when he traced my lips with his tongue.

He swallowed my whimper when I opened for him, pressing into me and tangling his tongue with mine. I'd expected him to be savage when he got his way, to take what he wanted, but he was the same as he'd been in high school when he finally got me in bed. He went slowly, taking his time, building my need through nothing but the feel of his skin against mine. I ran my hands over his chest, feeling the tightly corded muscles jump beneath my hands. When I curled my hands around his neck, twirling my fingers into the spot where his hair met the nape of his neck and pulled him closer, only then did he deepen the kiss beyond his initial exploration. Our mouths fused together, and I arched my back when his hand slid up my spine to find the clasp of my bra. He pulled away from me just enough to rip it off me, before he was back where he belonged, nibbling at my bottom lip. He smiled at me, cupping one breast in his hand until I arched further, pressing my flesh into his hand in a silent plea. He kissed the front of my throat, slowly kissing his way down until he hit my collarbone. Pulling back, he stared down at me for only a moment, and I watched those stunning blue eyes darken as he reached out his other hand to toy with my other breast. He pinched the nipples, worshiping the flesh while he stared at it like he couldn't believe he had his hands on me.

"Teo," I whispered, and I knew my voice conveyed every bit of my need when he growled at me. His hips slid further down the bed, and I immediately missed the press of him against me. Until he lowered his mouth to one of my breasts, sucking the peak inside and ravishing it with his tongue while he enveloped it in warmth. When he pulled away, the cool air of the room was a sharp contrast, making me writhe when he repeated the action to the other. "Please," I begged, and I immediately had a moment of hatred for myself.

He sensed it, erasing the logic when his lips kissed down over my stomach. His tongue found that spot, right in the hollow of my hip where I instantly squirmed beneath him. He sucked the flesh into his mouth, nipping and torturing it until I knew he'd leave a mark. Fingers grasped my underwear, and he knelt up and pressed my legs up so he could strip them off my legs. As soon as he released my legs, his mouth was between them. "Oh my God," I whispered, my legs thudding to the bed around him, and I stared down at his head as he worked me over.

Matteo didn't lick a woman's pussy because he felt obligated, or at the very least not mine. I might have argued he enjoyed it more than I did if he wasn't so damn good at it.

That talented tongue explored every part of me, thrusting in and out until I whimpered. When he turned his attention to my clit, it was so he could slide a finger inside me. I clenched around him on a cry, feeling the way he moaned in response vibrate through me. He withdrew that finger, only to add a second and curl them to stroke that spot inside me that made me quiver.

"Teo," I whimpered, and the sound of his name seemed to push him over the edge. He wrapped his lips around the bundle of nerves at the apex of my thigh, sucking gently. My legs tightened around his head; my hand buried in his hair to hold him exactly where I wanted him as I shattered in a blinding orgasm that stole my ability to function.

I laid there, panting and trying to regain my ability to move. When I opened my eyes, it was to Matteo shoving his own underwear down his legs and kicking them off. He pulled his fingers free of me and spread my legs wide from where they'd wrapped around his head. Sliding up my body, his hips lined up with mine so he could grind his length against my wet core. His lips found mine in a bruising, claiming kiss that seemed even more primal because he tasted like me. He reached down, sliding himself through my wet and notching his head at my entrance. Pulling away from my lips, he groaned, "Tell me you're mine."

Still recovering from my orgasm, I nodded in a daze.

"Words, Angel. Give me the words."

"Yours," I murmured, cupping his cheek with a delirious smile and tugging him down to kiss him again. He slid inside me slowly, filling me until there wasn't a single inch that couldn't feel him.

"Fuck," he groaned against my mouth. He reached down, wrapping my legs around his hips. Our foreheads pressed together; our mouths not quite touching as he started to move inside me. Even without his lips on mine, I could taste him, taste *me* in his breath on my face. One of his hands grabbed mine, our fingers intertwining while he wrapped his other under my shoulder to hold me where he wanted me. He slid in and out in slow, hard thrusts.

Matteo didn't fuck me; he'd never fucked me.

He made love to me, eyes on mine the entire time. There was no doubt who was inside me. No doubt about who owned me in that moment.

Matteo was all around me, an extension of myself.

The other half of me.

Tears stung my eyes again, and I buried my head in his shoulder to try to hide them.

He cupped my cheek, pulling me so he could see me. His face twisted in pain. "I'm here now," he murmured in what seemed to be a reassuring voice.

But it was just another reminder.

He was here now, but there would come another day when he wasn't. Another day when he broke me and tossed me aside.

I smiled at him and nodded, determined to guard my heart from everything my body seemed incapable of denying.

I loved Matteo, exactly as he was.

But he'd never be mine.

Seeming to sense my growing distance, Matteo reached between us, pressing fingers to my clit to bring me back to the place where I focused on the sensations between us. I moaned, not even trying to resist what he offered me. Tossing my head back, I came on another cry, clenching around him like my life depended on keeping him inside me.

Above me, Matteo groaned, sinking teeth into my shoulder as he flooded me with heat. We lay there for a few moments, neither one of us moving to disconnect. Because who knew what would happen when we did, and reality came crashing down.

Eventually, he had no choice but to pull free of me, and

the spill of fluid that followed made me glance down my body in horror. "You didn't wear a condom," I whispered. I couldn't believe I'd been so stupid. I'd just trusted that a man like Matteo would be smart enough to wrap it up.

"No," he said simply, not looking concerned in the slightest as he stood and strode for the bathroom. I laid there, feeling beyond lost until he returned.

Using a wet rag, he cleaned between my legs—his eyes fixated on the action. "What is wrong with you?" I whispered. "Why wouldn't you put on a condom?"

He looked at me, momentarily surprised, as if *I* was an idiot for expecting he'd wear one. "Nothing between us. Ever," he grunted, tossing the rag to the side of the room. "I'm clean. I know you are." I clenched my eyes shut, hoping he wasn't lying. Being on the pill, I shouldn't have had anything to worry about if he was honestly clean. "Really, Ivory. You're the only one I've ever had without a condom. You're safe. I would never risk you like that." I nodded blankly and stood. "Where are you going?"

"Bathroom," I said, and only partially because I needed a moment to myself. As oddly sweet as it was for him to clean me, I couldn't not use the bathroom after sex.

It was a convenient excuse to go hate myself in private.

12

MATTEO

It took Ivory too long to turn her brain off and settle into sleep. I could tell because she was still. I'd only spent one night with the woman, but there was no doubt in my mind that the way she thrashed in her sleep was a common occurrence. Even in sleep, she'd seemed relieved when my body pressed hers into the bed, holding her still. That beautiful face of hers calmed from the stressed, tense state it had been in when I'd entered her room.

Given how peacefully she slept with my weight on her, I was hesitant to leave her, but I needed to get her phone in case there'd been an emergency while we'd had our date, and the sun was already rising over the horizon. I hadn't bothered with the curtains, usually I was up before the sun. I removed myself from Ivory's body, silently hoping that her peaceful sleep would continue even without me. One day, I would understand the cause, but I knew better than to push too hard, too fast.

My Angel was stubborn.

And for whatever goddamn reason, I found that sexy as Hell.

I tugged the curtains closed quietly, slipping into my boxer briefs and stepping out of my bedroom. Making my way downstairs, I headed for my office. I'd put her phone on the nightstand before I slipped into the shower. I knew having it would comfort her, delude her into thinking it offered her any protection from me.

The truth was, I could do whatever I wanted to Ivory, and there wasn't a person on this Earth who would *dare* to stop me. Her endless bag of shit sat on my desk, and a quick glance confirmed that her phone wasn't sitting next to it conveniently. I had no choice but to dig into the monstrosity. It was a first for me, but I'd heard horror stories of what men found in their women's purses.

As soon as I opened it, I realized it wasn't on top of the pile of shit.

That would be too easy.

Rummaging through, my hand grasped a medicine packet. My heart leapt into my throat. Her file had shown no illnesses, so I tugged it out with growing horror. I should have been relieved to see the birth control. From any other woman, I'd demand it. But knowing that Ivory was protected from pregnancy didn't fill me with any relief.

A pregnancy was one more way to ensure that she was mine, completely.

In a way that no one would ever have with her.

I lifted my phone, snapping a picture of the front and the back of the packet before replacing it in her purse. It didn't matter that it burned me to do it. When I found her phone, I turned and went back to my sleeping woman, suddenly determined to experience my first morning sex ever.

13

IVORY

I'd been in a daze all morning. After Matteo had woken me up with his mouth between my legs, he fucked me until all I'd wanted to do was curl back up in his bed and sleep for the rest of the day. With a sexy as hell chuckle, he reminded me that I probably had work to do. Though he made it clear he didn't object to me staying in his bed all day.

I wanted to slap myself. I'd let him touch me, let him have me again, let him finish inside me without a condom. I didn't understand what it was about Matteo that turned me into an incoherent mess who couldn't string together two letters to say 'no.'

I was so distracted that I'd had to turn the stove off and walk away, because I would get nothing pretty enough to photograph unless I found an outlet first. I'd taken to cuddling with Smaug, running my finger over his scales and watching with amusement as he closed his eyes in contentment. He really was the weirdest, most affectionate lizard I'd ever seen. While I'd never really thought of myself as a reptile person, I melted the second I saw him at the pet store and brought him home.

Even if he ate mealworms and crickets.

Blech.

The knock on the door seemed like a welcome reprieve, even as I wondered who would drop by. Duke was pissed that I'd gone out with Matteo again and not answered my phone for nearly twelve hours, and I couldn't keep bothering Sadie with my emergencies while she was working at the gym. So, I hadn't told her about my sleepover yet.

The courier standing on my front porch wasn't someone I'd ever received deliveries from before, and I squinted my eyes at him in the bright sun. "Can I help you?"

"Miss Torres?" he asked, and I nodded. "Sign here."

I took the clipboard, scrawling my signature quickly and then accepted the small box. Carrying it over to my trusty island, I shrugged at Smaug's look of curiosity as he peered down at the box. With a sigh, I peeled back the gold wrapping paper.

A note rested on top, and I picked it up, reading the handwritten words with growing horror.

It reminded me of you.

Exquisite.

Adrian

His phone number completed the note that I set to the side like it was diseased.

It probably was.

My trembling fingers lifted the white gold necklace out of the gift box. I may not have known much about jewelry, but I knew the stones in that necklace were diamonds. *Fifteen* of them in a Y shape that would dangle between my breasts.

I swallowed nervously, dropping the necklace back into

the box and then wincing. That thing probably cost more than my car. The note followed, before I folded the box back up as best as I could.

Even if I'd been interested, I had no use for jewelry like that. But I *wasn't* even remotely interested in a man that would corner me in a bathroom and terrify me.

Picking up the box, I strutted my way outside to where Scar sat on guard duty in his car. He rolled down the window, looking on edge when he took in my bare feet. "You should go inside, Ms. Torres. It's cold."

I dropped the box in his lap. "I don't want this. Might as well make yourself useful if you must stalk me."

I turned and went back for my door. "Shit," he hissed, and I glanced back to see him already calling someone on his phone.

It didn't take a genius to guess who it might be.

14

MATTEO

I felt like my bones would burst free from the confines of my skin. Rattled in a way I'd never been, *pissed* in a way I couldn't recall ever experiencing. He'd touched my woman, and when I'd warned him, I meant business where she was concerned, he'd sent my woman a fucking gift.

As soon as I parked the Aston in Ivory's driveway, I shoved my door open. It felt like I should have run to where Scar stood guard on her porch, but my steps were careful, controlled. If I didn't contain the monster who was out for blood, I'd frighten Ivory beyond what a gift from Adrian must have already done. As soon as I was on the porch, Scar pulled the small jewelry box from his suit pocket, his jaw clenched tight and his nostrils flaring.

On anyone else, the display of anger over Ivory might have made me feel territorial, but I knew Scar. I knew him well enough to know that the man was trustworthy, and his interest in Ivory was purely related to his dedication to me and my family. He'd been nothing but a street rat when we'd taken him in, a little pickpocket who'd been abused in every way a man could imagine—just another victim of the failed system that let kids like him fall through the cracks every day. I took them in, gave them a purpose.

Even if it was one that the U.S. Government didn't agree with.

While I wouldn't say my crimes were without victims, I did my best to keep the innocent out of it.

The note crumpled in my hand as I read it and stared down at the necklace in the box. I hadn't even given my woman jewelry yet, and this fucker thought he could buy her affection with a predictable gift. I dropped the crumpled note back in the box, turning to Scar where he stared down at me. I nodded, and he pocketed it. "Keep it. Consider it your bonus for making sure he doesn't get near her."

"Yes, Boss," Scar smirked, and I knew the man was thinking how much it would piss Adrian off to line my man's pockets.

"She's permanent. Got any objections to being her detail long-term?" I asked, and his eyebrows raised.

"Permanent like—"

"Like a ring is being custom made at this very moment, and she'll have my kid as soon as I can swing it."

He chuckled, a rare sound for the more stoic man. "She know that?"

"Not yet," I shrugged, because Ivory's opinion on the matter was inconsequential. "Let's go."

I opened the door, not even surprised when I found it unlocked. I didn't suppose Ivory thought there was much point when I'd just break in as soon as I got there and she had her own personal security, but I added it to the list of conversations we needed to have.

"Is it safe to assume that you'll deal with him for me?" she asked, slamming around in her kitchen. There wasn't a food item in sight, so she wasn't cooking. I realized quickly that she was scrubbing the cabinets, as though she didn't already keep them immaculate for her blog. I, perhaps wisely, refrained from commenting. Next to me, Scar's lips quirked at the sight of the leopard gecko clinging to her shirt. She'd probably forgotten the poor thing was there, jostling him around in her cleaning frenzy. I sighed, stepping up to her and holding out a hand. It surprised me when the thing was more than happy to abandon Ivory in favor of the safety my hand offered. She stopped cleaning finally, glancing down at her lizard and pouting at him. "I'm so sorry, Smaugy," she cooed, taking it from my hand and bringing him to his tank while she whispered to him. "I forgot you were there, baby." She set him in the tank, and I fought the urge to laugh as the lizard glared at her.

Who could have known a lizard would have so much personality?

"I'll take care of it," I answered finally, like she'd been asking. We both knew I'd handle it. "From now on, you don't answer your own door," I said, and she leveled me with a glare. "Scar will be in the house with you, except for when he feels it necessary to check outside the house. You stay with him at all times. You do not drive yourself anywhere. You do not walk anywhere alone. He is always on you, understood?"

"That cannot be necessary—" she started to argue, breaking off when she saw the serious expression on my face. "I think you're being a little extreme over a bit of jealousy, Teo," she whispered.

My heart broke, hating that I would need to crush a bit of that remaining innocence in her. "He's not a good man, Angel. I've seen what's left of women after he's finished with them, and he's looking to pawn them off on the next asshole who wants to use them. He is *not* a man you want anywhere near you, and now he's fixated. I will make sure he gets over you real quick, but in the meantime, I need you to do your part and stay with Scar."

"He sells them?" She whispered, her voice cracking. "Like prostitutes?"

"Sex trafficking." She swallowed, nodding slowly as she closed her eyes in pain. I knew what question would be next; it was the only logical path her mind could take while she was still so in the dark about who I was and what I did. "You said he was a rival. Do you sell people too?"

"No," I said firmly, and even though it was true, the bitter stain of a lie twisted my insides. I ran women, but they were all paid for their services and chose to be there. It was a very different crime than what Adrian did.

I just couldn't be certain Ivory would see it that way when the time came.

"Okay," she nodded, relief making her chest swell with the inhale of breath she took.

"One day, you'll understand everything I do, Angel," I sighed, drawing her into my arms. "Just not today." She nodded, not even bothering to argue, and I knew that the reality of the threat Adrian posed to her was settling in. "You'll stay with Scar?"

"Yes." She nodded enthusiastically, and I felt my face harden at the bit of fear I'd put in my woman because of this piece of shit's determination to fuck with me. When I drew away, Ivory's eyes glanced down at my arms, where I knew my shirt sleeves were rolled up, ready to bloody Adrian for what he'd done. I had abandoned my suit jacket in my haste to get to Ivory, left behind in my office. I was only grateful I'd had the foresight to leave my gun in the car.

She didn't need to see that yet.

"Is that—" she started, and I knew she'd ask about the tattoo on my left forearm.

"I'll see you later. Stay with Scar," I ordered, nodding at the other man as I fled the house.

It was not the right moment to explain the tattoo I'd gotten the same day I broke her heart.

***

Adrian's home was a stone monstrosity right in the middle of the city. A complete and total attention-grabbing statement, like the man thought owning a home in it meant he owned the city.

He didn't, because it was mine.

I strolled up to the door, gun tucked in hand and not caring who saw me. This city was mine, and there wasn't a person in it who was stupid enough to fuck with me when I meant business.

Not a person except for Adrian Ricci. The stupid fuck.

Even his security didn't dare shoot me, not without direct word from their boss. Even in the unlikely event they killed me, my men would revolt, and the city would descend into complete and utter chaos. No one wanted that.

The door opened before I could knock, and I shoved it wide and shouldered the butler out of my way. "Where is he?"

"Mr. Bellandi, perhaps—"

I pointed my gun at his forehead, staring down at him with glacial eyes that showed just how little I would care if I shot him dead. "Where the fuck is Adrian?"

"Office at the end of the hall," the man whimpered. "Could you perhaps holster your weapon? There's no reason this needs to be a violent affair."

"I disagree." I stormed through the wood-paneled halls, a deception on Adrian's part to try to convince his business associates of the illusion that he came from old money.

Like them. *Like me.*

But Adrian Ricci was nothing but a motivated thug who thought because he made money on the backs of others suffering, that somehow entitled him to the luxuries that the old bloods enjoyed.

But we all knew the truth.

He was nothing. He lived as nothing, and one day, he would die as nothing.

I shoved his office door open, wondering how pretty his classical cream painted walls would look covered in his blood. "Matteo," he said, standing with a smile, even while I leveled my gun at him. "Come now, whatever it is you think I've done—"

"Stay the fuck away from my woman. I thought I made myself very clear that she does not exist for you."

"Ah, I see Ivory told you about my little gift then. How very disappointing," he sighed. "Really though, Matteo. Can you blame me? All is fair in love and war, and the woman is positively enchanting. Such fire!" he exclaimed. "I wonder what she'll be like when she's broken. How pretty those eyes will look when they're vacant. Like a beautiful, little doll."

I crossed the distance between us in favor of shoving Adrian up against the wall with my arm to his throat. "You will *never* touch her."

He grinned up at me, a direct challenge in his gaze. Drawing back my hand that held my gun, I used it to break his nose. "Fuck," he groaned, smiling again through blood-soaked teeth.

"Mr. Ricci?" one guard who'd undoubtedly followed me in asked from the door.

"It's all right, Jesse," Adrian assured him. "Matteo and I are just having a difference of opinion. Women. That trap between their legs makes all of us go a little crazy, isn't that right?" With a snarl, I repeated the strike, leaving no part of Adrian's face unbloodied. When my gun pressed against the underside of his chin, I knew that killing him would be the best thing for Ivory. I may not walk away, but she'd be safe regardless, and the calm in his eyes even as they swelled up told me he wouldn't be leaving her alone without my forcing it. Lowering the gun, I fired it into his right hand, the same one that had touched Ivory without her permission.

"Touch her again, and I'll shoot your dick off next time. You won't have much need of my woman without it."

He roared out a laugh, swaying when I released my hold on his throat and sucking in a full, unhindered breath. "I always knew I liked you, Bellandi!" he called as I turned and strode out of his office and home without another word.

I dialed Scar as soon as I was in my car. "She doesn't leave your sight if she's out of that house. Understood?"

"Yes, Boss. I guess it didn't go well."

That was an understatement.

15

IVORY

After Matteo left, I tried to ignore Scar's presence in favor of cooking. When he realized he was making me uncomfortable, an audience I hadn't asked for, he'd excused himself to go give himself a tour of the house, muttering something about needing to be prepared and know where everything was located.

Because that wasn't ominous.

I set to rolling out the dough, letting myself smash it a little thinner than I normally might have for sticky buns. I needed the outlet, and I'd just use this batch to test out the flavor for this replication. I rolled them mindlessly, shoving them in the oven.

I *never* left my kitchen a mess. It was one of the few things that had stuck with me from culinary school and my subsequent days working in a restaurant. I rebelled nearly every other way, because if I wasn't an *actual* chef than who gave a poop? But with cleaning my kitchen, I was a neurotic.

So, when I went to flop into a chair at my breakfast nook, I knew I was shaken even before my trembling hands touched my face. I lost track of how long I sat there, lost track of everything around me. It wasn't until the doorbell rang that I jolted out of my stupor, glancing at it nervously. When I was about to stand, Scar appeared from the hallway and shook his head at me. I remembered that I wasn't allowed to answer my door and flopped back into my seat in a sort of empty frustration. I picked a point on my wall, staring at it in fascination when I found the slightest of cracks in the paint. "It's Mr. Bradley. Would you like me to open the door?" Scar asked lightly. I nodded at him, hearing Duke's voice the moment it opened.

"What the Hell are you still doing here?" he asked.

Scar grunted; the sound oddly devoid of inflection. While he might have looked like a hard man, he'd been nothing other than polite and even warm to me. He seemed oddly capable of anticipating and dealing with my moods, like I was more than a nuisance his boss ordered him to watch over until he finished playing with me.

"Christ, Ivory," Duke said, striding past me and pulling my oven open. He cursed, hunting for a potholder and dropping the sticky buns on the stove top with another curse. "What were those supposed to be?"

"Sticky buns," I whispered.

"Well, they're burnt buns now." I must have forgotten to set the timer. He came to stand in front of me, after the beep of my oven turning off filled the too quiet space. "You all right?" he asked, kneeling so that his face filled my vision. I nodded, smiling at him slightly. Duke's hands rested on my bare thighs just above my knees, feeling too warm against my cool skin. "You're freezing," he whispered.

"Ms. Torres, I'm afraid I have to suggest that Mr. Bellandi won't appreciate Mr. Bradley's hands on you," Scar input, raising a brow at me. I glanced down at Duke's hands, confusion settling over me.

"He's my friend," I said, and Scar sighed and nodded. His expression communicated that he still didn't believe it would be something that Matteo would tolerate, but in that moment I couldn't have cared. Duke didn't appear to either, instead taking to rubbing his rough, artist's hands over my cold skin to warm me up. "I'm fine," I reassured him.

"This really has you freaked out," he whispered. "Why don't you come stay with me?"

Scar's face pinched into annoyance, but I took care of it when I answered Duke. "I think I'm safer here. This isn't the guy you can protect me from."

"What the Hell has he got you wrapped up in?" Duke hissed, and my eyes darted over his shoulder to find Matteo standing in the doorway. I hadn't heard the door open, and Matteo held a key in his hand. A key to my house, I presumed, though how he'd gotten it was beyond me.

"Take your hands off her," Matteo ordered, and Duke stood up quickly, turning to face Matteo for the first time since high school, I realized. Duke's attractive features that lent toward the boy next door all grown up were no match for the savage beauty that was Matteo Bellandi. He still didn't have a suit jacket, his sleeves rolled up to his elbows hastily, and a few splatters of red dotted the chest of his white shirt. He looked like a criminal which I was suspecting he was more and more with every day that passed. Ice-blue eyes glittered as he glared at Duke, sizing him up and finding him lacking.

"You don't get to come in here after twelve fucking years and put her in danger. She deserves better than you'll ever be able to give her, Bellandi," Duke hissed, all the vehemence he'd built up in the years of watching me fade into half a life wrapped up in that tone.

Matteo smirked at him, the blue eyes I loved to watch

warm for me glittering hard and cruel gems. "You still haven't made a move, huh?" he asked Duke, who froze solid in front of me. I turned my head to look at Duke, wincing when his shoulders sagged. The reality of what I hadn't seen struck me when he turned a sad glance my way.

"You broke her. I keep waiting for her to be ready for a relationship, but it never fucking happens, because of what you did to her," he spat at Matteo, confirming the truth that shook me to my core. "I love her enough to wait. Even for twelve years."

"Duke?" I whispered, staring up at him. He turned to me, looking down at me with a grimace.

"This isn't how I wanted you to find out."

I backed away a step, just knowing I needed space. "Why didn't you tell me?"

"Would it have mattered?" he hissed. "You've always been so wrapped up in him, that you never even saw me."

I winced again, hating that he was angry at me when he hadn't bothered to be honest. "Don't," Matteo growled. "You do not get to upset her because you were too much of a coward to make a move."

"Matteo!" I gasped, hating that he would be so cruel in a moment that was probably critical to my ability to maintain a friendship with Duke.

"Fuck you," Duke hissed, striding for the door. He paused, looking back at me with nothing but sadness. "Call me if you decide you want to be more than just a fleeting fancy for Matteo Bellandi."

I dropped into my seat as he left, wondering how the fuck my boring life had gotten so messy.

16

IVORY

Scar glared at me as we got ready for our morning run. The last week had passed with the same routine, a run in the morning, I went about my day, and then Matteo would show up in time for dinner. We'd either eat at my house and he'd spend the night, or he'd take me out and we'd end up at his. It was almost comfortable, predictable. I couldn't imagine Matteo's life followed that routine too often, but he gave me the distinct impression that he was doing everything he could to lull me into a sense of normalcy after I'd lost Duke.

It wasn't like he was dead or anything, and he'd answer my texts—mostly one-word answers—but the ease of our friendship disappeared. He hadn't dropped by since Matteo outed him, and I couldn't blame him. Not while knowing that at the very least Scar would be at my house with me. He'd been humiliated, his feelings for me revealed by the worst person in his mind. I knew that.

It didn't stop his absence from hurting me. Even Sadie had been mostly absent, likely spending a good deal of time with Duke and encouraging him to channel his emotions into his art rather than a less productive rage.

So in the face of all that, Matteo seemed determined to show me what a relationship with him could look like. I'd stopped fighting his presence, because until they resolved the Adrian issue, he was a necessity. I'd even stopped fighting his power over my body, because I might as well get some great orgasms out of the situation before he packed up and left my life without a trace. Again.

But I did everything possible to remind myself that it was temporary. That Matteo *would* leave me, and I'd be left to pick up the pieces. My resolve only strengthened with time, the more Matteo chipped away at my armor with his strong presence and made me want things that would never happen. I resolved to find some kind of solution to making him move on sooner than later when it would hurt more but had no idea what that would be.

"You need to vary your routine," Scar pointed out as I opened my front door. He turned with a copy of my house key in hand, locking up behind me.

I'd long since gotten used to everyone having a key to my house. If they'd wanted to hurt me, they would have already. "I like my routine."

"It makes you easier to track, easier to follow. Your predictability makes you an easy target for people who might want to harm you," he grunted, picking up a jog beside me. The massive, hulking man hated running with me, but he did it anyway. He even managed to not slow me down too horribly, given the length of his legs and the way one of his strides equaled two of mine.

"You want me to run at a different time of day?" I asked, slowly building my pace. "It wakes me up to start my day. That's the point."

My breathing was steady, my body going to that place of focus that running always brought me to. "At the very least you should change your route. Makes it less predictable."

I considered it. "I don't want to get lost," I admitted. Even though I'd lived in the area for a few years, I didn't venture off the main roads. There was still a distinct possibility that I'd wander somewhere I shouldn't be.

"You'll have me," he grunted, his own breathing far less steady than mine.

"I won't always have you," I huffed a laugh. "You can't spend the rest of your life looking after me. Matteo will need you to do something else, eventually."

"He won't leave you unprotected." We turned the corner, heading up the road that would take us by the park. I could feel his eyes on me, even as I pointedly kept mine fixated on the park next to me. "What exactly do you think this is?"

"What?"

"Your relationship with Matteo. You still think he will walk away?" Under any normal circumstances, I would have been grateful for the interruption that saved me from answering.

Those were not normal circumstances.

My body jolted as I crashed into a man who jogged out of the park entrance. He emitted an "oof," catching me with stabilizing hands on my hips when I nearly fell on my face. "Easy." My body stilled, horror crashing over me when I recognized the voice that spoke from above me. Tilting my head back, I came face to face with what I *thought* might be Adrian Ricci. In all honesty, it was difficult to tell.

His face was beaten, bruised with a gash through his cheekbone, a split lip, and a bandage over his nose where it had been broken. Two purple bruises surrounded his cruel looking brown eyes. "I—Adrian?" I asked, stepping back far enough that I forced him to release his hold on my hips. One of his hands was wrapped in a bandage as it left my body hesitantly.

He winced dramatically. "I realize I'm a sight at the moment, but I assure you I'm all right."

"What happened to you?" I asked against my better judgment. I didn't need to know the details of what happened to Adrian, not given his business.

If what Matteo said was true, he deserved everything he got.

"Matteo didn't mention he came to my home and beat me bloody for sending you a little gift? Went into a jealous rage, in fact. Most men wouldn't dare, but Bellandi is untouchable." He shrugged, as if to brush off the revelation.

Matteo had beaten the shit out of him.

I remembered the blood on his shirt that day when he'd come back and destroyed Duke. I'd been so distracted I'd forgotten all about it. "That's enough," Scar hissed, tugging me behind him and blocking me from Adrian finally. I wondered what had made him wait so long, deciding that Adrian didn't pose much of a threat to me with him right there and on a crowded street in the middle of the morning.

Still, his words about changing my route seemed even more necessary, given what couldn't have been an accidental meeting. Adrian had followed me, stalked me, and learned my routine. Exactly for this purpose.

It sent a chill down my spine.

"We were just talking," Adrian held up two hands, feigning innocence even as he winked a bloodshot eye at me.

"Think very carefully if this is a war you want to begin. There are plenty of things that Matteo lets you get away with when he can't be bothered to care. This will not be one of them." Scar nudged me, pushing me to turn back the way I'd come. I started walking in that direction, going slowly so I wasn't far from Scar's protection.

"To the victor go the spoils of war," Adrian said, a smile in his voice. I turned back to look at Scar, finding Adrian's eyes on me. "I look forward to seeing you again, little doll." Scar caught up with me, pressing a hand to my back and urging me to leave Adrian behind us. When I finally turned away from him, it was with mounting terror over what was coming.

He wasn't giving up.

***

Days passed, with my life a static, suspiciously routine pattern of events. But the constants in my life remained absent, until the day Sadie sat on my stool, finally back in the spot she'd been neglecting in favor of talking Duke down from the ledge. I felt Duke's absence fiercely, the text that I was making his favorite brownies going unanswered entirely, where he normally would have raced to my house.

"Did you know?" I asked her, pouring the batter into the brownie pan from my stand mixer.

She raised a brow at me, acting like it was ridiculous to think she wouldn't. "*Everyone* knew, honey."

"Everyone but me," I sighed, putting the pan in the oven and closing it. I stepped around the island, plopping onto a stool instead of immediately washing the bowl. Sadie looked at me with wide eyes, and I knew it didn't get past her as seriousness settled over her features.

"He never made a secret of it. You just didn't want to see it," she whispered, reaching over to pat my hand. "Now that you know, what do you plan to do with that information?"

I felt my jaw slacken, shocked she'd even suggest what I thought she was suggesting. "What do you mean?"

"Well, you could give him a shot," she suggested. "He loves you, Ive. Always has. He may not make you feel like Matteo always has, but he won't hurt you. You could do a lot worse."

I nodded, because she was right. "I know, but it's just—it's *Duke*. He's my best friend. It would be like dating you."

"I mean, I'm sure Duke and I have very different equipment. Can't say I've ever gone there, but—" she giggled, and I laughed with her. "He's not unattractive."

"I know, but we grew up together. How can I cross that line?"

"Kiss him. That's the best way to see if there's chemistry, find out if you can see him in another way," she suggested. My eyes bugged out of my head, envisioning the image of Duke touching me that way.

It didn't fit, no matter how much I might wish it did. I didn't want to hurt Duke, and I *had* promised I would find a man who could love me and give me a content life.

It just wouldn't be him.

"I can't do that to him. Subject him to a life with someone he knows will never—" I broke off on a whisper. "I need an easy, simple date. Something with no expectations, just to show myself that someone else can make me feel like Matteo does. Set me up," I begged. "That guy from the gym you were planning on before this whole Matteo mess started."

"No way in Hell! You do not need to involve another man in your mess right now," she laughed, standing from the stool and grabbing water from the fridge.

"It's exactly what I need! A distraction from unrequited love and dangerous sex machines. Pleaseeee," I whined.

She sighed, staring at me in disapproval. "All these years of having to force you on dates, and you choose now."

"Don't pretend you didn't keep Duke's feelings from me. You both kept something from me I should have known. You owe me." I wasn't beyond playing on her sympathy, because if I knew Sadie, I knew that the guilt of keeping that from me for so long had been weighing on her. It was probably part of what possessed her to stay away for so long following the revelation.

"Ughhh," she groaned. "Fine, but this makes us even. If Matteo kills him, I'll take it out on you," she said menacingly, the warning clear in every feature of her exotic face.

"Deal," I said. I couldn't contain my excitement even in the face of Sadie's threat, which I didn't take lightly. She'd beaten me up with fitness before, she knew how much I hated it. She'd get me in the ring again and kick my ass.

But the freedom of knowing I was my own woman, and I could do what I wanted, was worth it.

I hoped.

17

IVORY

It wasn't often that I got to see my uncle.

So, when he came to visit, I held that time as sacred. As his favorite, okay only, niece, it was my responsibility to him.

And so, it was tradition that riding in the car with him on the way to the restaurant, I claimed the front seat. I didn't even care that it stuck my parents in the back; they were used to it. Uncle Adam *always* drove, a consequence of whatever Rambo stuff he got up to when he took off to places unknown to do things most of the government didn't even have the clearance for.

My Uncle was a badass.

"Where were you this time?" He'd been a Marine, some special task force or something. I'd been only a teenager when he'd retired and opened up his own private security firm.

"Florida," he said, casting an amused look my way.

I chuckled. "Well, that's horribly ordinary."

"Oh, it was torture. Having plumbing, modern amenities, and a roof over my head to protect me from the elements. I tell you; I'll never take a job like *that* again." He shook his head, pursing his lips.

Sticking my tongue out at him, I muttered a quick, "Smart ass."

"Ivory! Don't call your uncle names. That's my job," Mom inserted from the back. Adam pulled up to the valet, and we all hopped out of the car. Mom and dad had never used a valet, like me, but Adam did things in style, and we'd learned long ago to just roll with it. Because when he was around, he paid.

That simple.

When the valet took his Mercedes away, we stepped up and into Angel's, the little Italian place Mom and Adam loved so much. It wasn't within Mom's price range normally, so she only got to have it when Adam came to visit.

We always came when he was in town. The name had been a bittersweet reminder in the first few years after it opened, but I'd eventually moved on over the term. The restaurant boasted some of the most authentic Italian food in the city, and that was saying something for Chicago.

Stepping in the front doors always felt like being transported to Naples, not that I'd ever been, but I could *imagine.*

What was different about that night from all the other nights, was the man who came striding in when my mom gave our name to the hostess.

"Angel," Matteo whispered, bending down and pressing a quick kiss to my lips as his hand cupped my elbow. I floundered, staring up at him in shock.

Because, please sweet lord tell me he hadn't just kissed me in front of my family.

Please.

A quick glance at my father's reddened face confirmed that he, in fact, had.

Well then.

Poop scoops.

"Uh, what are you doing here?" I asked, stepping back from him and hoping he'd release his grip on my elbow.

No such luck.

"I saw the reservation and thought I should reintroduce myself. It's been a long time since I saw your parents," he said with a polite, gentlemanly smile on his face.

"How did you know we had a reservation here?" I whispered. His stalking really knew no boundaries.

"It's one of my restaurants." He shrugged, because owning a restaurant was just a throwaway business detail in the great lineup of things the Bellandi family owned.

"Of course, it is," my dad snorted, echoing my sentiments.

"I don't believe we've met," Adam stepped up, holding out a hand for Matteo to shake. His face was hard, set in stone. Even though Uncle Adam had never met Matteo, I knew that he knew exactly who he was. My uncle made me his business, and there was no way he wouldn't have kept tabs on the guy who fucked me over.

"Matteo Bellandi. You must be Ivory's Uncle Adam." Matteo took his hand, and it was subtle, but there was obviously a struggle for dominance working between the two men as they stared each other down.

"I didn't realize you two were an item now," Adam said with a grimace.

"We're not—" I started, cutting off when Matteo's hand tightened on my elbow.

"It's fairly new," Matteo smiled. "But I recognize the real deal when I have it."

"You didn't the first time," my father muttered, his jaw clenched tight. My mom's eyes were wide, staring at where

Adam faced down with Matteo. She seemed to know there was something different from my uncle's usual protectiveness where I was concerned, something just *off* about the way Adam glared at Matteo but also looked at him like he might be a formidable opponent.

No one stood up to Adam.

Ever.

So that Matteo could and still smile while he did it, well, that was insanity to my mother. I could see the gears turning in her head, wondering about all the rumors that surrounded the Bellandi family. "Honey, you didn't tell me you were seeing someone," she said finally, a tight smile curving at her lips.

"It's new, like Matteo said. Didn't think it was smart to get you all excited," I lied, because the reality was, I never intended to tell my parents I was seeing Matteo. My father snorted at my choice of words, knowing damn well excited was a euphemism for pissed off.

Was that what they called it when someone inserted himself in your life and you couldn't escape?

Dating my stalker.

My parents would have been so proud if they'd known.

"Your table is ready, Mr. Bellandi," the hostess inserted, politeness stamped on every one of her features. I wondered if Matteo had slept with her too, but there was no trace of familiarity or jealousy on her face when her eyes met mine. If he had, he'd made sure she knew the score ahead of time and could be professional in the face of his girlfriend's family.

Regardless of how I felt about the temporary nature of Matteo in my life, I appreciated the discretion for my family's sake. They wouldn't take well to having my boyfriend's conquests rubbed in their faces.

Especially not with my history with Matteo.

"Lead the way, Ms. Favre," Matteo gestured, and it was a horrifying realization that he hadn't just stopped by but had every intention of staying for dinner.

"Matteo," I whispered, catching his attention as he guided me in to follow the hostess. "This is not an appropriate time. You can't just insert yourself to dinner with my family, especially not on the rare occasion I get to see my uncle."

"Ah, so you were intending to invite me to meet him another day during his visit?" he asked, guiding me to one end of the table. He sat me in the seat to the right of the head, smoothly lowering himself into the chair at one end. That in and of itself made a statement.

"Well, not exactly," I sighed.

"I thought as much. As you don't seem to want to make the introductions, I took the liberty myself." I could feel my uncle's eyes on me as he took his seat at the opposite end of the table. Normally he didn't care about posturing, and he would have taken the seat next to me.

I knew besides challenging Matteo; he took that seat precisely for the purpose of keeping tabs on me through the meal. Next to me, he might not see everything, but on the other end of the table, he saw Matteo and I perfectly.

I resisted the urge to bash my head on the table, staring at my empty wine glass in frustration.

I needed alcohol.

Lots and lots of alcohol.

My mom and dad sat next to Adam, leaving the seat between my mom and Matteo unoccupied. He didn't seem bothered when he took my hand in his, holding it openly on top of the table for my family to see.

A waiter came, delivering wine into all our glasses

without being ordered, and I narrowed my eyes on Matteo's high-handed bullshit. Then I took a few very unladylike swallows of the delicious bordeaux. Matteo's jaw clenched as he watched me drown my inhibitions in my glass.

"So, Matteo, how's business?" My uncle asked, his voice sounding cordial. I knew better. Knew that beneath that fake veneer was a man who would kill Matteo if he thought I was in danger.

And he'd never go to prison for it.

I realized that was why I couldn't let on to my family that I was anything other than a thrilled participant in the ruse of a relationship Matteo crafted. As much as my feelings conflicted over Matteo, I just couldn't live with him being dead either.

That was why I'd never even considered calling Adam in the first place, but his sudden, unplanned visit did suddenly seem all too convenient.

"Business is booming. I own several properties, restaurants, nightclubs. I do very well. Your niece will never want for anything." Matteo smiled, the edges fraying as he addressed my uncle. Knowing Matteo, he knew exactly who Adam was—knew what he'd done. He knew that Adam likely had a thorough understanding of whatever illegal dealings Matteo had, and I knew the two men were on opposite sides of the law. In Matteo's defense though, Adam had never truly operated within the realms of the law either.

How you went about saving lives was insignificant, as long as you did. That was his philosophy, and it always had been.

"What made you come visit?" I asked, turning a beaming smile Adam's way. "It's not like you to just drop in without planning." His lips crooked in a bemused smile, and he shook his head at me in the same way he did every time he told me I was too smart for my own good—too good at reading people to waste away in my own kitchen. He wanted me working for him, always had. Getting a feel on his potential clients. For the first time, I considered it.

I had a feeling I'd want to leave Chicago whenever Matteo decided he was done with me.

Too many memories.

"I had a case end sooner than planned. Figured I'd come surprise you all."

"Coincidentally, as soon as you could get away after I was involved in a robbery?" I smirked, and he grinned at me.

"Complete coincidence," he lied. "I would like to know what they have done about it. Have the police found them?"

My father snorted.

Ah that was where I got my refined behaviors from.

"I suspect you know more about that than us," Mom laughed.

"Wasn't asking you," my uncle said, turning raised brows to Matteo. I turned to face him too, watching as he lowered his Bordeaux to the table after a generous sip.

"It's been handled." He shrugged, and my father stilled at the table, taking it as further confirmation that Matteo was dangerous.

Mom looked to Adam like she expected him to protest, require information about how it had been handled. But Adam merely looked thoughtful for a moment, before turning his attention to the menu in front of him.

"Good," he murmured. "Good to see someone around here is at least capable of getting shit done." Mom's horrified eyes looked from me to Adam, finally stopping when my dad cleared his throat.

"I think I'll have the lasagna," he muttered, and the conversation ended there.

I turned to Matteo, panic coursing through me.

What the fuck did he mean it had been taken care of?

He shook his head, signaling me to hold my tongue for the moment.

For once, I listened.

I listened, and I guzzled more wine.

I didn't need alcohol. I needed to be shit-faced to deal with that hell of a dinner.

18

SADIE

My fingers hovered over the keypad on my phone.

Could I really do this to her?

The answer was easier than it should have been.

I could, and I would.

Ivory was far too stuck in her own little world to realize that she had two men on her hook. She couldn't just bury her head in the sand and pretend they didn't exist while she added another man to the mix.

Hopefully, this would be exactly what she needed to pull her head out of her ass.

I dialed the first number, tossing back a shot when it rang.

"Yeah?" Duke's voice grunted on the other end of the line.

"Ivory's going on a date," I blurted, determined to keep my voice strong. I knew Ivory would be pissed if she ever found out, but I would always do what it took to protect her.

Even from herself.

"I told you, I don't want to hear about that shit," he snapped and slammed something around. Undoubtedly some metal scraps in his shop as he worked off his rage.

"It's not with Matteo. It's someone else. You should go, stop her from doing something stupid. She doesn't see you that way; it just doesn't come naturally after being your friend for years, so you need to *make* her see you that way if you want it to go anywhere."

"Is this one of those grand gesture things women are always talking about?" he returned, a smile in his voice. The metal stopped clanging, and I knew he was considering it.

"Grand gestures, come to Jesus moment. Just get your ass to *Indulgence*." I hung up, giving him a ten-minute head start before I dialed the number Scar had been all too willing to give me.

"Bellandi," the voice on the other end said.

"Matteo?" I asked.

"Who is this?" His voice went taut, and I took it he didn't get very many phone calls from women. That pleased me.

"Sadie. I thought you'd want to know that I helped Ivory sneak out tonight. Scar's sitting downstairs, completely oblivious that she stepped out and took a cab."

"What?" he whispered, and that voice was menacing.

"I'm in her room pretending to be her to buy her time, but you should probably just head over to *Indulgence*."

"What the fuck is she doing in my club?" His voice went deep, menacing, and I worried about the guy that was on the date with Ivory. I convinced myself it would be fine. I'd warned him not to get touchy.

"She's on a date," I laughed, hanging up the phone. It rang when he called back, and I ignored it in favor of taking another sip of Ivory's wine. When Scar's phone rang downstairs, and I heard the front door slam, I considered how easy it would be to divert their attention and sneak her out again if the need arose.

I filed that bit of information away in case we needed it.

19

MATTEO

I didn't know what the fuck Ivory was thinking.

Had I not clarified that I'd kill any man who touched her?

And yet, I sat in my Aston, cursing traffic as I tried to get to her from the meeting that had occupied me later than I liked. I scoffed, the thought of Ivory challenging me by going on a date with another man insane to think. Nobody else would have dared, but if she'd made one thing clear with this little stunt?

It was that I'd been too gentle. Given her too much time to adjust to the reality of my return into her life.

That would change.

Effective immediately.

By that time tomorrow there would be no doubt in her mind that I meant every word when I told her she was mine. Every word when I explained I would never let her go.

Pulling up in front of the club finally, I tossed my valet my keys as I climbed out and strode off without another word. The Aston was inconsequential in comparison to Ivory with another man.

"Mr. Bellandi?" the boy asked, hushing immediately when I didn't spare him a glance. My bouncers threw open the doors, and I prowled into my club, ignoring employees vying for my attention.

I didn't give the first shit about any of them. My eyes scanned the dance floor, looking for my deviant little angel. People crowded into the floor, admittedly a security nightmare for Ivory, even if she hadn't been with another man to begin with. The pulse of bodies was too much, would make it impossible for Scar to protect her unless he was practically on top of her. I caught sight of the huge man, standing guard against the wall. Following his eyes toward the center of the floor, my heart stopped when the crowd parted to reveal my angel.

I froze momentarily as she threw her head back and laughed at something the man across from her said. He miraculously danced with her without touching, something I found odd given Ivory's metallic emerald green dress looked painted on. It left her legs bare, the length of them standing out in the stilettos she wore. Delicate straps led to a scoop neck that showed a hint of the beauty I knew was hidden just underneath.

I growled, flinching when Scar touched my shoulder reassuringly.

"He hasn't touched her once," he admitted and the sincerity in his voice took me off guard. Something in me loosed, knowing I wouldn't need to murder a man in front of Ivory.

Even I knew that might be just slightly too much at that point in our relationship.

But that wouldn't save my Angel from the wrath she incurred.

Especially not when Duke appeared in her space.

20

IVORY

It had been far too long since I'd been dancing.

I'd loved it, once upon a time.

And then I'd become a statistic. One of the millions of women who found themselves out of their depth in a dangerous situation with men who didn't give a shit about the word no.

I hadn't gone dancing since.

Hadn't been able to trust men or trust my recklessness.

That all changed the day Matteo came barging back into my life, even though I'd been the one to barge into his home. He was the most reckless thing I could ever do, not the alcohol pouring through my system or the way the music energized me as I moved to the sound of it. My date, Patrick, was nice. He kept his hands to himself, which, for a date in a nightclub, I had to say was surprising, but very much appreciated.

"You're the life of this club with those moves," he yelled, letting me hear him over the din of the music despite his respectable distance.

I threw my head back and laughed, because we both

knew it wasn't a compliment. I wasn't a horrible dancer, but I was too enthusiastic in my excitement to give in to the sensations pounding through my body. The adrenaline of feeling like I was part of something, part of a crowd, for even just a little while.

A figure emerged from the way the crowd formed, slipping through any gaps he could find. My eyes landed on Duke, watching as he panted with exertion. Whatever he'd been doing, he'd rushed it. His jeans were stained, his tee-shirt beaten and one I recognized from his collection that he wore only in his studio. Duke wasn't the nightclub type to begin with, but there was no way he'd show up in studio clothes if he decided to go out for a night on the town.

"Duke?" I asked, and he sucked back a deep fortifying breath. "What are you doing here?"

He didn't answer, suddenly crashing into my space. His hand caught me around the nape, sliding underneath the curtain of my hair. I knew he'd find it slick with sweat, but he didn't seem to care. I stared up at him with wide eyes, and I knew what was coming.

I wished I could stop it, but something in the look in his eyes prevented me.

He needed it. He needed to know.

The least I could do was give him that.

Because the truth was, I already knew I'd never love him the way he loved me.

It wasn't possible when someone else already owned me.

Heart and soul.

One more deep breath, his cornflower eyes staring into mine intently. They drifted closed, his lips touching mine tentatively at first. I didn't move, didn't dare do anything. I had to let him see, had to show him. He'd spent too long waiting, too long *wondering* what might be.

It was time for Duke to move on with his life.

When I didn't shove him away, his confidence grew, and his lips pressed into mine more firmly. The tip of his tongue traced my lips, and I opened for him just enough for him to kiss me. The art, the passion, with which he worked translated into his kiss. A skilled seduction where he used his mouth as the only conduit.

But there was nothing, no spark.

Because only Matteo could make me feel.

When he pulled back, his eyes opened slowly, a mix of awe and apprehension flitting through them. "You didn't feel it?" he asked. I shook my head, looking down as tears filled my eyes. "I'm sorry, Duke. You know that I'd change it if I could."

"It's because of him? You're choosing a criminal over me?" His voice sounded harsh, and I knew that the rough wrath of Duke's temper hovered just under the surface, waiting to unleash when he was alone and could show the real hurt.

"No. I know Matteo and I will never last," I explained. "I'm choosing you over me." His brow furrowed, and I stepped closer to his embrace, wrapping my arms around him supportively. "You deserve more that I'll ever be able to give you. I love you too much to trap you in a relationship with me, when I know I'll never be able to love you the way you love me. I don't want that for you."

His arms tightened around me. "What about what I want?"

"You'll find someone better for you." He stiffened, pulling away. His eyes darted over my shoulder, and he nodded silently with a huff of laughter before turning on his heel and disappearing into the crowd.

My spine tingled, something like apprehension sliding up it suddenly and pooling in my chest. The press of a body against my back came out of nowhere, making me stumble forward. A massive hand wrapped around my throat, trapping me, and panic flooded through me. My hands stretched up to claw at that hand, as Patrick stepped forward.

"Hey man, let her go!" he protested.

"It's quite fortunate that I think having his heart crushed is punishment enough. Otherwise, Duke would be a dead man. Get rid of the extra, naughty angel," Matteo's voice growled in my ear. I sighed in relief, my panic abating with the feeling of safety that came from Matteo. As pissed as he might be, and I imagined he really, really was, he wouldn't hurt me.

Not really.

"Let go of me, Teo," I whispered, giving Patrick a reassuring smile where he eyed us in a mix of fury and concern. "It's okay. I know him," I yelled.

"I suggest that you get the fuck out of my club while you still have all your limbs," Matteo grunted at him. His voice might have remained quiet, had we not been in a club. But with the music thudding overhead, he had no choice but to shout the command. Heads turned our way, watching the exchange. Patrick's eyes widened, but he nodded before abandoning me to Matteo.

I sighed, frustration mounting. I hated feeling owned, like property that belonged to Matteo and couldn't think or act for myself. "Did you forget about something?" he asked.

"Hmm, nope," I whispered, trying to ignore the way Matteo skimmed his free hand over my hip.

"You are spoken for, my love. Very much in a committed relationship. It is very fortunate for your date that he didn't touch you. Otherwise, it would have been the last thing he did."

I froze, feeling Matteo's grip on my throat tighten in warning. "Things are about to change. It's time for you to accept what is happening with us."

"There is no us! There will never be an us!" I yelled back at him, not even caring about the people watching.

"Ah, but you're wrong, *Cara mia*. There very much is an us. There has always been an us, and there always will be an us. You will never let another man touch you," he barked the order, releasing my throat in favor of taking my hand and yanking me toward the exit.

"Wait, I don't want to go anywhere with you!" I snarled, attempting to pry his fingers off my hand as I stumbled after him.

"That's most unfortunate for you. No one here will stop us."

"Matteo!" I shrieked, glaring at Scar where he took up his place behind us. The night air was cold as it hit my skin, the wind ripping through the street. The valet raced to get the car as Matteo draped his suit jacket over my shoulders. "*My* jacket is inside. At least let me get it before you cart me off like an animal."

Matteo nodded to Scar, who turned and stalked back into the club. When the Aston pulled up in front of the club, Matteo didn't wait for him. Instead, he shoved me into my seat and slammed the door closed before taking his own seat and stealing me away into the night.

✷✷✷

Matteo drove too fast.

He always drove too fucking fast, but nothing could compare to when he was full blown, *pissed off.*

"I cannot believe you were so stupid to go out without Scar. Do you care nothing for your safety?" he growled, turning blocks to head for the highway.

"I was fine!" I protested, shaking my head at his ridiculous behavior. I wasn't a reckless child, if I wanted to go to a club for once, then that was what I would do.

"And what would you have done if Adrian showed up?" Matteo asked, and I pursed my lips. I'd been confident no one could follow me since Scar hadn't even noticed me sneaking out, but there had been risk involved on that front.

It was just worth it, to have a single night of freedom from the confines of my life with Matteo.

"I can't have someone following me all the time, Teo," I whispered. "I need space, room to just be and the ability to do what I want."

"Yeah? Well, you can kiss that goodbye," he laughed, a dark, hollow sound that grated on my nerves.

"What does that mean?" He was silent for a moment, and I began to wonder if he would bother answering me or if I'd just wake up to some surprise restriction without asking my consent. He shoved the sleeves of his shirt up one by one, frustration written in every feature of his face. His bone structure was unique, sculpted, and radiated strength with his chiseled square jaw, and that *always* made him look intimidating to some extent, but the way he pursed his lips in that moment only aggravated it.

"Things are changing. You'll see what I mean once I make the arrangements." I considered asking but decided against it. If Matteo didn't want to tell me something, give me preparation, then he wouldn't. I could beat my head against a wall, or just accept that we would argue whenever he made those arrangements.

My eyes went to the tattoo on his forearm opposite me, watching the way the muscles corded as he gripped the wheel. "Why do you have that tattoo?" I asked.

His eyes darted down to it, and he veered off the road to pull into an empty parking lot of one of the many businesses lining the streets as we made our way out of The Loop.

"What are you—?" I stopped when he threw the car into park. He stripped off his seat belt, his body turning to face me ominously.

He took my hand in his, touching my fingers to the tattooed flesh of his forearm. I traced the lion's face with my fingers, circling the clock face that hid the face of a lamb in its intricate details. "I got it the day I broke up with you," he admitted, shocking me. "As a reminder."

"A reminder of what?" I whispered. I suddenly knew that I didn't want to have this conversation. My apprehension over it had made me procrastinate in asking, because why would I want to know why Matteo had immortalized the worst moment of my life on his skin.

"That the lion should never get involved with the lamb, because it's only a matter of time before the lamb is hurt." I huffed a laugh, pulling my fingers away suddenly. If I'd expected a sweet answer, something to hint that everything had been a lie, that had been anything but. "Not because I broke your heart, Angel. My life is complicated. It's dangerous, and it always has been. Walking away was the best way to protect you from the consequences of it. Every time I thought about going to you, about taking you back, that tattoo reminded me why I had to stay away."

Tears pooled in my eyes, and I shook my head. I

wouldn't let him in again, and I worked to rebuild those walls between us, the shaky ones that seemed to fail every day. "Don't."

"It was always you, Ivory. Always," he whispered, pressing his forehead to mine. "You're the only thing that could hurt me. The only thing they could use to break me. That is why you need to do what I tell you. You must stay with Scar. It's the only way I can keep you safe."

I nodded, numbness flooding my system as I fortified my walls. Matteo sighed, aggravated. He'd always known when I worked to build up my walls, always sensed them the second they went up.

It was what made him so effective at tearing them down.

"Fuck it," he grunted, shoving open his car door. My eyes opened, staring around us. The lot was dark, not a car or a person in sight. I flinched when my door opened, and Matteo unbuckled me hastily.

"What are you doing?" I asked as he pushed me to lie over the center console. Maneuvering my legs, he twisted me about until I knelt on the seat. "Teo?"

"Hush, Ivory," he whispered, sliding my dress up my thighs and over my hips to reveal my black thong. "Fucking Christ, you're beautiful." His hand came down on the cheek of my ass in a loud smack that made me cry out, and I felt the searing pain immediately. He repeated it to the other side, and I whimpered. "You do not let another man touch you. Never again, Ivory. I gave Duke a pass because he won't be a problem again, and because I know you would hate me. I will not be that generous going forward." His hands stroked over my hot, burning skin, and I resisted the urge to squirm when that heat shot straight to my core and transformed into a deep, dark arousal that should have humiliated me.

Instead, I thrust my ass back at Matteo, letting him know just how I felt about his spanking. "Shut up and fuck me."

He chuckled, "my little angel likes being spanked? I'm not surprised. You'll take everything I give you, Cara mia."

I nodded, whimpering when his hand gripped the waistband of my thong and pulled it down my legs as far as he could until it got caught at my knees. He left it there, two fingers thrusting inside me and finding me already wet and waiting. The sound of his zipper broke the silence behind me, and only a few seconds passed before his fingers withdrew and the smooth, velvety head of his cock replaced them. A hand wrapped in my hair, making me arch my back to take him deep as he surged inside in a single, hard thrust that I felt bottom out against the end of me.

"Teo," I gasped, the fingers of his other hand bruising my hip with the force of his hold on me.

"You'll take it," he ordered, using his grip on my hair and my hip to tug me back until I fell out of the car. With his cock still planted firmly against me, he positioned me so that my hands supported me on the seat. My heeled feet hit the ground, feeling all too shaky to support myself, but Matteo didn't give me any reprieve. He pulled out and snapped his hips back in quickly, releasing his hold on my hair finally in favor of keeping my ass tipped up the way he wanted it. The skin of my ass tingled, something more than the recovering sting from his strike against me. A glance over my shoulder confirmed his eyes were fixated on where we connected, watching himself sink in and out of me in a fast rhythm. I knew I must have looked obscene, standing and bent at the waist to the point I nearly folded in half, and it wasn't easy to hold still and let Matteo take what he needed. His palm slapped down on my ass again, and I screamed, tossing my head back. "This pussy is mine."

"Yes, Teo," I whimpered, and in that moment, it couldn't have been a lie. I clenched around him, my body loving the domination in his voice and the way he gripped me.

She was a traitor when it came to Matteo.

Just like my heart.

"Your mouth is mine. You will never let another man put his lips on you again. Understood?" he barked an order, shifting his hips so he dragged over that spot inside me with every thrust.

"Yes, Teo," I repeated on a whimper. My body tightened, my orgasm crashing over me. He never stopped, never even paused, just forced his way through my orgasm with punishing thrust after thrust.

"This ass is mine," he whispered, and one of his hands abandoned my hip in favor of pressing his thumb to the part of me that no one had ever touched. I whimpered, wiggling against his grip on me. "I'll claim it soon, Angel. All of you belongs to me. I was the first man to take your mouth, the first man to take that sweet little pussy, and I'll be the first man to claim your ass too."

He slowed his pace, and I glanced back to watch him stare at the dirty way he touched me, *claimed* me while he fucked me with his monster of a dick.

"Shit," I moaned, not wanting to reveal that the strange, foreign pressure against me felt *good*. It was dark, forbidden, something I'd never thought to like.

But I did.

"Do you want to know a little secret?"

"Hmm?" I hummed, exhaustion claiming my calves from the angle and the heels.

"I'll be the last man to take all those things too," he groaned, finding his own climax within me. His hand hit the roof of the car, supporting his weight as he lost his control for that one moment where Matteo ever let go. The one rare moment of vulnerability he only showed when he came. I couldn't see his face, but I felt it all the same.

When he finished, he helped me slide my thong back into place and straighten my dress. Then we went home.

21

IVORY

When I'd gotten in the car with Scar, I'd *thought* we were just going home after letting Sadie work me over at the gym for two hours. She was itching to kick my ass after the scene with Duke, and I couldn't particularly blame her.

I wanted to kick my ass too.

What was wrong with me I couldn't feel chemistry with my admittedly handsome best friend who I knew would do whatever he could to keep me from being hurt?

Ugh.

So, when Scar turned the wrong way and merged onto the highway, I cursed and turned to look at him. He'd tried to convince me to sit in the backseat of the SUV more times than I can count, but I never wanted to feel like I was being chauffeured around. It made me feel like a rich man's mistress, which wasn't far from the truth, but I detested it all the same.

"Where are we going?" I asked him, groaning and flipping my head back into the seat. He didn't answer, just sat there all stony and silent with his eyes on the road. "Did it maybe occur to either of you I don't feel like going to Matteo's? He rarely summons me this early, anyway. What's going on?"

"I think it's best I leave it for him to explain," Scar grunted and the muscles of my body tightened.

"Oh God, is it bad? Did something happen?" More silence. "Whatever," I sighed, trying to calm myself. "He's probably just done with me. Ready to end this bullshit."

Scar snorted out a laugh, and I realized I'd rarely heard the man laugh. Even though I was comfortable with his presence, and I knew he found me amusing, I'd never once made the man laugh.

That was unacceptable.

"I'll miss you; you know. You're always welcome to come over if you need food. I'm good at feeding people, if you couldn't tell. You eat a lot. Who feeds you when you aren't stuck with me?"

He shook his head like I was ridiculous.

Now *that* he did all the time.

"I'll have plenty of your cooking, Ms. Torres."

Well, *that* sounded ominous.

I crossed my arms over my chest, watching as the city streets turned to the slightly less urban streets that led to Matteo's estate.

I was a sweaty mess, going to Matteo's where I didn't even have clothes to change into.

The drive passed in stony silence, Scar knowing damn well that I wanted to ask questions, and me knowing he wouldn't answer them. He was a loyal bastard; I'd give him that.

Besides, I had a feeling asking questions about Matteo was a slippery road. I'd taken to the strategy that burying my head in the sand and waiting until he was done with me was the best way to walk away without being completely shattered when it was over. Whatever he did for a living, I didn't want to know.

Nope.

Ostrich I was.

Scar rolled down the window as he pulled up to the gates of the estate, and the guard stepped up to the window. He stood outside, unusual as they normally stayed in their little house until we pulled up.

"Busy day," he muttered to Scar, glancing at me across the car. "Good afternoon, Miss Torres," he smiled politely. It was the same guard who had been working when I'd first naively come traipsing into Matteo's domain. I had since learned his name, after he'd returned from vacation, anyway.

"Hi, Christian," I said with a hesitant smile. He'd been nothing but polite since the first time, abnormally so, but I hadn't been able to shake the reminder I looked like all the other girls Matteo banged.

Euw.

He cleared his throat, turning an oddly amused look Scar's way, and the sullener man only glared back. "Go on in," Christian said, stepping back from the car and hitting the button to let us into the estate. As we drove up the long, winding drive, it became obvious what Christian had meant by a busy day.

Someone was moving.

My heart thudded in my chest, unable to believe that Matteo wouldn't have mentioned he was moving, unless he planned on dumping me or he was in trouble and had to get out of dodge.

But why would he have me brought to the house?

A moving van passed us on the drive, another sitting in

front of the house as two men hopped out of the front. We pulled up behind them, and they opened the rear doors to reveal a van packed with boxes.

"Uhh kay. Did Matteo get married or something?" I asked Scar, who smirked at me from the side. He was out of the car the next moment, and I followed him, albeit hesitantly. I did *not* belong at Matteo's house under the best circumstances, but my dirty running shoes were particularly unsightly against the opulent tile of the foyer. My high-waisted running shorts and sports bra weren't much better. Boxes covered the foyer, and two staff I recognized in passing collected things from the foyer and brought them up the stairs or to the living area and kitchen as we made our way to the hall to go to Matteo's office.

Scar knocked on the door, turning to murmur to me. "I really don't feel like chasing you. Keep that in mind, yeah?" he grinned, shoving the door open at Matteo's command. I froze at the threshold, staring up at Scar.

"Why—why would I—" I broke off when Scar shoved me into the room, and I barely caught myself before I stumbled. The door closed behind me, and I eyed Matteo as he stood from behind his desk. "What's going on?" I asked him, crossing my arms over my chest and preparing to harden myself. Matteo wouldn't know that he hurt me.

Not the second time around.

"Come sit with me," he gestured to the couch against the wall and facing his desk. I eyed it warily, knowing it hadn't been there before. It was white, modern but a light contrast to all the masculine grays and browns of his office. A little coffee table and ottoman hybrid sat in front of the couch, looking like a perfectly cozy space to curl up and work if I ever saw one. I went as he took my hand and guided me to the couch, plopping down next to him. I didn't even care that I might dirty up the fabric, since I'd likely never see it again.

"The issue with Adrian is proving to be more difficult to solve than I originally foresaw. Given your stunt last night," he broke off, eyeing me in frustration, "I no longer believe it's safe for you to remain in your home for the time being."

"I knew—," I paused, feeling everything in my body tighten as his words sunk in. "What?"

"Adrian remains as fixated as ever, and you're determined to put yourself in dangerous situations by sneaking out past your security. I need you to remain where I can keep a closer eye on you." I tugged my hand free from his grasp.

"What the fuck does that mean?" I whispered.

"Angel," he whispered, and I stood from the couch. Darting to the door, I raced for the foyer and threw open one of the boxes. The staff stared at me, and I vaguely knew of them snickering when my jaw dropped, and horror settled over me.

My stand mixer sat there, gleaming like sea glass in the light streaming down through the massive skylight.

Backing away a step, I stared at it, blinking while I wrapped my head around what was happening. With a shake of my head, I made for the front door.

This was *insane*.

He was insane.

Scar stepped in front of the door, crossing his arms over his chest and looking formidable as he blocked my path. "Move," I ordered, walking into him and trying to shove him aside.

"Can't do that, Ms. Torres," he grunted. "Told you, I don't much feel like chasing you."

"Angel," Matteo said somewhere behind me, and the

sound of his footsteps against the tile made my body jerk with every step closer he came.

"You can't do this," I whispered, feeling like I might break.

"I'll do what I have to do to keep you safe," he murmured back, a hand reaching out and brushing my hair away from my shoulder.

I whirled on him, shoving at his chest to the sound of gasps around me. "You do not get to move me out of my home! What is wrong with you?!"

"You should have thought of that before you went out alone last night."

I shoved him again, hating the fact that his body barely budged. "I'm going home. I expect my things will be returned today."

"You really think Scar is all that stands between you and freedom? You have no car. The only exit from the property is guarded, and there is a guard on each door of the house itself. You no longer go *anywhere* without my permission, *Cara mia*." His voice dropped low, dancing over my skin like a caress.

"You can't do this!" I yelled, tears welling in my eyes. I'd expected Matteo to break my heart, but I never would have thought he'd do it like this.

Never like this.

"Ah, my love, I believe it is already done." Matteo turned and strode for his office, leaving me floundering in the middle of the foyer with an audience.

"Ms. Torres?" Donatello asked, stepping up to me and putting a hand on my shoulder. "Do you have any specific requests for where you want things in the kitchen? I'll see to that personally. Normally the kitchen is my domain, but I very much look forward to having company."

I shook my head, feeling the first tear fall as he patted me on the head and stepped away. I turned, eyes connecting with Scar's where he stood at the door.

"You knew," I whispered, betrayal making my heart clench. I meant it when I said I'd miss the sullen man who had come to mean something to me.

And he'd brought me to a prison.

His face contorted briefly, as though the sight of my tears bothered him.

But it didn't.

None of them gave the first shit about me.

"He'll keep you safe," he whispered, and each word was like a blow to my gut.

"Ivory," a vaguely familiar voice whispered next to me, and I turned my head to look up into Lino's familiar brown eyes.

"Lino?" I asked stupidly, wincing when he wrapped an arm around my shoulders.

"Come on, sweetheart. Let's sit you down."

He guided me to the living room, settling me on the couch next to him. Donatello delivered a glass of wine a moment later, giving me a sad smile and eying me warily.

"How are you?" I asked Lino after chugging the contents of my glass. Donatello took it, refilling it in front of me and handing it back.

"Better than you at the moment, I expect." The sheepish smile he turned my way was a welcome sight, and I even returned it.

"Samara?"

He winced. "Going through a rough divorce."

I nodded. It had been years since I'd seen her, but the man she'd gotten herself hitched to had never been a good man. "I'm surprised it took so long."

"You know her, she's stubborn." I nodded. "Like you," he added.

I glared at him. "I just want to go home."

"You *are* home," he said, tucking me into his chest when fresh tears welled in my eyes.

※※※

Lino had long since gone back to Matteo's office, doing whatever it was the two of them called work where Matteo's employees were completely content to watch me cry over being trapped in his house. Staff moved around me, unpacking my things without regard for what I might want. They didn't even ask me where I wanted everything to go—the only person who had bothered with that being Donatello.

I suspected they knew I'd say to keep everything in boxes.

Locking myself in the bathroom, I thought over my options.

I only had two.

Let it happen.

Or call Adam.

The phone in my hand rang when I pressed his name on the screen, and I had to wonder if I knew what I was doing.

I just wanted to go home, but alerting Adam might be like declaring war. He was unpredictable and there was absolutely no way to know how he might react to me being a prisoner in Matteo's home.

"Hey pretty girl," he answered, affection always in his tone. When I was silent, I could feel the way he radiated tension through the phone. "Ivory?"

"I need your help," I whispered, sobbing over the line.

22

MATTEO

*I*vory knew the moment her uncle arrived, if the wide eyes she threw my way when I stormed out of my office were any sign.

"You think you're clever, don't you?"

She didn't respond, staring at me silently as she stood from the couch and making her way to the door. I blocked her, stepping into her path and catching her up in my arms. "He will *not* take you from me. Do you understand?"

"You already lost me, so what does it matter," she hissed, the wildcat in my stubborn little angel rising to the surface after her temporary shock.

I looked forward to her wrath when I took her to bed later.

But in that moment, I needed to remind her who called the shots. I stepped back from her, going for the door. Her sneakers squeaked against the floor behind me, a reminder she hadn't changed after her arrival although all her clothes were being unpacked systematically. "She doesn't step foot outside," I ordered Scar, passing through the space he allowed before he closed it to block Ivory in.

"Yes, boss," he grunted, absorbing Ivory's slap to his chest.

"Let me out! Matteo!" she yelled, and I closed the door behind me to drown out the sound.

I didn't need her uncle thinking she was being tortured.

"Bellandi," Adam greeted, crossing his arms over his chest and attempting to stare me down. He knew I wasn't so easily intimidated, but he still had to try. "I'm taking Ivory with me."

I knew there was a gun in his holster, the man went nowhere unarmed. But I didn't even consider needing to proceed with caution. He was too smart to pull a gun on me in my turf.

If he did, he'd be dead. Shot down by any of the guards undoubtedly on edge after I gave the order to let him in the gate.

"Ivory is with me now."

"I know your reputation. I know what you do. Ivory isn't the woman you involve in that kind of shit, Bellandi. You know that and I do."

"She's mine. Always has been," I grunted.

He sighed, nodding. "I know, but you threw her away. Now she wants to leave, and you have to let her."

I pulled the tiny box from my pocket, fingering the velvet and holding it up so he could make no mistake about what it contained. He eyed it warily, a deep sigh rattling in his chest. He hung his head, knowing what it meant for a man like me.

Men like us didn't let go of what was ours.

Not when it came to wives.

"Fuck," he whispered, and the way he warred with himself almost made me feel bad for the poor guy.

"If you hurt her or let anything happen to her, I'll make her disappear, and even you will never find her. Got me?" Adam asked, glaring at me.

I nodded. I could live with those terms; after all, it was much easier than I'd anticipated it would be to convince him.

"She loves you," he sighed. "Always has. She's scared, but I have to believe she'll find a way around that."

"I'll make sure she does," I said, reassuring him. I'd always envied the relationship Ivory had with her family. The way they loved each other and wanted what was best was admirable.

"Can I see her?" he asked. I nodded, stepping back to the door and watching as Scar opened it.

Ivory raced out, flinging herself into her uncle's arms. "Thank you!" she said, breaking my heart when she took solace in him. Solace from me.

"You call me if he hurts you, yeah?" Adam grunted; voice thick with emotion. Ivory backed up, staring up at him in confusion.

"Wh—what?" she stuttered.

"This is the safest place for you, honey. Adrian Ricci is no joke. You do what Matteo tells you," Adam grunted, wincing when she tugged fully from his grasp. "Love you," he murmured, turning and going for the driver's side of his car.

"Adam!" she yelled as he climbed in. "Adam!" she screamed when he started the car and inched down the driveway.

I stepped up behind her, wrapping arms around her waist and containing her when she lunged for the car with horror in her eyes.

My angel broke, crying while I held her in my arms and

wished there'd been another way. That she'd let me ease her into it.

But it didn't matter.

We'd always end up with her living with me.

I couldn't regret it being sooner than I planned.

23

Waking up trapped underneath Matteo's weight had become far too comfortable. Normally he woke up before me and stayed with me until I woke up. It was an unspoken thing between us, that he insisted on doing it so I could get my first quality rest in years. I didn't want to talk about it—didn't want to acknowledge the fact that Matteo was far too astute not to suspect there was a reason for my restless sleep.

Not when the reason felt so insignificant. Some women survived much worse. Some women dealt with the true trauma that came from horrific circumstances.

They were stronger than I was. Stronger than I would ever be.

So, when I woke up the next morning to the familiar press of his chest against my back and his leg draped over mine, I revolted against the feeling of comfort. Even with how angry I'd been yesterday, how broken I'd felt knowing he would completely disregard my wishes, I hadn't been strong enough to resist when he rolled me underneath him and made love to me.

At least that's what I would have called it, if Matteo was capable of love.

He wasn't. The day before had made that clearer than ever.

"It's time we talk about this," he grunted, pulling off me and rolling me to my back. My sleep camisole revealed more than it hid, and I brought my arms up to cover my silk covered breasts.

"Talk about what? That you've completely ignored what I want?"

"Ivory," he warned, and I blinked up at him with the most innocent expression I could muster.

"We're not doing this," I mumbled, rolling my eyes and moving to escape the bed.

Grabbing me around the waist, he shoved me down onto my back again, inserting himself between my legs and pinning my arms to the bed by my head when I struggled. "Whatever the fuck happened to you fucked you up. You thrash around in your sleep. You fucking beg for it to stop."

"Don't—" I warned, turning my head from side to side.

"I want to help you, and I can't do that if you don't tell me who to kill," he growled.

"Matteo—"

"Who, Ivory?"

"I don't know! Okay. I don't know who he is." My voice trailed off, unable to meet Matteo's gaze.

"Tell me what happened. Every time he bothers you at night, you bring another man into our bed." I turned furious eyes to him, finding him looking at me apologetically. "I didn't mean that the way it sounded. Our bed is ours. Just you and me, Ivory. Let me help you erase whoever he is."

"It's your bed, not ours," I snarled instead, determined to

hold on to my anger over being moved in without permission.

"Are your clothes in the closet? Your toothbrush at the sink?" His face turned to stone as he spoke.

"Teo," I whispered.

"Am I inside you every night and wake up with you in my arms?"

"Teo, that's not—"

"Answer me, Angel."

I grimaced. "Yes."

"Then this is *our* bed. That will not change."

I sighed, finally relenting. I so did not want to have a discussion with Matteo about his lack of boundaries and his ability to lie. We both knew it was only a matter of time before he kicked me out of his home when he got bored. Maybe the reality of cracking me wide open would prove I wasn't worth all the intrigue he seemed to think I was. "You know that moment when you first fall asleep? Where you're still aware, but everything is fuzzy and warm. Little bits of reality filter through the fog, but most everything is lost."

He tensed above me, staring at the side of my face since I refused to look at him. "Yes," he whispered.

"That's the best way I can describe what being drugged felt like. It reminds me of how that felt and what happened, so when I hit that part of sleep, it makes me panic, but I'm just so used to it that I guess I don't wake up anymore," I admitted.

His forehead touched my temple, and from the corner of my eye I saw his eyes slide closed. "Drugged?" His voice was a hoarse whisper along my skin. I nodded. He couldn't possibly mean to make me discuss the gritty details. "What happened?"

The breath that rattled out of my chest was rough, filled

with disbelief and fear. "I went to a club alone. Sadie hadn't turned twenty-one yet, and Duke just hated the whole club scene. One minute I was fine, drinking and dancing, enjoying myself. The next thing I knew I was stumbling and fuzzy. Someone caught me, said he'd find me a place to rest it off. I was too out of it to protest. I just didn't understand what was happening."

"Jesus. *Fuck*," Matteo groaned, his face contorting in pain.

"He didn't rape me. He didn't have a chance. He propped me up against one of the walls in a darker corner of the club and supported my weight. I was in and out of consciousness, but I know he moved my underwear aside. *Touched me.* Someone caught on to what he was doing and chased him off, she said he had his pants undone when he ran off, and I just fell to the floor. She and one of her friends who was a bartender set me up in a back room and saw me through it. I didn't want to involve the cops, not when I'd been so stupid, and they respected that."

"He touched you," Matteo growled. "Drugged you and planned to rape you."

"It wasn't that bad. It's silly. I just, that feeling of losing control over my body was the worst thing. I couldn't even fight him. People surrounded me, and I still had no way of making anyone know that I was in trouble. Falling asleep reminds me of that, and I know that's a ridiculous association. But it's never gone away," I explained with a shrug.

"What did he look like? What club?"

"It doesn't matter, Teo. It was a long time ago, and I remember nothing about him. Everything was blurry. I barely even remember what Verona or Evie looked like if I'm honest." That was one reason it would have been so stupid to involve the police. There was nothing to go on. Even Evie hadn't gotten a very good look at the guy, and it wasn't like a rape kit would have been productive. Just traumatizing.

I hadn't dated for over a year after that. Hadn't gone to my gynecologist. I'd only touched myself when necessary for hygiene.

"No one will ever touch you again," Matteo promised. I smiled at him sadly even though I believed him.

Matteo would let no one else touch me as long as I was his.

We'd been here before.

And one day soon, I'd have to relearn how to live life without him.

***

Several times over the two days since Matteo had moved me in, he'd suggested I do my blog posts and such from the couch of his office. Apparently it was the purpose for it, but he also clarified that there may be meetings where I needed to vacate when he and Don or Lino or when one of the countless other guys who worked for him needed to have private conversations about the business.

I wasn't the type to be forced to move once I'd settled in for the more tedious back end stuff of my business. I hated doing it to begin with, so I wasn't about to move once I motivated myself to do it. Because of that, I'd neglected to join Matteo in his office while I worked, preferring to sit in the kitchen with Don for company. I was coming to associate Matteo's office with bad news anyway, between the day I stupidly strolled in there like I had any control and the day he told me he was moving me in.

I was happy to avoid the misfortune that happened in there, thanks.

So, when Lino finally emerged from the office after a long two-hour meeting, I barely looked up at him when he strolled into the kitchen. "He wants you," he said, and I assumed he was talking to Don. Matteo didn't summon me to his office regularly, as opposed to the other man who appeared to handle many matters for Matteo. "Ivory, sweetheart. Talking to you." There was a smile in Lino's voice, and my eyes darted up to meet his in shock. I closed my laptop slowly, smiling at Don.

"Will this bother you if I leave it for now?" I asked.

He glanced at it and shook his head. "No worries, Ms. Torres." I brushed my hands over the fabric of my easy sage dress as I stood and made my way down the hallway.

Foreboding crept down my spine as I walked down the hall, and I took deep breaths and tried to convince myself it was only because of what happened the last time Matteo called me to his office. I wasn't a child. Wasn't about to be reprimanded by the principal. This was a man I slept with every night. Yes, he was a man who admittedly did things I didn't approve of without concern for my thoughts, but he wouldn't hurt me.

Not so soon after the stab of betrayal of moving me out of my own home and trapping me in his estate.

Knocking on the door, I waited for the familiar voice to summon me in before opening it. Matteo wasn't alone, a middle-aged man stood next to the desk. I walked in, smiling for him when he nodded.

"Ivory," Matteo said, standing and wrapping an arm around my waist. He pressed a chaste kiss to my cheek, turning his attention to the strange man. "This is my personal physician, Dr. Marchesi."

"Are you sick?" I asked him, and he chuckled at me. His eyes didn't meet mine, and that foreboding feeling slithered through me again. "What's going on?" My eyes turned to the corner when the doctors' eyes darted there. A massage table sat in the corner, and my brow furrowed. I didn't understand why a physician would give me a massage.

"He's here for you," Matteo said.

"But I'm not sick," I whispered.

"He's going to help me keep you safe. Just in case." Matteo's voice dropped to a whisper, and my eyes darted to the medical bag sitting on the coffee table where Matteo intended me to work.

"I don't understand."

The doctor pulled something from his bag. He held it between two gloved fingers, so small I could barely see it from across the room. "It's a microchip. Just a little tenderness for a day or so following insertion, much like a flu shot, then you won't feel a thing."

Horror dawned on me, and I backed up a step only to have Matteo tighten his arm around my waist and plaster me to his side. "No. No fucking way."

"Angel," Matteo whispered, and I turned wide eyes to him.

"You can't be serious! I'm not letting you put that thing in me!" Struggling against his grip, I shoved at him to let me go.

"You need to be still. We don't want to hurt you more than necessary," Matteo warned. My eyes returned to the doctor, watching as he loaded the chip into a syringe with a fat needle.

"No! Teo, please!" I begged, backing away. I couldn't explain the dramatic reaction, but in the face of being microchipped like a dog after being taken from my home, it was too much.

I felt trapped.

Trapped in a way I'd never been before, like I might never know freedom again.

"Lino!" Matteo yelled, and my panic increased. Matteo's grip tightened on me, and I thrashed in his arms as he hauled my back against his chest. Lino, Don, and Scar rushed into the room and made their way toward us.

"No!" Matteo maneuvered us to the massage table, letting Scar help guide him until my stomach pressed to the table gently.

Even manhandling me, they were gentle about it.

I screamed again, wincing when Lino pressed a hand to the back of my head and stroked it affectionately. "It will be alright," he murmured, pressing my face forward into the face cradle. His other hand pressed to my left shoulder, holding it down firmly. Matteo's hand took up residence on my right shoulder, and the other two men grabbed my legs and held me perfectly still. I felt my chest shaking with the force of my crying and wished I could stop, but I was so angry that there was no stopping the tears.

Another hand pressed against my back, and the sound of scissors snapping together reached my ears before my dress suddenly loosened around me slightly. "I recommend here," the doctor said, pressing a finger into the fleshy part to the right of my spine. "It makes it impossible for her to remove herself."

I mumbled against the pillow. What the hell did this guy think I was? A superspy?

I was n*ever* cutting anything out of my skin.

Good God.

"That works," Matteo grunted as I wiggled in their hold. "Get it done." The needle pressed to my skin, and I whimpered.

"Shhh, sweetheart," Lino comforted me, and I didn't miss

the fact that it wasn't Matteo. He knew there was no forgiving this.

Especially not after our conversation the day before.

With a slow glide, the needle pressed in, dropped the microchip under my skin, and pulled back. A hand pressed something to the entry point, no doubt to stop the bleeding until the doctor taped a bandage to it. When the sound of latex gloves being removed from his hands caught my attention, the pressure at my legs and shoulders finally relented.

I didn't move.

"Get out," Matteo barked, and I heard footsteps as they all hurried to do just that. When the door closed, Matteo finally turned all that intensity on me again. "Angel," he whispered. His hands wrapped around me, pulling and rearranging me until I sat on the table. I still didn't look at him, seething behind my tears. He reached out a hand to cup my cheek, wincing when I flinched back from him.

"Don't touch me," I hissed.

"Ivory—"

"I'll never forgive you," I whispered, finally looking at him. I had to wonder why it had been necessary—why he'd needed to break whatever good we'd had in our fucked-up history.

"You don't have a choice," he murmured back, icy eyes staring into mine.

"That seems to be a common theme with you," I huffed a laugh. Guilt flashed across his features momentarily, before he wiped all expressions from his face. "You were right. I never should have come here. I was happier without you."

I stood, forcing my way around him. He didn't move, didn't follow.

But his roar of rage echoed behind me as I escaped. Glass shattered, and it sounded like something flipped. I emerged into the kitchen, snatching up my laptop and ignoring Donatello's apologies. I couldn't even meet his eyes as I fled the room.

I hurried to one of the guest rooms upstairs, locking myself in and collapsing onto the bed.

I couldn't even go home.

24

IVORY

Our interactions with each other had been fleeting for two days. I worked in the kitchen. He worked in his office. We ate dinner in silence. He went back to working while Donatello and I cleaned up.

Then I ran to the spare bedroom and locked myself in. Somehow, I woke up in his arms in his bed the following morning both days. How he maneuvered me there without waking me, I'll probably never know. As soon as I woke up, he wordlessly stood from the bed and got ready before burying himself in his office again.

I stood in the kitchen, staring at the ingredients set out in front of me and preparing myself for the experiment I was about to undertake when Matteo's yell echoed through the house.

"I don't fucking care what you do with it! Just get it out of here!"

I hesitated. His office was officially on my no-no list of places to go, but there was *something* so *broken* in his voice as he shouted, that my feet moved on their own accord. I rounded the corner, passing people who stared at me in horror.

My eyes landed on the doll as soon as I walked in the room.

The size of a child's doll, she almost looked like she could actually be a child's plaything.

If you only looked at her face.

And ignored the lace teddy that adorned her body.

My eyes darted to the scrap of red lace sitting next to her, an identical, life size match of what she wore.

"Ivory," Matteo whispered. "Go back to the kitchen, Angel."

I only spared him a moment's glance before it drew my eyes back down to the doll. Her sea-green eyes were vacant and empty, surrounded by ivory skin and perfectly layered chestnut hair. Freckles dotted her cheeks and nose, and it didn't take a genius to figure out exactly who she was supposed to look like.

Me.

"What is that?"

"Go, Ivory."

"Where did you get that?" I snapped, ignoring the sympathetic way he stared at me. I knew Matteo well enough to know when he was protecting me, and that expression on his face was answer enough about where the doll came from.

"Everyone get the fuck out," he grunted, and the office cleared instantly. The door closed behind them, and Matteo strode to me and caught me up in his grasp. "He won't touch you," he murmured, as if it would distract me from the missing doll. One of his security people had snatched it up as he fled the room, no doubt the one who messed up and brought it into the house.

"Teo," I whispered, feeling raw in the face of the way that doll made me skin crawl.

Hefting me up into his arms, I barely protested as Matteo carried me over to the couch and sat with me in his lap. I buried my face in his neck, breathing in the familiar scent there and letting it comfort me.

The thing about Matteo for me?

I couldn't be near him and not want him.

Ever.

It was why I kept my distance from him. I knew I had zero self-control where he was concerned and being pressed up against him—feeling him harden beneath me as I straddled his hips—only proved that the feeling was mutual.

Nothing should have been sexy in that moment. Not after being given a creepy doll and lingerie from a man I'd given no indication of interest.

But Matteo was a different story.

He always had been. I pulled out of his neck, crashing my lips to his in a torrent of need. His hands worked my dress up my hips as my hands went to the zipper of his trousers.

I wanted him.

I needed him.

And in that moment, I would not question it.

I needed the reminder I was alive.

Not just a thing to be used and discarded, but a real, live person with feelings and thoughts. I needed to exist, and Matteo was the greatest adrenaline rush I'd ever had.

I freed him from his pants stroking him as he shoved my panties to the side. Rising, I notched him at my entrance and slammed down onto him so hard he groaned. "Easy, Angel."

He knew as well as I did that taking him, even with foreplay, wasn't an easy feat. Taking him with no preparation after zero sex for two days was just plain foolish.

But I needed that pain, the feeling of being ripped open from the inside.

I needed my body to match what he did to my heart. To my soul.

I needed him to understand what he did to me, and I wasn't foolish enough to think I'd ever hurt Matteo the way he hurt me. He'd have to have a heart for that to be possible.

His hands at my hips tried to steady me, but I swatted him away and rocked my hips back and forth quickly. I knew my pace was frenzied. I knew I was acting like a crazy person as I used him, but I couldn't be bothered to care.

Eventually, he settled, seeming to sense that I needed *exactly* what I was taking. He put his hands back on my hips and slid them up and under the fabric of my dress, not stopping or encouraging me so much as just wanting the contact with my skin.

I chased my orgasm, loving the way my clit rubbed against his pubic bone in that position, and feeling like maybe, just maybe, for one moment I was in charge of something. My hands on his chest steadied myself as I exploded into an orgasm, trembling around him and feeling him find his own release inside me.

I didn't let the intimacy of our simultaneous orgasms touch me. Not the way it normally did.

As soon as I caught my breath, I stood and smoothed my dress back down. "Ivory," he whispered, reaching for me. Something in my expression seemed to make his own darken.

I knew what he saw as he looked at me. Something I expected I hadn't been able to achieve since the moment he came back into my life.

But in that moment?

I was safe within my walls.

Not even Matteo Bellandi could touch me.

I turned and strode out of the room, going to the guest room and taking a shower to scrub myself clean. Matteo didn't bother to follow me.

❋❋❋

For a couple of days, the distance between Matteo and I remained firmly planted like a void. I ended every day with him inside me despite it, with him trying to force me from my shell with the intimacy of sex and the sensations only he could wring from my body.

But that's the thing about sex. It could only be intimate if I allowed him to touch more than my body, and after the way he'd betrayed me that wasn't happening.

For the first time in my life, it felt like my heart was safe from Matteo.

I *hated* it.

It should have been a comfort, should have reassured me I'd walk away unscathed when he decided he was finished me. Instead, it just left me feeling cold.

Alone.

Again.

So, when Matteo had suggested I could go to *Indulgence* with Sadie while he handled some business with Lino, I jumped at the chance. I was desperate to get out of that house, desperate to have some semblance of freedom. Going dancing with my friend was a welcome change.

I didn't always expect Matteo to have me surrounded by security.

I never expected to be trapped in the VIP area where he could watch me from his tower of an office.

I decided right then and there as I watched that I really, *really* hated any offices where Matteo was concerned. Watching brunette after brunette strut her way up those steps and act like she had a right to Matteo, listening to them tell Simon that he'd want to see them.

That they're special.

Newsflash.

They weren't. Not even one of them.

After the first few, Simon took to pointing me out and informing the girls that Matteo was spoken for with a live-in girlfriend, and just like that, women glared at me from every corner of the VIP. When I glanced down at the regular part of the club, for ordinary nobodies like me, I wished I could go be anonymous with them. Until I saw women pointing up at me with harsh expressions and speaking in one another's ears.

"Why am I here?" I asked Sadie, flopping onto an empty seat.

"Beats me. This sucks," she groaned. They allowed Sadie to go down to the dance floor. Just not me.

"What the fuck is the point of a club if I can't dance?" I snarled, catching Simon's attention.

He shrugged at me with a smile. "Boss' orders, Ms. Torres."

I groaned, flopping back against the cushions dramatically. A new girl wandered into the VIP, easily admitted access for whatever reason.

If I had to guess?

It was because she was *gorgeous*.

Inhumanly gorgeous.

I wanted to hate her but staring at her clear blue eyes

and chestnut locks only gave me a different idea. I waved her over, patting the seat next to me. She took it with wide eyes, seeming entirely grateful to be saved the awkwardness of being on her own.

"Thank you!" she gushed, perching next to me.

"Have you ever met Matteo Bellandi?" I whispered, and Sadie eyed me curiously. Simon's eyes rested on mine in fixation too, but I didn't care.

"No. I've heard he's beautiful," she whispered, as if Matteo's looks were a secret.

As if.

It seemed the entire brunette female population of Chicago was very well acquainted with Matteo's appearance.

And his dick.

I fought back the surge of possessive jealousy. He wasn't mine, and never would be.

"So, this might sound weird, so bear with me," I laughed. "But do you want to fuck him?"

"Oh, for fuck's sake," Sadie groaned, smacking my shoulder. I winced, turning a glare her way.

"I—what?" the girl asked.

"I live with Matteo, girlfriend by force, I guess. Anywayyyy," I noted her shocked expression and realized I needed to save this conversation from crazy town. Stat. "He's a cheater. Already cheated once, but says he's changed. Blah blah you know the spiel."

"And you want to prove he'll cheat again?" she asked.

I nodded, opening up just enough to admit that Matteo had gotten to me before everything went to shit. "I want it done, before it hurts more, you know?"

"Oh honey, I mean. If he's as good looking as I've heard,

then it's not exactly a hardship, is it? Are you sure you can handle knowing—?"

I nodded, though I knew there was a grimace on my face. "I want to know if he gives you *any* sign of interest. If he takes your number, gives you his. Whatever. I need to know."

She nodded, and I forced Simon to let her up the stairs. He played along, smirking the entire time like he was in on some huge joke.

Sadie took my hand, pulling me from my seat. "Let's go."

"Go where?"

"Dancing." She shoved past two bouncers who just trailed after us in dismay. "They won't touch you. Matteo would cut off their hands if they did. So we will not sit here so you can wait and watch him be seduced."

I swallowed, nodding. As soon as we hit the dance floor, I made it my resolution to *not* look at Matteo's tower. I didn't want to know. Didn't have any interest in finding out how Matteo liked to fuck the girls he took in his office. He'd admitted he didn't have sex in beds except with me, but the office saw some action.

I hated it by extension.

I threw myself into the action of dancing, trying actively to lose track of time. Song passed after song, and when there was no sign of the gorgeous girl returning to the VIP room from Matteo's tower, I felt something inside me shrivel and die.

There would be no doubt in my mind about what happened in that office, not with the time she'd spent there.

When my eyes slid away from the tower slowly, I met Simon's eyes briefly. Even his gaze was knowing, all traces of amusement gone from his features as he stared down at me. I didn't expect the anger making his face tense; the disappointment making his shoulders drop.

Hands touched my waist from behind, and barely a second passed before Scar stepped into my space and physically separated the guy from me.

I forced my best, most convincing, *bullshit* smile to my face as I turned to look at whoever had been brave enough to touch me with bouncers and bodyguards all around me. He was cute, if not oblivious to the *off-limits* aura my guys gave anyone who got too close. "It's okay," I said to Scar, stepping into the stranger's orbit. I took his hands and placed them back on my hips as I resumed the rhythm of the music.

"Ivory—" Scar started, and I smiled at him. He didn't seem to know what to do with that smile, faltering in whatever he'd been about to say. My eyes darted back up to the Tower, and Scar winced when my eyes found his again.

"It was only a matter of time, Scar," I whispered, and his face twisted with confusion.

Like Matteo had really convinced his guys I mattered— that I was important. He probably had to, if he expected them to risk their lives to protect me.

But the secret was out. I was just another in a long line of forgettable women who would mean nothing to Matteo. His jaw tensed, but he nodded, stepping back and letting me turn my attention to my stranger.

I smiled again, shoving down that broken part of me. I didn't get to be upset.

This was my doing.

The stranger smiled at me, and once we had room to move, he picked up the sway of his body and moved in tune with mine. Sadie found her own dance partner, moving close to me in the crush of bodies so we all enjoyed the music as a group.

A prickle of unease tingled down my back, but I was

determined to ignore it. Until people dancing around us froze, and Sadie's hand grasped my arm. Turning to look at her, I saw her face etched with horror. "Ivory," she whispered, grabbing the stranger's hands and shoving them off my body. My eyes met Scar's next, and he smirked at me and crossed his arms over his chest.

My body pivoted slowly, eyes tracking through the crowd where they stared at me.

Matteo stood on the stairs that connected the VIP area to the main dance floor. His hand gripped the railing tightly, so much that it looked painful.

His face was etched in rage.

Those beautiful features looked monstrous in the flashing lights of the club as his darkened gaze found mine. Lino followed behind him, dragging the girl I'd sent down with a tight grip on her arm. Her eyes found mine, wide and full of fear. Her lips mouthed the words, "I'm sorry."

"He didn't take the bait," Sadie whispered in horror. "So, what was he doing up there?"

I glanced over at her, wondering the same thing. When Matteo took the first slow step toward us, it was not the body language of a man who'd fucked up and fallen for a woman's tricks and gotten laid.

It was the movement of a man who'd been wronged.

A man hell-bent on destruction.

I turned, shoving at the stranger. "Go," Sadie whispered, and the poor fool just stared at her. "If you value your life, you'll leave this club right now and never come back." That caught his attention, and he backed away slowly before picking up his pace and fleeing for the door.

I felt Matteo's presence. Felt every step he took until he stood directly behind me. He didn't touch me, didn't speak.

But I knew he was there, heard the ragged intake of each breath.

"Matteo," I whispered, glancing to the side to look at Lino and the woman I'd selfishly sent into a situation I'd never had a hope of controlling.

"Do you think this is a game?" he whispered with a dead voice that probably concealed his rage from anyone who didn't know him. I watched with wide eyes when my stranger was stopped at the doors, bouncers ushering him toward a hall at the back of the bar.

"You're taking this too far, Bellandi," Sadie hissed. "This is too much."

"Do you know who I am, Sadie?" Matteo asked her slowly, and I watched as my friend gulped and nodded. "And you knew this when you called to inform me that Ivory had a date, no doubt?"

Pure, unfiltered betrayal rushed through me, and I turned to stare at her. Not only had she kept secrets from me, but she'd been the one to tell Matteo I'd gone on a date?

"Ivory," she whispered, stepping into my space. Matteo blocked her with an arm at her chest, forcing her to keep her distance.

"Ivory does not exist for you. Not until she understands the severity of what is happening here."

"You can't do that!" Sadie shouted.

"How could you?" I whispered to her, and I thought for sure the sound would be lost to the music. By some miracle, the music was nothing but a dull pound in the background, lost to the potent silence and the crush of people staring at us.

"I can, and I will."

"He doesn't have to. I don't even want to look at you," I hissed, flinching when Sadie winced. She nodded as if she'd expected that and turned and walked away. The bouncers didn't stop her and shove her into some back room to wait for their boss' wrath.

Matteo finally touched me, his fingers brushing the hair off the back of my neck delicately. "The next time you send me a woman," he paused, and my breath hissed between my teeth in anticipation of the crash. The admission that he would touch her, the pain that would break me all over again. "I'll make her and whoever the fuck you think to let touch what's mine, watch me fuck you," he hissed, wrapping his tight grip around my arm and pulling me into his body. I staggered, lost for words, because that had *not* been what I expected him to say. When he turned and pulled me toward the staircase, I fought against his hold.

"Teo," I whispered.

"Shut the fuck up, Ivory," he snarled. He kept pulling me until I stumbled in my heels on the third step. Then he looked at me, grasping me around the waist and tossing me over his shoulder. I shrieked, my hands going for my ass to make sure I wasn't hanging out of my dress. He smacked the back of my thigh, and I whimpered in shock. "I wouldn't expose you. That pussy is mine."

I gasped, smacking at his back in outrage. We passed Simon who chortled despite Matteo's glare.

Up and up we went until we stood outside the door to his tower of an office. "I don't want to go in there," I whispered, and he paused.

"Why?"

"I'm not naïve. I know you've had women in there before. They were all looking for seconds, and it was obvious you'd invited them up."

"I wasn't a saint, Ivory."

"I don't want to be another one of them, Teo." My voice broke, and I buried it in my hands.

"You could never be one of them." He stepped into the office against my wishes, kicking the door closed behind him and locking it. He didn't hesitate to bring me straight to the wall of glass overlooking the club, a King in his kingdom. He set me down, turning me to face the glass. Security convinced everyone to return to the fun, and the music cranked up loud again, but I didn't miss the way everyone's eyes seemed to fixate on the glass even as they drank and danced.

His hands grasped the bottom of my dress, tugging until he revealed my thong. Shrieking, I shoved his hands away. "What are you doing?"

His hand came down on my bare ass in a hard slap, and I screamed. "Matteo!"

"He had his hands on you." His voice went deathly quiet, and it took everything inside me not to tremble. Those strong, somehow calloused hands stroked over the sensitive skin where he'd struck me, and heat bloomed in my core in response.

I hated how much I liked it—hated that I had to resist the urge to arch my back and press my ass into his touch. "I thought you fucked that woman. I didn't think you'd care."

Wrapping his hand around my throat, he slowly guided me back until I had no choice but to support my weight on the glass with my hands and the back of my head touched his shoulder. His free hand fidgeted with my thong, shoving it down my thighs one side at a time and inching it down like he couldn't bear to release his hold on my throat. "Teo," I rasped.

"Shut up, Ivory. Just shut the fuck up and listen for once." I stilled, snapping my mouth closed. The sound of him unzipping his pants behind me made me whimper, anticipation of what was coming like a pulse in my veins.

I thought I'd had everything Matteo had to give. I thought I made him lose control sometimes.

I'd been wrong.

He shoved inside me in one hard thrust, not giving my body time to adjust to the feeling of fullness that came with him being inside me. "This is where I belong," he groaned, keeping me still and keeping himself planted deep.

So deep.

It felt like I could feel him in my soul. Etched there permanently in some strange tether that tied us together through the years.

Over lifetimes.

Like nothing could ever keep us apart.

"I will n*ever* touch another woman again, Angel." His words were soft, menacing beneath the surface. The real Matteo that few ever got to see playing at the surface instead of hidden down deep. "I'm yours, Ivory." Tears stung my eyes when his lips touched my cheek, the soft pressure too much to handle at that moment. "And you're mine."

I nearly sobbed.

Because I wanted that.

I wanted to be his, and for him to be mine.

But to love Matteo was to be broken. I knew that better than anyone.

And I couldn't do it again.

"I'm not a good man." He pulled his hips back, thrusting in so hard he rammed against the end of me. A mix of pleasure and pain shot through me, and I gasped in his hold.

"Teo."

"I don't care if you want to leave me. I won't let you," he

growled in my ear as he fucked me in slow and deep, hard strokes. "Do you know why, Angel?"

I shook my head, too incoherent to form words as he worked me over. His free hand wrapped around my front, pressing between my thighs to feel the place where we connected. He cupped me, touching himself as he slid in and out of me and made me mindless. The palm of his hand pressed against my clit and threatened me with an orgasm that hovered just out of reach.

"Because I love you. I have loved you since the moment I laid eyes on you." He shoved deep, pausing there and letting me think for just a moment. "Nothing will ever take you from me."

"Stop," I pleaded on a whisper, and from the way he slid out of my pussy and then glided back in, he knew I didn't mean to stop fucking me.

"I'll never stop," he whispered, that hand abandoning my throat finally in favor of cupping my cheek and turning my head so he could look at me. "Tell me you understand."

"Please, stop," I begged, clenching my eyes shut, so I didn't have to look into the piercing blue of his eyes. Even his eyes told lies.

Even his eyes deceived.

"Look at me," he commanded, and my eyes snapped open of their own accord. "You will be my wife." My body acted on its own, fighting in his grasp until his length slid free and I stumbled forward into the glass. "You will be the mother of my children." He stalked toward me, gathering me up in his arms even as I slapped at him like a cornered animal. He spun until my ass hit his desk, and he shoved everything onto the floor as he pushed me onto my back. Forcing my legs wide, he plunged inside me again and my back arched in pleasure despite the panic flooding through me. When I moved to rise, his hand went back to my throat, pinning me to the desk with pressure that threatened instead of hurt.

This was not the Matteo I could fight. It wasn't the Matteo I could plead with.

This was the criminal who took what he wanted without remorse. His face came into my space, staring at me and our breaths mingled. He shoved one knee high, keeping it positioned with his hand on the back of my thigh.

And then he fucked me.

Brutally.

Until I sobbed beneath him, and I would have sworn I would feel him imprinted inside me for the rest of my life. "Teo, please," I whimpered.

His lips crashed to mine, ending my halfhearted protest. Even as I feared the man staring back at me as he ravaged me, an orgasm built between my thighs. I tried to reach for it, wanted it to wash away the taste of pain Matteo gave as he slid in and out of my tender pussy.

He pulled his mouth away, glaring down at me. He pressed his thumb to my clit, but didn't move it, just tormented me with the promise of what could be. "Tell me," he growled.

"Tell you what?" I whimpered. "Teo, please."

"Tell me you're mine."

"I'm yours!" I shrieked, willing to admit just about anything in that moment.

"Tell me you love me." I froze, staring up at him in horror. "Tell me, *Cara mia*." His face softened, something in the beast receding as he stared in the face of my panic. "Tell me," he pressed.

"I love you," I cried, tears falling from my eyes to tickle my ears. "I never stopped," I admitted and hated myself for it. His thumb made a single circle around my clit, and I erupted beneath him to the sound of his arrogance.

"I know," he murmured, and after a few more slow, languid thrusts he flooded me with his heat.

Even after we both caught our breath, Matteo made no move to separate from me, pressing his chest against mine and cradling me.

It was like he knew my foundation had been rocked.

That he'd changed my world with three little words.

I just hoped they weren't lies.

25

IVORY

The smells from the kitchen made even my nose tingle with excitement.

The Ragu Napoletano was something I'd made occasionally, but never for a true Italian like Matteo.

Arms wrapped around my waist, Matteo's face nuzzling into the crook of my neck. "That smells delicious," he murmured, nipping at my skin softly. "But not as good as you."

I swatted him away playfully. "Get out!" I giggled when the scruff on his face tickled my jaw. "I mean it! You'll make me overcook the Strozzapretti."

"So make more." He shrugged, his shoulders jostling me as if he truly didn't care.

"Are you insane? No. Be gone, you slut."

"Your slut," he smirked, and one of his hands took mine in his. He turned me to face him, staring down at me intently in a way that scared me.

"Is everything okay?" I asked, biting my lip. His free hand left my waist, darting into his pocket. The thumb of the hand that held mine captive stroked over my left ring finger as he stared at it in fixation.

The smile he gave me when our eyes met again was breathtaking. A full, disarming smile that stole the air from my lungs. He held my eyes with his, and the cool touch of metal against the skin of my finger made my body freeze.

"What—what is that?" I asked, eyes darting down to the huge teardrop shaped diamond settled around my finger in two intricate, diamond studded bands of rose gold.

"Pick a date. I want to know by tomorrow."

"I—what?" I asked, feeling like my jaw was on the floor.

"A date, Angel," he chuckled. "I'd prefer a summer wedding, so we need to make arrangements quickly."

"A year is plenty of time—" I started to explain, because I had no need for a big wedding.

Wedding.

"You misunderstand me, *Cara mia*. I'm not waiting until next year to make you my wife."

"But it's already the end of May!"

"As I said, pick a date." He gave me that beautiful smile again, and I almost wanted to smack him for the way he enjoyed my floundering.

"You can't just put a ring on my finger, you know? You didn't even ask me if I would marry you!" I argued, shrinking back into the counter as much as I could.

"Asking would imply you have a choice." He smirked, giving me a glimpse of that dark possessiveness that always seemed to linger beneath the surface.

"Matteo," I warned. "I think we should slow down."

"I'll not waste another moment of my life without you as my wife, Ivory. Pick a fucking date," he growled, and I winced. With a sigh, I nodded. I was learning. Maybe I wasn't the fastest learner, but I knew well enough to know when to push and when not to. This was clearly one of those moments I shouldn't touch.

He smiled again, pleased with my concession. "Thank you. Don't overcook the Strozzapreti," he said, turning and striding back to his office like he hadn't turned my world on its head again.

Like marrying me had always been a foregone conclusion, and I suppose for Matteo it had. After all, he didn't care if I said no.

We were getting married.

His wife.

Ivory Bellandi.

Fuck.

26

IVORY

"Where are we going?" I grinned at Matteo as he swerved the Aston through the highway traffic just outside the city. We'd spent a few days in bliss, ignoring the world and getting lost in each other whenever we could manage. Matteo still worked, I had a feeling that would never change, but I'd finally set foot in his office long enough to work from the couch.

Offices no longer seemed terrifying.

Was he perfect?

Absolutely not.

He was dominating, controlling. He manipulated me to get his way and forced my hand when I didn't do something he wanted, but I realized that everything he'd done was to protect me.

Could I really be angry that he loved me enough to keep me safe?

He was all I'd never dared to dream for.

I didn't want to waste any more time.

He eyes met mine across the center console, his hand

tightening around mine briefly. He glanced at an exit sign before moving into the right lane to take it. "Don't freak out."

I froze solid. "Why would I freak out? What did you do?" I'd only just come to terms with the last time; I did not need a new thing to be pissed about.

"We're going to my uncle's house for dinner," he admitted, and everything inside me tightened. I'd never met his uncle before, but I'd caught snippets of information from conversations Matteo and Lino had. I knew enough to know he wasn't a kind man.

"Say what now?" I asked, turning to him and feeling my eyes harden when he glanced at me in amusement.

"You had to meet him sometime, Angel," he laughed.

I glared at the corner of his eye, that spot where just the faintest trace of crow's feet were forming on his face. Even the tiny trace of aging only emphasized his dangerous features. "You're right. I probably did," I agreed, and the relief in his face was comical. He seriously thought he was off the hook. "But not today! Not without knowing what's coming. You blindsided me, you asshole!"

He barked out a sharp laugh, reveling in my growing comfort with him. In Matteo's words, it often grew boring having people just do what he said all the time.

I was anything but boring.

"Can you blame me?" he asked.

"Why was this necessary? Now I'm panicking!" I groaned, tearing my hand out of his grip.

"Which is exactly why I didn't tell you until we were almost there. I didn't want you fretting all day when you could be happy with me."

"That's almost sweet," I admitted. "But mostly selfish I think."

"It was completely selfish," he consented with a rogue

grin. I smacked his arm, trying not to think about the time before we'd left the house where he'd ambushed me in the shower.

Where I'd gone to wash the sex off me.

That had been an exercise in futility.

"What if he hates me?" I whispered, and Matteo winced.

"He won't be your biggest fan," he returned, and I groaned.

"Why?"

"You aren't Italian. He wants me to marry a friend's daughter, and he thinks—" Teo paused, thinking over his words, and I knew the next statement would be about whatever his secret business enterprises entailed. "He thinks love is a weakness. That I should marry someone I'm prepared to lose one day."

I widened my eyes at him as he turned down a long driveway. "What's the point?"

"To have children." He shrugged. "That's the entire point of marriage to my uncle, after Lino's mom died, anyway."

"What happened to her?" Lino never talked about her. I hadn't known for sure she'd died but had guessed as much.

"There was an accident. Men targeting my uncle ran them off the road. He lived, she didn't."

"God, Teo," I whispered, horror rolling through me. "What are you involved in?"

He didn't answer, pulling up to the security gate in front of an estate slightly smaller than Matteo's. The driveway wasn't as long, not as winding, and the house itself was boxier than the sprawling structure that Matteo lived in.

But whatever the family business was, Matteo's uncle benefited from it greatly.

"Go on through, Mr. Bellandi," the guard said when

Matteo rolled down the window, and the Aston rolled through the gate as it opened.

"Breathe," he chuckled. "My uncle not liking you has *nothing* to do with you. Being sweet won't change his opinion. Looking your best won't change his mind. And I don't give the first fuck what he thinks of you, because I choose you. That's all that matters." We pulled up in front of the house, and something unwound inside me. There was a lot less pressure when I knew his dislike of me was already a foregone conclusion. "I won't let him disrespect you."

"Okay," I whispered. Matteo turned to me, inspecting me. Satisfied with whatever he saw, he climbed out of the car. Regardless of what Matteo said, I was grateful I lived in dresses. My sky-blue wrap dress was timeless and classy, and probably the one thing I might have contemplated wearing to meet Matteo's uncle, anyway.

With both his parents gone, the disapproving Uncle was the closest thing to parents he had left. Lino liked me, I thought. So, there was just the Uncle left to sway. Maybe he'd come around eventually, right?

I couldn't imagine spending my life with a man, to have half his family hate me for the entirety of our time together. "About me being your wife," I started as soon as he opened the car door for me. He pulled me out, tucking the hair behind my ear on one side.

"Mhm," he murmured, shutting the car door with a soft thud.

"I don't want to be a problem for your family. You don't have to feel obligated to make me promises, Teo. Not every relationship is built to last, maybe—"

"Don't," he hissed, the hand that closed the door staying planted firmly so he trapped me against the car. "Nobody obligates me to do anything. Ever."

"But maybe this is better off as a short-term relationship. We don't have to muddy it up with things like divorce and kids—"

"There will never be a divorce," he grunted, grasping my hand in his and tugging me away from the car. "I will only marry once, Ivory."

"So, let it be with someone—"

"Enough." His voice was a whisper, but the warning was clear. I didn't even know why I bothered to argue with the man sometimes. So stuck in his own way that he'd never consider when someone else offered him a viable option.

"Okay," I whispered back, knowing fully well I'd resume the conversation another time.

I plastered an easy smile on my face, determined to make the best impression despite whatever Matteo's uncle might think of me. Matteo knocked on the door, as cool as ever, and I snuggled into his side. The last thing I wanted when his uncle formed his opinion of me firsthand was for Matteo to be distant because I'd pissed him off. A bit of his coolness melted as he grasped me around the waist and smiled down at me momentarily, but I knew the rest of his attitude wouldn't change. He was in work mode, the same calculated way he behaved the moment he set foot in his office or when talking with one of his guys who he didn't trust as much.

At first, the persona had terrified me, especially combined with my residual hatred of his office itself. But after being around him in that mode more often, I was insanely attracted to it. The dark waves of dominance that poured off him appealed to something in me, the part of me who had floundered on her own and worked to find herself loved the comfort in which Matteo just was who he was.

When a middle-aged Italian woman answered the door,

she nodded to Matteo respectfully before turning surprised eyes to me. "Mr. Bellandi. We weren't aware you were bringing a guest." Panic crossed over her features, and Matteo continued as if he wasn't bothered by it. Stepping into the house like he belonged, he dragged me with him. The woman's eyes darted toward the living room, and voices sounded from the space. Matteo's eyes narrowed at the sound of a woman's tinkle of laughter.

"What did he do?" Matteo growled, clasping me tighter around the waist.

"He invited Mr. Morelli and his daughter," she whispered, eyes clenched. Her tension racketed up my own until I gasped when Matteo used the hand at my waist to guide me into the living room without preamble. Lino stood off to the side, totally and completely devoid of all the playfulness I was so used to seeing in him. His serious mask had been in place before we'd even entered the room, but it faded momentarily when he approached us.

"Ivory, sweetheart, you look beautiful as always," he said, pressing a kiss to my cheek affectionately. He and Matteo exchanged a look, and it was clear who Lino would side with when the battle lines were drawn. Judging from the disbelieving glare the three other occupants of the room leveled me with, I had to guess that moment was approaching.

Quickly.

"Matteo." His uncle grimaced. "What's this?"

"I could ask you the same thing, Gabriele. I'm fairly certain I made it very clear the last time we saw one another that I was not interested in your arrangement regarding Elena." I felt the wince that went through my body as my eyes met hers, knowing that the beauty on the couch with the big brown eyes was my competition as far as she was concerned.

She smiled, completely unconcerned with Matteo's dismissal. Whatever arrangement Matteo's Uncle Gabriele had in mind; love wasn't a part of it. She stood from her perch on the blue velvet sofa, crossing the distance between us to press her lips to Matteo's cheek in greeting. I fought to maintain my composure, knowing I needed to appear unconcerned with the beauty before me. If Matteo wanted her, he would have her, no doubt.

I didn't want to think about the fact that he could have already.

"It's always lovely to see you, Matteo," she practically purred. "Who is your friend?"

I bristled at the blatant dismissal, feeling murderous as she reached out a hand to touch his forearm in familiarity. I didn't understand how I'd gone from trying to shove a woman at him to feeling possessive, but I suspected it had something to do with the heavy, weighted ring sitting on my finger.

"Elena," Matteo said coolly. "This is my fiancé, Ivory."

Her eyes widened, and she turned her back to us momentarily to shoot a meaningful glare to Gabriele. "You assured me I would be his wife."

"You will be," the Uncle reassured her, ignoring the glare Matteo shot him. "She is merely a passing fancy. You know how men are."

"The ring on her finger tells a different story," she spat, eyes darting to my left hand where Matteo used it to drag me into his side. "Such a pity. Come daddy, I believe we've been misled enough for one day." The other man followed his daughter out the door.

"Lino, take Ivory into the dining room," Matteo said, and

my eyes turned to him. I wanted to argue that my place was beside him, but the menace on his face communicated that this was exactly one of those moments where I just needed to get the Hell out of his way.

"Of course," Lino agreed, holding out an arm for me to take. I stepped away from Matteo, letting him guide me to the door at the back of the room.

"Not one more step, son," Gabriele snarled with a vicious bite that made me want to shrink into Lino for protection. "If she's so worthy of being your wife, then she will need to get familiar with situations like this. Will she not?" he turned to Matteo.

"Don't you dare," Matteo returned, and his hand went behind his back.

Both men moved so suddenly that I couldn't possibly follow the movement. All I knew was one moment they glared at each other, the next they each had a gun in hand and pointed at the other. I gasped, and Lino cursed under his breath.

"She is a weakness. I should have gotten rid of her the first time she distracted you from what's important." He shifted his gun to the right, taking his aim off Matteo and leveling it on me where Lino guided me to the door.

I winced, feeling Lino shove me behind him so I wasn't staring down the barrel of the gun. "Killing her now would be a mercy compared to what they'll do to her to hurt you."

"She's not mama, father," Lino begged. "Matteo won't let anything happen to her."

"Put down your fucking gun before I kill you," Matteo threatened, and the quiet rage in his voice sent fear through me.

What the fuck had I gotten myself mixed up in?

Gabriele huffed. "You'd shoot your own uncle? For pussy?"

"I'd shoot you for calling her that. I'd make you suffer if you hurt her," Matteo growled. Gabriele lowered his gun, tossing it onto the coffee table and raising a hand as if he was no longer a threat.

I exhaled a sigh of relief, releasing the desperate grasp I had on the back of Lino's suit. I didn't even remember grabbing him, remembered nothing aside from the terror that I'd lose Matteo.

I couldn't lose him.

"She had better be fertile," his Uncle grimaced, staring down Matteo's fury. I had to admit, it took a brave man to push his luck in the face of all that was Matteo.

Matteo's features twisted, and the sound of the gun going off was deafening in the living room. My hands flew to my ears, covering them instinctively. "Fuck," Lino grunted, staring at where his father clutched his arm in agony.

"You fucking shot me."

"You ever threaten my woman again, and it will be far worse than a flesh wound. Come Ivory," Matteo demanded, and I rushed into his side. Even though I was terrified of the glimpse I'd gotten into that beast that lurked under the surface, I knew Matteo wouldn't hurt me.

I felt that in my soul.

It didn't stop me from trembling as I burrowed into him though. He guided me out of the house, and I resisted the urge to ask questions. I got into the car, Matteo in the driver's seat, and didn't even argue when he pulled me over the center console and crushed me to his chest. "Teo, what—?"

"When we get home. I'll explain everything when we get home." He set me back to my seat, and I buckled up.

"Why not now?" I asked when he put the car in gear and started down the driveway. The gate opened at the end, and we escaped Gabriele's manor in one piece.

Or two.

"I can't have you trying to run. I need you locked down first," he admitted, and my heart clenched.

"It's bad, isn't it?"

"Do you love me?" he asked.

"You know I do."

"Then that's all that matters."

I hung my head, tears threatening to fall. Matteo had shot someone.

His own uncle.

And he didn't seem the least bit remorseful. "That's not the first time you've shot someone, is it?"

"When we get home."

I released a quiet sob, turning my attention to stare out the window.

I was so fucking screwed.

※※※

The door to Matteo's office closed behind him with a quiet click. He turned to face me, a thousand emotions flitting across his normally impassive face. "You need to understand that what I'm about to tell you will change nothing."

"Teo, you're scaring me," I whispered, stepping back as far as the space would allow when he prowled toward me. He caged me between him and the desk, touching my cheek so gently I might have thought I imagined it had my eyes been closed.

"Anyone but you would be right to be afraid. Anyone but you would have to be stupid not to be, but I'll never hurt you, Angel," he whispered. "I wish I could be a better man for you, but I'm not, and I can't be."

"Why can't we just leave? Go somewhere and be someone else?"

"This is all I know. They raised me to run the family businesses, and I can't abandon that legacy. I'd always be a threat to whoever tried to take over, and we'd never be safe. Not really."

"I don't understand." I shook my head, staring up at him with glassy eyes.

He sighed, touching his forehead to mine. It felt final. It felt like he knew, no matter what he demanded, that whatever came next would cost him.

That it would cost him *me*.

"My family has run this city since my grandfather was in charge. Nothing happens here without our say so."

"You make it sound like you're some kind of mob boss." I shook my head with a dark chuckle, my smile fading when his eyes caught mine. He didn't laugh. Didn't flinch. "No. That's ridiculous."

"We call it more of a syndicate, but the premise is the same," he said, voice low.

Quiet, as if waiting for me to scream.

"But mobsters deal drugs and sell weapons!" I whisper hissed. "They sell women, and you told me you didn't do that."

"I told you I didn't take part in sex trafficking. The women who work for me are willing and very well compensated—" The sound of my hand striking him across the face echoed through the otherwise silent office. I stared at him in horror, waiting for the beast to strike. But to my amazement, he only nodded. "I deserved that."

"You think?" My eyes went to the ring on my finger, staring at it as tears slid down my cheeks.

"Don't even think about it," he snarled at me, pulling my attention away from the ring that suddenly felt like a shackle to a life I didn't want.

"I don't want to be a mob wife."

"Too fucking bad. I told you, this changes *nothing*," he stressed, pressing into me tighter. "I do what I can to keep innocent people from getting caught up in this world, Ivory. I'm not a good man, but I'm not the worst there is. Me in charge is what's best for the city."

"You shot your own uncle!" I protested.

"He disrespected you!"

"Was it the first time you've shot someone then?" I asked with a grimace, because he and I both knew that I didn't want to know the answer to that question. I needed to bury my head in the sand and pretend the day never happened.

"No," he admitted.

"Have you killed before?" I whispered, and his face shuttered as he stared at me.

"Don't ask me questions you don't want the answer to, Angel."

"Oh God," I cried, flinching away from him. But I had nowhere to go. Nowhere to run. "You're a murderer," I whispered.

"In my life, it is kill or be killed. I have done what I need to do to survive."

"This is why you left me, isn't it? You need a good little Italian wife to make your mob happy. Fuck, I'm so stupid," I winced.

"No. My uncle believes that women are a weakness. People only use the ones we love against us, and to protect Lino and I he forced us to stay away from the women we love. He threatened you, and I had no choice but to walk away to keep him from hurting you, Angel. Believe me. Nothing else could have ever made me leave you."

"You expect me to believe you *broke me* to protect me? I wasn't worth walking away from this shit?! You chose this over me, Matteo. You do not get to sugar coat that. The wealth, the power, God. Is that all that matters to you?"

His hands grasped me around my waist, twisting me around until he bent me over his desk.

I gasped, swatting at his hands behind me as he hefted my dress up over my ass. The hand at the back of my neck kept me pinned in place, unable to even begin to fight him. "Stop it!" I shrieked, flinching when he tore my thong down my legs.

"And what about you, Angel? What happened to my adrenaline junkie who couldn't get enough of the rush of doing something wrong? Who loved to drive my fast cars without a license and dared any cop to fuck with her?" His fingers pressed between my thighs, finding me already growing wet in response to his skilled manipulations of my body.

"I was a stupid child!" I yelled. "I did stupid shit, and it got me in a stupid situation."

"No, the only thing you did that was stupid," he said, releasing himself from his pants and pressing inside me slowly until he filled me to the brim. "Was doing something like that without me to protect you." He groaned, and I heard him fumble around in a drawer of his desk.

"What are you doing?" I whispered; my head turned the wrong way.

"Before you go accusing me of shit I didn't do, I've never fucked anyone but you in this house. This is for all those nights when I'd sit here, working late, and imagining your pretty fucking lips wrapped around my dick." I had no clue what he was talking about, but it came a little clearer the moment a bottle uncapped, and cold liquid trickled down between my cheeks.

"Matteo!" I gasped, squirming away when he pressed his thumb against that forbidden place.

"I'm going to show you just how good it can feel to be bad, *Cara mia*."

"Teo!" I screamed, wincing when that thumb popped inside the outer ring of muscle and pressed inside me. His cock worked my pussy, sliding in and out of me in slow, intoxicating strokes that teased my g-spot without ever sending me over the edge.

"You are mine. This pussy is mine." His thumb left my ass, leaving me with a bizarre empty feeling until he replaced it with a long finger and pressed in mercilessly.

"It hurts," I whispered.

"This ass is mine," he continued as if he hadn't heard me. "You say it hurts, and yet your pussy is strangling my cock and so fucking wet I can hear it." He added another finger, making me burn from the inside out. That same dark pleasure I got when Matteo did things, I shouldn't like set me on fire, coiling in my core and waiting to explode.

"Let me come," I begged, not even recognizing the deep rasp of my own voice.

"You come when you take my cock in your ass." He gave another teasing roll of his hips, tormenting me in all the best ways. "You ready for that?"

"Just do it already," I hissed, feeling strangely brave in the face of what I was so sure would tear me in two. That dark side of me craved the things Matteo did, the way he took control of my body and demanded what he wanted without preamble.

He groaned, pulling his fingers free. He abandoned my pussy in favor of rubbing lube all over himself if the squeezing sound of the bottle behind me was any sign. With both his hands used, he finally had no choice but to let go of my neck. I turned my head to look back at him, watching him. For the first time when I looked at him, I knew exactly who he was. Exactly what he did.

It changed nothing. Didn't change the fact that I loved him with every fiber of my being.

I hated myself for it, knowing I could love a monster capable of such unforgivable sins.

When the head of him pressed against my ass, I tried to relax. While I may not have had anal before, I knew enough to know tensing up was not in my best interest. He stilled me with a hand at my hip, guiding himself inside slowly and making me whimper beneath him. The stretch was uncomfortable, outright painful even, but the way pleasure built with every minuscule thrust into me was undeniable. Wrapping a hand around me, Matteo worked his fingers at my clit in slow, tantalizing circles, adding more pleasure to the mix to overwhelm the pain. He paused, pressing his forehead to my back momentarily when his balls touched my pussy. "You like this," he groaned, and the slickness coating his fingers was undeniable. He pulled back, pressing back in slowly.

"Fuck!" I moaned, wiggling my hips to get more friction from his fingers.

"Not yet," he ordered, stilling me with a slap to my left butt cheek.

"You said I could come when your dick was in my ass. Did you not get the memo that it's in there? Because I sure as fuck did," I argued. He chuckled, humor in every little inflection of that deep voice.

"Oh, I sure as fuck got that memo, Angel." He pulled back, picking up his pace when I didn't protest. His strokes were still soft, downright delicate compared to the way he normally took my pussy, and I could feel his eyes watching the spot where he entered me so gently. "You look so fucking beautiful taking my cock in your ass."

"Fuck you, Teo," I groaned, and his fingers left my clit in favor of pressing two inside my pussy. "Oh God," I cried, thrusting back against him. "Please."

That thumb of his pressed to my clit, and I detonated around him on a cry. Heat scorched my insides when he followed me over the edge, and we stayed in place long enough to catch our breaths.

Matteo pulled free and brought me to shower without another word.

I felt like I'd changed. Like the Ivory I'd been before was gone, replaced by a woman who would let a murderer fuck her ass and love it.

It left me feeling numb.

Because I didn't recognize myself when I looked in the mirror. Matteo was content to hold me close, smothering me so he knew that I hadn't left. He didn't say it, but I could see the panic in rare moments. I knew he didn't want to lose me anymore than I wanted to lose him, so one of us would have to concede.

I knew it would be me.

It always was.

27

MATTEO

Ryker stood just inside the door, welcoming me inside with a nod. "Is he alive?" I asked.

Another nod in response, but the tension pouring off him was tangible. It impressed me the man was still alive.

The dealer who had shot his woman's husband had been a very idiotic man.

There was no doubt in my mind that he wouldn't walk away with his life. Even if I'd been so inclined, which I wasn't, there would be no way to talk Ryker down from the cliff. Not after I'd seen the pictures of Calla sobbing with her two children clinging to her.

"What are you going to do about the woman?" I asked as we walked toward the freezer. Her husband hadn't been a good man, the crooked cop that he was, but she hadn't had the slightest clue about that. So wrapped up in the picture perfect life they lived, she never saw the darkness that lurked beneath the surface in the man she'd married and shared a bed with. She didn't know him. Not in the slightest. The reality made me grateful that the truth was out with Ivory. No matter how much the truth of who I was had hurt her, the pain was done. She could heal, and there would be no more secrets between us.

Not that she'd ever find out about, anyway.

"She needs time," he answered gruffly, one of the rare twinges of emotion crossing over his face. Only that woman and those kids could bring out anything that even remotely resembled humanity in the enigma that was Ryker. "They aren't ready."

"No, they're not," I agreed. "It would take a cruel man to uproot them right now."

He nodded. "She hasn't worked in years. Never needed to. I'll send money. Take care of them until they're ready to understand."

He opened the freezer door, schooling his harsh features back into the mask of indifference that he was so gifted at. I wondered if it was conflicting for him. He didn't want Calla and the kids to suffer but having Chad out of the way undoubtedly freed up the place he wanted to fill more than anything.

I stepped in behind him, glaring at the beaten pulp that remained of the overzealous street dealer who worked for me. His eyes were nearly swollen shut, but even with all that, he still recognized me the moment I walked in. "Mr. Bellandi," he sobbed.

"Who gave you permission to kill the cop?" I asked.

"No—nobody, sir. He saw me dealing, was gonna arrest me. I didn't have no choice!" the guy sniveled, greasy hair hanging down to his shoulders in a matted mess of blood and his own filth.

"Tell me, what do you think is more valuable to me? A low-time street dealer who buys more of his own product than he sells or a cop on my payroll who makes evidence disappear? Hmm?"

He winced, fat tears rolling down his blood-stained cheeks. "I didn't know!"

"Even if he wasn't on my payroll, do you think it's more of a hassle for me to get you out of prison for dealing? Or for killing a cop?"

"I'm sorry. I didn't think—"

"Clearly," I spat. "His wife and kids are important to my friend Ryker. I'll let him decide what to do with you. But allow me to make one thing clear. You'll never see the light of day again, so you can save your apologies. I'm not in the habit of employing idiots." I turned, striding for the freezer door. Ryker nodded at me, a little satisfied smirk playing at his lips.

However, he ended the dealer's life, one thing was for sure.

It wouldn't be pleasant.

The dealer's screams started before the freezer door closed behind me and cut the sound off completely.

As soon as I was out of the warehouse, I climbed into the Aston and went home.

It would be the first time I did something unsavory after Ivory learned the truth. She'd given me a look when I left the house at ten at night that communicated exactly what she suspected.

I guess the good thing was that I didn't need to fear she'd think I was having an affair.

Bright side.

I drove in silence, hoping she'd be sleeping by the time I got home. If she asked, I'd tell her the truth. But I still wanted to keep her as sheltered from that side of my life as possible.

She was everything good, soft, and sweet. I loved that about her and intended to do anything I could to protect it.

Even if it meant keeping her in the dark.

When I finally pulled up in front, the house was quiet, nobody but my security moving around the property. I nodded at one of the door guards, moving into the house wordlessly. The sight of Ivory curled up in the center of my bed, tangled in the blankets, made my heart heavy.

I couldn't stand it when she tried to sleep without me, the way her brain felt the danger that came with not being wrapped up in me.

I stripped out of my clothes, showering as efficiently as I could. Even though I had done nothing, hadn't even put hands on the man, I couldn't sully Ivory with the filth of my decisions. I wore my bloodied hands like armor but would never allow them to stain her.

When I was finally clean, I climbed into bed with her, my boxer briefs on just for safety. I didn't tolerate Ivory sleeping naked if I could avoid it and didn't do it myself either. With my lifestyle, the risk of there being an emergency in the middle of the night was too great. I pulled her into me, rolling her under my body like every other night. Her brow immediately settled, relaxing into a content expression even in her sleep.

I knew exactly how Ryker felt about Calla.

Because Ivory was the only thing that made me feel human.

I breathed her in, savoring the humanity that only she could give me.

And fell asleep faster than I ever had after leaving the warehouse where all my greatest sins happened.

28

MATTEO

"Matteo. Mr. Atticus Revere is here to see you. Shall I instruct Pete to open the gate?" Donatello rarely interrupted when I was working, particularly after Ivory started spending her computer time in my office with me.

He never knew when we might be preoccupied.

I wasn't even sorry.

"Yes." I nodded, concern pooling in my stomach. There weren't many men who had my respect enough to worry me when they dropped by unannounced.

"Atticus Revere?" Ivory asked, her lips pursing as she thought her way through the name. "Why do I know that name?"

"He's a pro-football player. Quarterback for Minnesota." I stood, helping Ivory gather up her notebooks. "You can meet him, if you like, but we'll need a few moments. I'm sorry, Angel. I wasn't aware he'd be dropping by."

She shrugged. "I should start making lunch, anyway. How do you know a Pro-football player?"

"My father put him through school. Even when he was

in high school, he was an incredible athlete, apparently. But his grades weren't good enough to land a scholarship. My father always loved football. Wanted to see the kid do well, give him the chance he wouldn't have if he hung around Chicago." My father had been a cold man, uncaring most of the time. But God help the man who tried to come between him and his football.

I set Ivory's things on the coffee table when Rev swaggered into the office with an easy smile. I returned it, moving forward to shake his hand. "Good to see you, Bellandi."

"You too. This is my fiancé, Ivory," I introduced, holding out an arm and inviting my angel into my side. She accepted, gladly pressing herself into me.

"Fiancé?" Rev raised an eyebrow in surprise with a huff of laughter. "I didn't think it'd been that long since we spoke."

"It hasn't," I agreed. "I suspect you'll understand one day."

"It's nice to meet a friend of Teo's," Ivory murmured, pressing a kiss to my cheek and gathering her things. "But I suspect you came to talk business. I'll get out of your hair. Would you like to stay for lunch?" she asked, bringing a smile to my face.

"You're an idiot if you say no," I informed Rev, and he chuckled in that easy, laid back manner he learned from his Southern daddy.

"She a good cook?" he drawled, and Ivory smiled at me smugly.

"A chef actually. The best, but I might be biased."

"Then shit yeah, I'll stay. Won't pass up a good, home cooked meal."

"Great," Ivory agreed with that smile that made my breath catch. She retreated from the office, closing the door behind her and letting us get down to business.

"So, what brings you by?" I asked, sitting down behind my desk and leaving Rev to get comfortable in a chair in front of it. He steepled his hands over his knees, leaning forward to look at me intently.

"I'm retiring."

"Okay," I nodded. Thirty-five wasn't an unheard-of age to retire from pro-sports, and I wasn't an unreasonable man. While Rev's contract with my father had ensured a small cut of Rev's pay came to me, I by no means required it.

I had plenty of money of my own.

"That's it?" he asked, and I chuckled.

"You've more than paid off your school loans at this point. Out of curiosity, what prompted the retirement? I thought you'd play until you dropped dead."

He sat back in his seat, a smile of disbelief flitting across his face. "My kid's in high school, man. My ex just moved to this new town in Colorado, and I ain't gonna miss another minute of his life, you know? Time to settle down."

"Admirable," I agreed. "I wish you the best of luck, Rev. You deserve it. Let's go see what my woman is cooking up."

I wasn't a good man. Was far too hard most of the time. But for a man who did everything he could to hold up his word? A man who worked his ass off and just wanted to spend time with his son?

I could pretend for an hour or two.

29

IVORY

I was going crazy.
Literally.

I could feel my sanity slowly slipping away the longer I spent in that house. The more days I spent cooped up like a prisoner.

I hated feeling like the world wasn't a safe place and wondering if I'd ever look at it the same. How could I? When I was set to marry a mob boss of Chicago.

Fuck, that still sounded insane.

I shook my head, snapping out of my trance when my engagement ring clinked against the mixing bowl I pulled from the cupboard. I slipped it off my finger, setting it on the bottom shelf of the cabinet for safekeeping while I cooked.

Wearing jewelry was one of those things that I couldn't overlook, even if I rebelled against my culinary training in a lot of ways. Because it was unsanitary and made me feel gross.

Matteo had a sick sixth sense about when I took that ring off.

If I didn't think it would make me paranoid, I'd suspect him of putting a sensor in it.

But that was crazy, right?

Sure enough, he stepped into the kitchen and snatched my ring out of the cupboard in favor of shoving it back onto my finger. He stared down at me, eyes full of rage that we were about to have that damn conversation again.

Yeah, well, I was sick of it too asshole.

I tore it off my finger, shoving it back into the cupboard. "It bumps into everything," I protested. "Not to mention it's gross. Do you know what germs get on rings like that? Nope. Not happening."

Matteo's eyes narrowed on me, studying my face. "You're pissed off today. Are you feeling okay?"

I squinted back, daring him to comment. I'd been hit with sudden spells of nausea the last couple days, at the most random moments. Nothing severe, and the moments passed almost as quickly as they appeared, but I could see the control freak in Matteo rebelling against the notion that something could be wrong with me.

"I told you, I'm fine. I just need fresh air. I need to run, but you won't let me leave the fucking property!"

"Christ, Ivory. The property is huge, you act like you can't run out there."

"It's not the same," I whined. "Please, Teo."

"Not yet," he sighed. "I haven't heard shit about Adrian in over a week. I don't trust it."

"Fine," I groaned, turning back to the counter to mix. If I couldn't exercise, maybe dark chocolate brownies could fix it.

"If you're looking for a workout, I can help with that," he chuckled, stepping into my back and running his lips behind my ear.

"Oh how convenient," I laughed. "I don't think sex is safe anymore. I mean, I could get hurt, you know?" I mocked him, testing his limits. He and I both knew that sex with him wasn't such a workout for me. He put me where he wanted me and took it.

"You can run the show," he whispered, and I froze, turning to face him.

I narrowed my eyes in suspicion. "For how long?" He twisted his lips in thought, and I fought the rising chuckle. "Don't hurt yourself."

"Ten minutes," he offered.

I chuckled, "thirty."

"Fuck woman, what the Hell are you going to do to me that will take thirty minutes?"

"Should we find out?" I whispered, giggling when he turned for the stairs to our bedroom.

***

Matteo lasted thirty minutes *on the dot* before he hauled me up from between his legs, rolled me underneath him and slid inside me. He fucked me until I came on a scream, only then finally letting himself find his own release.

"I wasn't done," I protested with a pout.

"Woman, thirty minutes was up. You were done."

"What were you, counting the minutes?" I giggled, but the serious look he leveled me with made me roar with outright laughter.

"How the fuck else do you think I managed not to come down your throat?" I bit my lip. I never liked blowjobs, never enjoyed swallowing, but something about Matteo was intoxicating, and I wanted him everywhere I could get him.

His gaze darkened, and he cursed. He rolled off me,

muttering about how I would drain him dry as he went to the bathroom. I got dressed, deciding that while my jaw had been the only thing to really get a workout, I would make those brownies, anyway. By the time I made my way back to the kitchen, a tiny, delicate trinket dish sat on the counter. I bit my lip, resisting the urge to smile. Gilded in gold around the edges, it was hand painted in a marbled pattern of icy blue and sea green.

Slipping my ring off, I dropped it in the bowl before washing my hands and starting to work on my brownies. When Matteo emerged from his office a few minutes later, he whispered in my ear briefly. "Back on your finger as soon as you finish, yeah?"

I nodded with a smile.

It wasn't about the dish.

It was about him listening to me, respecting my wishes on something, even if it might seem small.

First, he let me be in charge for sex, at least for a little while, then the dish.

Matteo was learning to compromise, and I knew our relationship would be all the better for it.

✳✳✳

The funny thing about boundaries is that they constantly fluctuate.

I should have known Matteo would let me leave the house if it suited his needs.

Evidently, informing my parents of our pending nuptials qualified as important enough to venture off the estate. With two bodyguards anyway.

I'd wanted Matteo to stay home. Knowing my parents' hatred for him, it seemed like the most natural solution to delivering what they would never consider to be good news.

So when I knocked on the front door, it was the only sign that my parents might get that something was off. Usually if they were expecting me, they'd leave me to let myself in. And I would.

I'd wanted to take off the engagement ring, give us some time to settle them into Matteo's unexpected presence before they were blindsided with the sight of the massive rock on my finger. Matteo had put his foot down, claiming that the woman who would soon be his wife wouldn't be hiding her engagement ring *ever*.

"Ivory, honey, what are you doing knocking—" My mother broke off, staring wide eyed at Matteo. "Mr. Bellandi."

"Matteo, please." He smiled, and I watched my mom melt in the face of it. When we'd been in high school, my mother had adored Matteo and loved the way he doted on me.

She'd been nearly as crushed as I was when he broke my heart. My father had always disliked him, as most fathers hate their daughters first real boyfriend, and the way things ended set the tone for every other relationship in the future. No one would ever be good enough for me in my father's eyes. Men only used and abused and hurt.

It was why I'd never bothered bringing anyone else home to my parents.

"Of course," my mother smiled. "Would you like to come in?"

"Please." There was no hesitation in his voice, only the slightest edge of victory. He knew as well as I did that, he'd be able to win mom over again. She was the easy one.

"Martim?" Mom hollered, stepping back to let us move into the small home they'd lived in all my life.

"What, woman?" Dad yelled back, and mom rolled her eyes at me.

"Ivory brought a friend!" We moved into the kitchen, following mom to where she was finishing up with dinner. "Can you test the pasta for me, sweetheart?"

I stepped away from Matteo, moving to the stove and scooping out a piece of spaghetti to taste. I felt mom's eyes on my finger nearly immediately and tried to ignore them. She reached over, snatching my hand in hers. "Ivory," she gasped. "You're getting married?" I nodded shyly, preparing for the tirade. Instead, she wrapped her arms around me and clung to me tightly. "Oh, my baby. I'm so happy for you!"

I gave Matteo wide eyes over her shoulder, wondering what the Hell kind of twilight zone I'd landed in. "You are?"

"Oh, sweetie, I know he hurt you. But no one else ever made you happy the way he did, and that's all I want for you. Besides, I'm ready for some grandbabies." She turned her excitement to Matteo. "You will give me grandbabies, right?"

He grinned happily. "As soon as I can manage it, Mrs. Torres."

I choked on my spit, hacking up my lungs like the lady I was. "We haven't talked about kids yet, mom."

"Well, that's all right. You have time before the wedding to work those things out." She waved us off and the other reality sat heavy on my chest.

"Actually, Mrs. Torres, we're getting married July 6th."

"But that's like a month away," she whispered, and my father chose that moment to step into the room. He narrowed his eyes on the ring on the hand my mom still clutched in hers, his face turning red.

"No offense, ma'am, but I've spent too much of my life without Ivory as my wife. I plan to remedy it as soon as possible."

"Like Hell you will," my father growled.

"Martim!" Mom hissed.

"You broke my daughter. I won't let you do it again."

"With all respect, that's not your decision to make," Matteo said calmly, matter-of-factly. He knew as well as I did that my father's approval was not something he would have for years.

"Daddy," I whispered. "I'm not broken. I never was. Broken-hearted, yes, but I wasn't broken."

He hung his head. "I watched you. For years I watched you keep every man at a distance, because of how he hurt you."

I stepped away from my mother, touching my father's shoulder affectionately. "I didn't do that because I was broken," I admitted, saying the words I had never even dared to speak to myself. But they were the truth, regardless. "I knew, even back then, that what I had with Matteo was special. I knew that I'd never find it again, because I was only capable of falling in love like that once. Not looking was just easier than being disappointed constantly."

"He hurt you," Daddy whispered.

I nodded, feeling tears sting my eyes. "He did," I agreed. "But we were just kids, Daddy. If I can forgive him, why shouldn't you give him a chance to show you why I did?"

My father nodded slowly, turning to Matteo and holding out a hand for him to shake with a sigh. "You hurt her again, and I'll have Adam make sure they never find your body."

Matteo nodded solemnly. "I'll die before I let anything hurt her ever again."

They released hands, helping mom carry things to the table while I checked the pasta.

And we settled into our slightly awkward, first-of-many family dinners.

***

There were two more people who needed to know about the wedding, and one of them needed to be the one to approach me.

No matter how things may have turned out, what Sadie had done in calling Matteo to inform him of my date had been a betrayal.

It was one I knew I would forgive her for, but not before she apologized for it at least. My two best friends not knowing that I was getting married, when I'd always seen them every day, was proving to be too much for me. I was an emotional mess, the isolation mixed with the frantic questions from the wedding planner at odd times throughout the day, were going to my head. I needed a brief reminder of someone who had always been a constant in my life.

So naturally, I took to harassing Duke like a maniac. I called him five times a day, even knowing I looked like a crazy person. He'd ignored my calls and texts for long enough, and it was time for both of us to grow up and face the conversation like adults so we could work on mending our friendship.

He'd finally caved, relenting to my emotional plea over the phone for him to come to the estate. I'd completely expected him to refuse to meet me here, but given the security threat from Adrian, Duke seemed more concerned with my safety than with his pride. I figured that had to be a good sign, coming from my hotheaded friend.

Still, when Donatello escorted Duke into the kitchen where I stood wringing my hands in nervousness, the cool expression on his face made me flinch. His normally perfectly styled dirty blond hair was a mess, his smooth face covered in stubble. He shrugged, glancing down at the work clothes he didn't normally wear out of his studio. "I've been working," he explained. "Turns out getting your heart stomped on is good for the muse."

I winced, stepping around the island to stand directly in front of him. "I'm sorry," I said, throat tightening with the threat of tears. "I don't want to hurt you."

He stared down at me, cornflower blue eyes tormented. "Then don't. We can leave town until things die down. Go somewhere Adrian can't touch you." He reached out a hand covered in cuts and scars, calloused and rough, to touch my cheek. I leaned into it briefly, drawing in a deep breath to try to gather my strength to deal with the outcome of my admission.

"We're getting married," I said, steeling my spine.

I watched as his brow furrowed, realizing that given his offer to run away with me, those words had been insensitively vague, but I didn't know what else to say as he stared at me. I stretched up my left hand, taking his hand in mine and squeezing it supportively. I knew the moment he felt the band around my finger, watched as the confusion melted off his face. His eyes landed on the ring, his lip trembling briefly as shock widened his eyes. "You're *marrying him?*"

"In July."

"Ivory." He croaked, leaning down to press his forehead to mine. "How am I supposed to deal with this? I can't watch you marry him, sweetheart. You're making a mistake."

"Then it was my mistake to make," I whispered back,

hating the way his eyes hardened at my words. He pulled his hand back, taking his face from mine and stepping away.

"You don't know what he's capable of. He's—"

"I know everything," I said shortly. I might not have been privy to all the details, but I knew *more* than I ever wanted to know about Matteo's businesses.

"You what? Do you hear yourself? The Ivory I know would never be okay sharing her body with a criminal! He hurts people for a living," Duke rasped, staring at me in a way I'd never felt from him.

Judged.

Less.

Somehow, he'd built up this fantasy in his head where I was perfect.

I wasn't. I was a mess, a shell of a woman too afraid to love, because no one would ever live up to the real deal.

No one would ever be Matteo Bellandi.

"You're one of my best friends, Duke. I don't want to lose you, but I won't let you treat me like there's something wrong with me. I love him. I have always loved him, and you know that. What he does for a living"—I paused, shrugging and flopping my ass onto one stool at the island.—"It's not ideal, but I'm not doing it. My part as his wife is just to love him, and I'd be lying to myself if I said that having his love wasn't enough for me."

"Christ, Ivory. I've *never* been your friend. I've always been waiting for you to come to your senses and *see* me."

I closed my eyes, drawing in a ragged breath. "One day, you will meet someone who makes you feel the way I feel with Matteo, and suddenly you'll understand. Finding *that* is what you should have been doing all these years, not waiting on someone who'd already found her person."

"I'm so sorry I wasted my time then. Hopefully this other

woman is too smart to fall for some guy's bullshit. Are you so naïve to think he loves you? Christ."

"I do," Matteo's voice announced from the hall that led to his office. I looked to him, watching as Duke spun quickly to face the man he'd always treated like an enemy. In high school, I hadn't really understood.

But hindsight was everything. Duke had been jealous, chasing a relationship he'd never have for over a decade.

"If you did, you'd let her go. She's better off without you," Duke accused.

"Hmm," Matteo mused. "And why do you think I spent so many years without her in my life?" Duke's head jolted, like me, he never could have guessed that Matteo might have been anything other than a cheating dog back then. "As much as you might hate me, I understand it. Losing Ivory is like losing the sun. You had a decade to claim her, Duke. A decade with me out of the picture where you could have made Ivory yours. You could have been married, started a family in that time. But you never told her how you feel, and that's because you *knew* she didn't feel the same."

Duke winced but surprised me by nodding solemnly.

"I want you in our lives. I want you to be Uncle Duke to my kids. Please," I begged. "Don't make me choose."

Duke turned, crushing me into his chest and hugging me tightly. Lips touched the hair on my head as I broke down in tears. "I won't make you choose, sweetheart," he whispered. Matteo let him hold me as I cried, but I felt his eyes on us every moment.

Thinking. Calculating.

Protecting me always.

30

IVORY

"I'm all for you working here whenever you want, you know that," Matteo grunted, and I smirked into my laptop, not even bothering to glance up at him. "But for the love of God, could you let me work, woman?"

I broke into giggles, crossing my ankles over the arm of the couch where I'd draped them to give Matteo a perfect view as my sundress rode up my thighs. "I don't know what you're talking about. I'm minding my own business, working myself."

He gave me that panty-melting grin that literally no woman in the world would be immune to. "Is that so?"

"Mhmm," I hummed in response, crossing and recrossing my legs so that my thighs rubbed together in a desperate bid for friction. I didn't know what the Hell was wrong with me, but I'd wanted sex constantly in the few days since we'd told my parents about our engagement. I almost felt bad for Matteo.

"I can't have sex with you again, Angel. You've drained me dry." I pouted at him, finally turning to face him and the unbelievable happiness written plainly on his face.

I smiled back at him. "I can't help that I want you so much. Maybe you should stop working out. Eat more of my brownies," I teased.

"Oh, so you'll stop jumping my bones every ten minutes if I lose my abs. Is that what you're saying?" I chuckled, setting my laptop on the coffee table and prancing over to plop my butt on his desk in front of him.

"Like you wouldn't be upset if I changed my body," I accused.

"Angel, I love you. Your body is a bonus, yes, but I'll love you however you come."

I tried not to melt, because an admission like that for a man like Matteo, who could have anyone, meant so much to me. "Hmm, it's a good thing, really. Marriage is forever."

"It is," Matteo agreed, capturing my lips with a sweet kiss.

The door opened behind us and Donatello cleared his throat. "I'm sorry to interrupt."

"What do you need, Don?" Matteo asked, leveling the man with a stern look. I knew Donatello had never had to knock before I'd come to the estate, and everyone was having some adjustments to the changes in rules regarding privacy. I forgave him for the awkward moments when he forgot, but Matteo was a little less lenient.

"Ms. Hicks is here for Ms. Torres. Should I have the guards let her in?"

I glanced to Matteo, daring him to say no. I knew at the club in his anger he'd told Sadie she wouldn't see me. I'd honestly mostly forgotten about it in all the drama that ensued after that, given her betrayal and the fact that we weren't speaking, anyway. Him refusing to allow me to see Sadie would violate my trust, another heavy-handed attempt to control me, and with the way he looked at me, he knew that. He knew if we would have a real chance at this marriage, then I needed to make my own decisions so long as they didn't endanger me. "Do you want to see her?" Matteo asked me on a whisper.

I nodded to both men, giving Matteo a relieved smile that he'd made the right choice. "I'll let the guards know," Donatello said, bowing out of the room to give us a moment of privacy.

"You and me, Angel. I know Sadie comes along with you, just don't let her talk you out of this." It almost sounded like an insecurity, a question of whether my friend could convince me that the relationship we were building was unstable. There was a time when a stranger could have convinced me it wouldn't last, but that time had gone.

Somewhere along the line, I'd started to believe that Matteo loved me as much as I loved him—needed me to feel whole. Maybe it was in the way he clung to me at night and slept later than he should so he knew I could rest peacefully. Maybe it was the way he had called my Uncle to let him know he'd made things official and invite him to the wedding. Maybe it was the way he'd agreed to bury the hatchet with Duke so he could be a part of our lives, despite Matteo's possessiveness.

Whatever it was, I knew without a doubt that it was *real*.

"Just yell if you need anything," he murmured, leaning into my space again to give me an affectionate kiss.

"Always." I stood from the desk, smoothing his papers for him and retreating from the office. By the time I made it to the kitchen, Sadie sat in one stool waiting and Donatello was nowhere to be seen. She'd taken Smaug from the tank Don had set up for him against the wall where the kitchen connected with the dining room, snuggling him in the way she didn't like me to see. Nobody could resist the tricky little bastard. Even Matteo was growing fond of him, and Don was a goner.

"So, this is the great Bellandi Estate," she sighed, eyes darting around the room as she took in the pristine, gourmet kitchen.

"Did you come to sightsee?" I said, every bit of the bitterness I still felt over her betrayal coming through those words. It was enough to make her wince.

"You know I didn't," she sighed, finally turning to look at me. When our eyes connected, relief seemed to flood through her. "I was half worried I'd come, and you'd be miserable. Heaven knows that he's intense and controlling enough to smother you."

I crossed my arms over my chest to stare her down. "And yet, you called him when I went on a date. Did you call Duke too?"

"Yes," she admitted. "You did that thing where you just bury your head in the sand and keep digging your hole! You needed someone to force you to deal with the problems instead of just pretending they didn't exist."

I sat down on the stool next to her with a sigh. "I needed to do that," I agreed. "But that wasn't your decision to make. I should have been able to come to that on my own."

"I'm sorry," she whispered. "I wanted to tell you a hundred times, but you're never home anymore—"

"Matteo moved me in here the day after the club," I sighed. I didn't want to remember those days and the tumultuous storm of emotions. Having my will stripped away, locked up in a glorified prison, was not a feeling I wanted to relive.

"God, I'm sorry, Ive. I'm sorry it hurt you, but you look good. You look happy. So I don't regret it. The way he looks at you...." she trailed off with a secret little smile. "I hope one day I find someone who looks at me like that."

"Intense? Like he wants to eat you alive? Is that what you mean?" I giggled, and the tension broke as she burst into laughter along with me.

"I guess so, yeah. Things are good?"

I grinned. "Yeah, you could say that. He's...intense. I don't think I've ever met someone as strong-willed as Matteo, like everyone in his vicinity just has to do everything he says. I know he has power, and that's part of it, but there's also just that something about him, you know?"

She laughed. "Yeah, he's dangerous. Not just because of the title, but he just gives it off."

I fiddled with the ring on my finger, turning to face her finally with tears in my eyes. "It's a good thing you finally came to your senses and came to apologize. You were running out of time to pick out a Maid of Honor dress."

"I was, what? What?!" she shrieked, snatching my hand to stare at the ring. "You're getting married?"

"July 6th," I grinned.

"Holy shit!" I could hear Matteo's chuckle drift in from the office.

"Eavesdropping creep!" I hollered at him, and the chuckle transformed into a roar of laughter. "Come on, let's go for a walk outside where the stalker can't listen in."

I took her out the front door, going around the rose garden on the side of the house. I'd never spent much time in it, mostly just run past it in the mornings. I knew I'd need to remedy that, because it was gorgeous. "So, tell me about the sex. I need to live vicariously through you. I'm in a dry spell."

I rolled my eyes, Sadie had always been a little more open to casual sex than I had, but the recent dry spell had lasted six months. Her opportunity for sex hadn't changed. What had changed was her willingness and desire for something more, but she wasn't ready to hear that. "It's pretty much constant. I mean, I always knew we were attracted to each other, obviously. But lately I swear all he has to do is look at me, and I'm dragging him off to bed."

Sadie laughed her ass off. Her voice was teasing when she spoke. "You're sure you aren't pregnant, right?"

I smiled back at her, even though I knew my body froze solid. "Of course not. You know I'm on the pill."

Except I'd been due for my period the day Matteo proposed. I'd spotted a teeny bit a few days after, so hadn't thought anything of it. I'd gotten so wrapped up in the wedding and being happy that I never realized it didn't come.

"You okay?" Sadie asked. I wanted to hide it, wanted to pretend that my world wasn't crashing down around me, but I couldn't. I had to know, and since I couldn't leave the house, she was my only chance.

"No. I don't think so," I whispered.

"Woah, what happened?" Sadie was suddenly in my face, but I forced a smile in case one of Matteo's men were watching us. I didn't doubt it in the slightest.

"I missed my period. I didn't—I didn't even realize."

Sadie stilled next to me, her face breaking out in a grin. "Holy shit!" she whispered. "You're pregnant! I'm going to be an Auntie."

"Would you be quiet? We don't know for sure—"

"Honey, when has your period ever so much as been late?" Her voice turned more somber when she realized I wasn't as excited as her.

"Can you go to the pharmacy? Get me a test? I don't want Matteo to know until I *know.*"

"I'll be right back, okay?" I nodded, and she walked calmly to her car. I knew Sadie enough to know by the tensing of her shoulders she wanted to run. She wanted to fucking sprint, but she wouldn't risk outing the secret before I was ready.

Matteo telling my mother he wanted kids soon was a very different thing than me getting pregnant before we were even married. He would kill me. I couldn't imagine there hadn't been situations in the past where women tried to trap him with a baby. Even in high school, people joked about it.

As soon as she left, I made an excuse to Matteo that she just had to run a quick errand and would be right back. I faked a smile the entire time, leaving him to his work meeting with Lino and Donatello in favor of baking my stresses away.

✳✳✳

Sadie came back, disguising her purchase with a bag full of all my favorite chocolates. "I thought you might need them while we wait," she blurted, and I gave her a grin before breaking out into laughter when her eyes landed on the double chocolate chip cookies waiting on the tray to go into the oven. She brought her purse into the bathroom with her to wash her hands, conveniently slipping back into the kitchen without it.

God, I loved this girl.

"I'm just going to use the bathroom," I said after I put the cookies in the oven. "Make yourself at home."

"Always do," she grinned, catching my hand briefly as I made my way to the door. "No matter what happens, we'll figure it out, okay?" I nodded at her, tears pooling in my eyes.

I already knew what the test would say. All the symptoms, the missed period, every thing was a glaring point of evidence against me.

I couldn't believe I'd missed it.

So when I closed myself in the bathroom, I tore open the test without hesitation. I'd chugged two bottles of water in the brief fifteen minutes it had taken Sadie to run to the pharmacy.

Because I was desperate to know the truth.

Whoever decided that it was a great idea to pee on a stick was an asshole.

Sadie had even been generous enough to buy me an ergonomic one.

Because I was obviously at risk of developing carpal tunnel in the five to ten seconds I had to pee on the damn thing.

I rolled my eyes as I capped it and set it on the counter, proceeding to wash my hands too thoroughly. I counted in my head, an endless cycle of seconds that never seemed to end.

It didn't seem possible that two minutes could be so long.

It brought me back to all those speeches in high school, the torment of required time frames when all you wanted to do was race through the words as quickly as possible and get it over with.

When I finally counted to 120, I did it again. Just to be safe, I mean, who knew how fast I'd counted? Right?

With a few deep breaths, I looked in the mirror, fixating on how pale my face looked compared to the deep wood tones and amber tiles. I hated this bathroom, and if Matteo and I made it work, I decided I'd immediately change it. I spent more time in that bathroom, positioned between the kitchen and Matteo's office, throughout the day than I did in the gorgeous master bathroom upstairs.

Finally deciding I couldn't distract myself anymore, I glanced down at the test on the counter.

Digital, it left absolutely nothing up to interpretation.

Not with the way the word glared up at me in stark, bold letters.

Pregnant.

Even having known what the test would say, I swallowed my sob. I'd never felt so conflicted, never wanted something so badly despite knowing it had the potential to ruin my relationship with Matteo. He was all I'd wanted for so long; it was completely disarming to realize that for the very first time, there was something I wanted more.

This baby. Even knowing it was nothing more than a tiny collection of cells in my womb, even knowing there was likely nothing resembling a baby to it yet, I wanted that baby more than anything.

I loved it in a way I'd never known could be possible.

I made sure the test was clean, carrying it out to Sadie.

"Oh my God," she whispered, her eyes filling with tears of joy. I nodded back at her, feeling beyond happy. "He's an idiot if he isn't over the moon, but I don't think you'll have that problem," she whispered, taking the purse I carried out to her.

"I hope you're right."

"You going to tell him now?" I nodded. "Okay, call me if you need me." She crushed me to her in a tight hug that I felt in my soul. No matter what happened, I'd always have Sadie.

And I hoped Duke.

I'd be okay.

I just hoped I'd still have Matteo.

***

As soon as she left, I took a few deep breaths and started my way down the hallway, pregnancy test still in hand. It was fairly unusual for Matteo to work with the door open, let alone have meetings, but the light streaming through the crack in the door was there, regardless. I realized with a start that I'd been the last one to leave the office, and it must have been me who left it open. I hoped they hadn't heard any snippets of my conversation with Sadie, but my hopes dashed when I heard Matteo's annoyed tone as he snapped at Lino.

"I don't understand what's taking so long!"

"These things take time, Matteo," Donatello soothed him, that fatherly tone to his voice. "We've talked about this. It will happen. You're both young and in your prime. Without the pills, you just have to be patient." I froze in my steps, the first inkling of something being horribly wrong making me listen to know for sure.

"How long has it been since you swapped out her pills for placebos?" Lino whispered to him. "It can take months. Some people are just less fertile than others."

I gasped, covering my mouth quickly as my body started to shake.

It couldn't possibly be what it sounded like.

There was no way Matteo could do something like that to me.

And yet, it made too much sense. I wasn't naïve. I knew that the pill wasn't foolproof, but I'd never so much as had a pregnancy scare before. To get pregnant within weeks of Matteo returning to my life?

"Six weeks," Matteo grunted in response to Lino's question, and it felt like something within me shriveled and died.

Any chance we'd had at having an open and honest marriage, any chance I'd felt I might have had where he respected the boundaries of a normal relationship.

Just gone.

Having heard enough, I shoved open the door and stepped into the office. Three sets of shocked eyes turned my way, Matteo's icy blue ones closing briefly as he clenched his jaw. "Please tell me it's not true," I whispered, watching as his eyes drifted down to the pregnancy test still clutched in my hand.

"Get out," Matteo muttered, and neither Lino nor Donatello put up a fight, taking the opportunity to happily flee what was no doubt about to devolve into something ugly. "Angel," he murmured softly, stepping around his desk and looking like he might touch me. He reached out a hand, slipping the test from me so he could read the damned word that changed our lives.

That he'd changed without my consent.

"Did you change out my birth control pills?" I whispered, and his eyes darted up to look at me finally, so much joy swimming in them as he clutched the test tightly. "Please, Teo. Tell me you didn't do this." My voice broke, devolving into a sob.

He reached for me, cupping my cheek in his strong hand. "I can't," he whispered solemnly despite the happy little smile that continued to tip his lips up. His eyes went to my stomach, and his hand followed. He stroked it over my dress, acting like he could already feel the life growing inside me.

The life he'd put there, without a single thought for what I might want. "How could you do this?"

I stepped back, and he snapped a tight jaw and weary eyes back up to me. "I did what I had to do. I told you, I'm not wasting any more time. We both want a family together."

"We never talked about it!" I hissed. "I never gave you any sign that I'm ready to be a mother! What if I didn't even want the baby?"

"I know you, Ivory. I knew as soon as you were pregnant, there would be nothing anyone could do to keep you from giving that child everything. Please, just try to understand—"

"When did you do it?" I asked, shaking my head and closing my eyes. I couldn't listen to him rant about how he'd known I would want this. I tried to think of what our relationship was like six weeks ago, but all I could think was that it was different. I fought the relationship at every turn.

"The morning after you first spent the night here, I saw your pills when I went to get your phone. That was when I put it in motion, and I replaced them within a few days."

"That was the first time we had sex," I snorted in disbelief. "You fucked me once and thought it entitles you to knocking me up? What is wrong with you?"

I ran my hands over my face, trying not to see the way his face tightened, that familiar possession running over his features as he stared down at me. He stepped into my space, and I winced at the feeling of his chest touching mine. "You have always been mine," he growled. "I wanted you bound to me in every way. I have done nothing but *be* clear that I would not lose you this time. I wanted you to be the mother of my children. I knew that in high school! Now, I'm a thirty-year-old man. I made it fucking happen, because I'll be damned if I waited for you to come to your senses. If I'd left you to come to terms with our relationship on your own and hadn't pushed you every step of the way, we'd have been forty before we got married."

I winced, stepping back out of his space and shaking my head. "You're wrong. If I trusted my instincts, we wouldn't have gotten here at all. And all you've done with this is prove those instincts right! I can't trust you, and I won't marry a man I can't trust, Teo," I whispered, moving to slide the ring off my finger.

"Don't you fucking dare," he hissed, making me stop. I turned on a huff, striding through the house to pack a bag. "Ivory!" he yelled, behind me. I passed Scar in the hallway, and he gave me wide eyes at whatever pissed off expression he saw on my face.

"We're leaving in ten minutes," I told him.

"Uh, is that cleared with the boss?"

"Fuck your boss," I spat. "So help me, Paolo, if you don't take me I will make your life a living Hell." I raced up the steps to the master, ignoring the sound of Matteo thundering after me.

"What the Hell are you doing?" he asked, hauling ass into the bedroom behind me as I hauled out my suitcase.

"I'm leaving. I can't do this with you." I tried to focus on the angry. Tried not to break down into tears as his betrayal felt like it stabbed right over the same scar tissue from the last time he'd ruined everything we had.

Sniffling against the tears making my throat ache, I ignored him in favor of shoving random clothes into my suitcase. "You can't leave," he whispered, the first sign of real regret coloring his tone.

"I can't even look at you right now. What you did, I—I don't know if I can ever get over that."

"You don't want the baby?" he whispered.

I spun around, staring him down fiercely. "Of course, I want the baby! I don't want you!"

He flinched, as if those words hurt him as much as I'd

intended. But they couldn't because he didn't care what I wanted. "You don't mean that," he murmured, stepping into my space slowly, hesitantly.

"You hurt me," I whispered. "You promised you wouldn't hurt me again."

His face crumpled. "I'm sorry, Angel. I'm so sorry I hurt you. I just needed you to be mine completely. I couldn't bear the thought of losing you. Don't go. Just stay, and we can figure it out."

"You have to let me go home. I just want to go home for a while and think things through."

He sighed, nodding reluctantly and pressing his forehead against mine. "Take Scar with you."

"Okay," I whispered, turning and zipping my suitcase hastily.

"Ivory?" he asked when I reached the bedroom door. "I love you, Angel. I love the baby. More than anything else in this world. Take some time, think things through. But you'll come home. I won't accept anything else."

I swallowed, darting out of the room and down the stairs. Somehow, Scar knew I was cleared to leave, and he hustled me to the car where he let me break in silence.

31

IVORY

The sound of my doorbell was jarring against the classical music playing in the background.

I hated it, but Sadie had read it was good for the baby.

I fought down the vomit that threatened at the smell of bacon as I made Scar breakfast. I didn't want him to know that cooking has become a chore. That I couldn't even enjoy that anymore, because the smell of food made my stomach roll. I couldn't have him reporting how ill I'd gotten to Matteo.

Despite hiding it, I knew the moment the doorbell rang, knew my time was ending.

The problem was, I was no closer to deciding what to do with myself. No closer to deciding if I'd ever be able to forgive Matteo for what he'd done. My hand rubbed my stomach out of habit, as if the baby could give me all the answers.

It surprised me he'd given me a few days. I didn't know if that was a sign that he was having second thoughts, or if I should look at it as a gift he gave me out of true remorse.

Scar nodded at me when he looked through the hole in

the door, confirming what I already knew. I nodded back, even though I knew it was pointless. Scar would always do what Matteo told him to, no matter how I might care for the broody man. He'd quickly joined the ranks of people I love, and it hurt to know that when it was all said and done, I'd always be second to Matteo.

It shouldn't have hurt. He'd been Matteo's first.

But everything hurt.

He opened the door, leveling the man behind it with a glare I didn't expect and standing directly in the way so he couldn't enter. "Are you here to fuck it up again?" I startled, removing the bacon to a paper towel lined plate and turning off the stove in disbelief. I'd never heard Scar talk to Matteo with anything but respect.

"If you're stupid enough to stand between me and my woman, then maybe I need to think about cutting you loose. I don't employ stupid people," Matteo warned, and then his footsteps came into the house and the sound of the door closing followed. I didn't turn around, didn't want to look at him.

I wasn't ready. Not for this.

I still didn't know what I was doing.

"How are you feeling?" he asked, and I heard him tap his fingers on the island behind me.

He was too close, only a couple steps away, and even just the vague sense of him being there was enough to weaken my resolve.

I missed him.

So fucking much I wanted to strangle myself. There had to be something wrong with me. "She throws up about a hundred times a day," Scar answered helpfully, and I winced.

I guessed I wasn't as stealthy as I thought I was.

"Shut up and eat your breakfast," I teased, putting a plate in front of his usual seat at the island. He took it, digging into his eggs with vigor.

"Is that true?" Matteo asked, and I finally had no choice but to face him. The dark circles under his eyes came as a surprise, I'd never seen Matteo look anything other than perfect. It shouldn't have surprised me though, they were flawless copies of mine. The return to not sleeping well had not been kind to me.

"They should rename morning sickness something like all day misery," I answered with a little smile. It never stopped, even as early in the pregnancy as I was. I really hoped that wasn't an indicator of a rough pregnancy.

"Have you been to the doctor? Did they say there was anything they can do?" he asked, and his eyes darted down to my stomach where the island hid it.

"My appointment isn't until next week, but it's normal, Teo," I whispered. "Some women don't have morning sickness at all, and others just get hit hard."

"Come home, Angel." He rounded the island until nothing separate us but a few inches of space. "Let me take care of you. Let Don do the cooking. It can't be helping."

I eyed Scar warily, noticing the tension in his body. I knew it would be easier for him if I returned to the estate, knew he wouldn't be so stressed about making sure I was safe.

I wanted to go home, but how could I just forgive something that was so unforgivable?

The way he'd broken my trust, it wasn't something I would have tolerated from anyone else. I didn't have the answer to the question that I had to ask myself. Did I love him enough to forgive it?

The thought of a life without him was terrifying, going

back to being that void of all the feelings only he gave me. "I am home," I said instead, and watched from the corner of my eye as Scar's entire body locked solid.

"Your home is with me," Matteo scolded, stepping into my space until he wrapped his arms around me.

"I'm not ready for that. I'm not ready to forgive you."

"So come home and let me prove to you I'll take care of both of you! Christ, Ivory. I just want to give you the world." He whispered the words, and Scar took that as his sign to abandon his plate in favor of doing a perimeter check.

"I don't want you to take care of me! I never wanted that."

"Then what do you want, Angel? Tell me, and I'll give it to you. I swear!" I almost melted at the desperation in his voice, almost caved into the way he curled into me like the possibility of losing me brought him to his knees.

"I've never chosen you," I whispered, finally feeling like I had the words to explain the conundrum that tore me in two. "Every decision, every step to be together or not be together, you've made it. You decided we were going on a date in high school, and that was that. Then you dumped me, and I had no say in that either. When you claimed me again, you didn't care that I told you I hated you. You didn't give a shit that I was terrified of you and wanted to run for the hills. You pushed and pushed and moved me into your house against my will. And I forgave it," I whispered. "I tolerated it. But now, you took away my right to choose this baby. I'll never have that moment where the man I love tells me he wants to have a baby. I'll never get to make love to you and hope that *that* was the moment we made a child together. So now what do I have? I'm just a woman living a life that she didn't *choose,* Matteo! I want to choose you. That's what I want."

He pressed his forehead to mine gently, his face

scrunching up in pain. "So I can't pick you up and drag you home?" I chuckled at his attempt at what I assumed was a joke, but I never could tell with Matteo.

"No," I sighed back, letting him press his lips to mine softly. I resisted the urge to lean into him. It conflicted me enough for both of us, the last thing he needed was me showing him just how desperate I was for him.

He nodded, letting his hands touch my belly. "I'll be back to check on you in a couple of days. Call me if you need me for anything." Then with a deep sigh, he turned and strode out of my house. Scar replaced him within minutes.

He went back to eating his eggs even though they were cold. "You okay?" he asked.

"You want fresh eggs?" I asked him, ignoring the million-dollar question that I felt a little closer to answering.

"Nah. These are fine." I shook my head and turned to scrub my pans.

※※※

That cleaning continued. I'd made the switch to all-natural cleaners we picked up at the store when we'd fled Matteo's house. Just enough supplies for us to survive.

And for me to clean relentlessly, if we were being honest. I didn't have enough cookware to go crazy, had no baking dishes to speak of. If I'd thought Matteo wouldn't have had a coronary at the prospect of me bringing more belongings to the home, he didn't want me in, I might have asked for some. But that was not a battle I thought worth fighting.

My thoughts plagued me as I scrubbed, wondering if I would *ever* really have a choice where Matteo was concerned. Obviously, the choice with the baby was gone. It was coming whether I was ready for it or not.

But if I decided that I didn't want to marry Matteo? Didn't want to raise our child together?

I knew he'd take away my choice again. He made it very clear that he would do whatever it took to have me as *his* in every sense of the word.

Did it really count as having a choice, if I'd lose the opportunity to choose if I made the wrong decision?

I didn't think so, and that thought plagued me.

Could I raise a child with a mobster? Could I bring up a child in a world as dangerous as the one Matteo inhabited, where I couldn't leave the estate without a bodyguard for safety?

It seemed impossible. It wasn't the life I wanted for my baby, and as much as I might love Matteo, my child's life had to be the most important consideration.

But the only way for the baby to be safe from Matteo's enemies would be to leave Chicago, sever all ties with Matteo permanently. No one could ever know he had a child.

And that made my heart hurt.

Car doors slamming outside made Scar's head snap to attention, and he instantly went alert. "Call Matteo," he ordered as more cars slammed. I grabbed my cell, dialing Matteo quickly as Scar pulled his gun from his holster. My fingers shook, but I dialed him as quickly as possible. "Get down, Ivory." Scar whispered, going to the window to peek outside.

"Angel?" Matteo said over the line.

"Matteo, there are people here—" I started, but Scar snatched the phone.

"Adrian and about a dozen men are outside. Ivory is going out the back," he snapped, handing the phone back to me. "Go, Ivory. Keep your head down but fucking run."

Matteo's voice shouted in the phone, but I stared up at Scar in horror.

"I won't leave you!" I protested.

"Yes, you will," he announced, touching a hand to my stomach delicately. "Go, Ivory," he whispered, shoving me toward the back hall that led to the back of my house. I scurried, keeping my head down so no one would see me through the windows. The phone in my hand echoed with the furious sound of Matteo's voice calling for me, and I brought it up to my ear.

"Teo," I whispered as the first tear fell in my terror.

"Fuck, *Cara mia*. We're on our way. Just get out of there."

"I love you. I'm sorry. I'm so sorry," I whispered as I hit the back door.

"Don't you dare. I love you, Angel. I'm coming for you, and I'm never letting you out of my sight again, you understand me?" The door crashed open, the sound of it carrying through the house. I was out the back door when the sound of yelling carried through it, followed by gunshots. "Fuck! Ivory!" Matteo shouted, but I didn't answer.

With tears streaming down my face, I got to my feet and ran through the yard. "I've got her!" a male voice shouted, and I sobbed.

Weight hit my side, and I went flying and landed sprawled out on my back with my hands curled around my stomach protectively. "Matteo!" I cried, reaching for the phone I dropped.

A male hand reached down, plucking it off the ground and I followed it up to stare into Adrian's crazed, dark eyes. "Goodbye, Matteo." He grinned, dropping the phone to the ground and stomping on it until it crunched, and the call disconnected. I gaped up at him in horror. "Hello, beautiful.

Fancy seeing you here." I started to stand, getting to my knees warily and eyeing him.

"Adrian, what are you doing?" I asked, and then he was wrapping a hand around my upper arm and dragging me through the yard. "Help!" I screamed. "Somebody!"

He made no move to stop me. Didn't seem to care that someone would have heard the commotion. He hurried me through the house, because there was one person, I knew he wouldn't want to face.

Matteo.

God, what if I never saw him again?

Bodies scattered my living room, and the sight of Scar lying motionless among them was enough to make me collapse despite his grip on me. I barely touched my fingers to his face, shaking at the sight of all the blood covering his chest. "Scar?" I asked, hoping like Hell he'd wake up and just look at me. "No. No, please," I begged, fighting off Adrian's arms as they wrapped around my waist. "No! Let go of me!" I shouted, twisting to claw at his face. When a nail broke the skin of his cheek, those eyes darkened, and I froze in horror. I didn't even see the fist he aimed for my temple.

All I knew was the sudden explosion of pain.

And then black.

32

MATTEO

My blood roared in my ears, drowning out the sounds of Lino shouting at me from the driver's seat as he navigated through traffic. My men's SUV's surrounded us, racing for the only thing that mattered in my life.

My angel and my unborn child.

In the hands of that mother-fucking sadistic piece of shit.

I should have never allowed her to leave the estate. I should have never *touched* her.

"Matteo!" Lino shouted, finally drawing my attention away from the dead silence coming through my phone. "Talk to me, man. What's going on?"

"He has her," I answered, feeling a deadly, killing calm settle over me. I knew it wouldn't last, knew that as soon as I saw for myself that Ivory was gone from her house the rage would return.

But until that moment I embraced the monster. Let it take over me as I coordinated with my men.

The second we pulled up in front of Ivory's house, the

house I'd left only an hour before, I was out of the car before it even stopped. "Matteo!" Lino shouted, throwing the car into park and following me. I didn't know what he was so worried about, it was obvious that Adrian and his men were gone. Not a single vehicle remained, just random bodies left to rot on Ivory's floor as I threw myself in the open front door.

In the middle of the chaos, Scar laid there—entirely too still. Lino went to him, checking for vitals, but a few of the men went to check the rest of the house. "Ivory!" I yelled, racing for the backyard, unsure if it should relieve me that I didn't find Ivory laying there.

She was alive but being with Adrian was far from a blessing. As soon as he put his hands on her, she'd wish she was dead.

He would hurt her. He would *break* her.

I couldn't let it happen.

Lino stepped out into the yard, looking around in dismay. "We'll find her," he said.

"She has a tracker," I reminded him, never more grateful that I'd disrespected Ivory's wishes than in that moment. "Get the guys ready."

"Scar's alive," he said, making my head jolt in shock. "Riddled with bullets, but somehow the stubborn fuck is still alive. Bruno and Marino took him to Doc."

"Good," I nodded, pulling out my phone and opening the app that would show me Ivory's location. They were still moving, but it would take me time to assemble enough of a team to stage an invasion wherever they landed. "I want every man we have."

"You've got it. I'll call Don, get him on it too." I gave a last nod, calling the one other man I wanted at my side. The one man I could trust to make sure Adrian suffered a very slow, painful death while I tended to my angel.

As much as I wanted to deliver his punishment personally, I knew Ryker would be a far worse punishment than I could ever dream to be.

And that would have to be enough.

"Yeah?" he asked when he answered the phone. Simon stood at the front door and nodded to me as I made my way back to the car, hopping in the driver's seat to be ready to go with me wherever I went.

"Adrian Ricci took Ivory. I need you to give him the worst death imaginable," I hissed into the phone as I made my way back inside her mostly empty house.

"When and where?"

"Get your ass to her house," I said, rattling off her address. "We're mobilizing now." I kicked one of his men's bodies for good measure, wanting to make even their corpses suffer for the part they played in taking Ivory from me. The number of them was a sign of just how hard Scar had fought to protect her, taking out half a dozen men on his own before they took him down.

"On my way."

33

IVORY

I woke up.
        Slowly.
Disoriented.

The pillow beneath my face wasn't mine. It didn't smell like Matteo, and the fabric of the pillowcase was far too luxurious to be the cheap set I'd picked up at the store with Scar. My face throbbed as I moved, and my head swam the moment I peeled myself off the pillow.

Deep wood-paneled walls stared back at me from the edges of the room, a navy comforter draped over me. I touched the side of my head, wincing at the pain radiating from there and the dried blood that seemed so coarse against my fingers.

I ignored my swimming head, shoving the comforter off me and got to my feet slowly. I swallowed my nausea as my stomach rolled once I was standing, determined not to vomit until I figured out where I was.

The first door I came to was a bathroom, and I stared into the mirror at the huge, mottled bruise at my temple that covered my brow bone and the top of my cheekbone.

The blood seemed to be from a minor cut, and I ignored it in favor of finding my way out of the bedroom.

Seeing the bruise, I knew without a doubt Adrian must have knocked me out. Everything came back to me in a rush of panic.

Scar was dead.

I swallowed back my tears, knowing I needed to find a way out of that sadistic fuck's home. That was what Scar would want. I could mourn him once I was safe, could tell him how sorry I was that my stupid decisions had gotten him killed.

I liked to think he would forgive me.

But I didn't think I'd ever forgive myself.

The door opened quietly, and I slipped out into the hall. For once, I was pleased my feet were bare. It let me slip through the house silently. The hall was an endless parade of closed doors, and I found my way to the staircase easily. I sprinted down it, the front door in sight.

I did not understand what might wait for me outside. I couldn't imagine Adrian would lock me somewhere and leave me unguarded.

All I knew was that I had to try.

My hand was only an inch from the front door when Adrian's voice made my skin crawl. "Going somewhere, my love?" he asked, and I froze in place. I spun to face him, noting that he looked more manic, more crazed than normal. His normally slicked black hair was a mess, sticking up at all angles like he couldn't keep from taking his frustrations out on it. "Ah, sweetheart. Your beautiful face," he whispered, stepping toward me with an expression of concern. Like he hadn't been the one to hurt me. "I wish I hadn't needed to hurt you. I never want to hurt you, Ivory."

"Matteo told me you like to hurt women." I stepped away, retreating until my back hit the door, and I was trapped.

Reaching out a hand to run his fingers over the bruise, his brow furrowed when I whimpered at the pain it sent shooting through my skull. "Whores. I like to hurt whores. You are not a whore, my little doll. You are pure. Innocent in a world of filth."

"I'm not innocent," I argued, shrinking further into the door. "I'm not some virgin—"

"You are loyal. Loving. Warm. All the things that made Bellandi choose you as his wife, yes?"

"Matteo chose to marry me because he loves me," I argued, probably stupidly. I shouldn't argue against the points the man gave for not wanting to hurt me, but I also figured he wouldn't risk Matteo's wrath over someone he thought of as a common whore. My eyes darted around the entryway of the house, taking in the oversized windows that reflected the woods surrounding the house.

Nothing but woods.

Where the fuck was I?

"And there is a reason he fell in love with you, out of all the women who throw themselves at his feet. Something about you, little doll, that just draws men like us in like moths to a flame." Those dark eyes of his glittered as he stared at me in fixation, an intensity that might have rivaled Matteo's, if not for the unhinged quality that Adrian had.

Where Matteo's fixation always felt like coming home, even in his darkest moments, Adrian's was nothing but haunting. "Matteo will come for me," I whispered.

"He'll have to find you first." He grinned, looking confident in his intention to hide me away. I felt my lips twitch but disguised it with a grimace. I owed Matteo an apology for fighting him so intently on the tracker he'd put beneath my skin.

I felt nothing but gratitude for it in that moment.

"And what is it that you plan to do with me?" I let my lip tremble, because I knew it didn't take long to break someone. And having Adrian's hands on me might be my breaking point.

"I want what he has. I want his businesses, his control of the streets, you as my wife, and to see you swell with our child." He stepped back from me, moving to the couch visible from the door, completely unconcerned that I might try to run out the door. He raised a brow, as if daring me to try it.

I knew I wouldn't get far. Not with how arrogant he was, and I knew in that moment that my best odds laid in waiting for Matteo to come.

And I knew he would.

He would always come for me, that I knew.

"I can't give you Matteo's businesses."

"I think you underestimate what he would do to see you returned to him safely. Once he has signed everything over to me, I'll kill him." He shrugged, as if Matteo's death didn't truly matter.

My lungs seized in my chest. "You can't," I begged finally stepping away from the door and approaching him somewhat. I kept my distance, stayed away from the couch and stood on shaky legs. "I won't survive if you kill him."

"You'll do whatever I tell you to do," he barked as he lit up a cigar and poured himself a scotch. "Because if you do, I'll let you keep your baby." I flinched, staring at him with horror-filled eyes. My hands wrapped around my waist on instinct, protecting the baby from the monster who would threaten something that hadn't even *lived*.

"H—how?" I stuttered. It didn't seem possible. I'd told only Sadie, Duke, and Scar about the baby.

"I bugged your friend Sadie's home." He grinned, pride in every feature of his exotically handsome face. If he hadn't been so deranged, he might have been attractive, but as it was, he just couldn't ever be anything but terrifying. "Imagine my surprise when she went on and on about being a godmother to her best friend's baby."

"You can't—" I started.

"I've no desire to hurt your baby, my doll. It is my insurance to be sure you do as you're told. If you behave, you can keep it, and I'll even claim it as my own. If you don't, well, I could sell it for quite a hefty sum. So many sick people in this world that would love a baby."

I blanched, and I knew my face must have paled when I dropped into the armchair with a gasp. "Please," I whispered.

"As I said, I have no desire to do that. Hopefully, the child will be a girl, and no one need know she's not mine since she won't cause problems with the succession." He stood, smoothing his suit as if he were some classy, elegant businessman and not a monster who trafficked women and children. *People.*

He sold people, and for the first time in my life, a lust for blood pumped in my veins. I wanted him to suffer, wanted to watch him bleed out for the children he hurt. For the threat to *my baby*. I knew Matteo would have plans to handle it and probably be able to ensure he suffered more efficiently.

But it didn't stop me from wanting to be the one to do it when he approached me with an arrogant swagger to his hips. He'd thought he'd trapped me. Cornered me in a way that I could never escape.

He didn't know I was a survivor, and he didn't know I'd promised myself a long time ago that I would *never* be somebody's victim again.

His hand tilted my head up to look me in the eye, his thumb stroking over my injured cheek gently. "Come to bed, my doll," he drawled in a voice that was nothing but a mockery of men who knew how to seduce a woman to their beds.

I stood, trying to rein in my venomous glare when he smirked at me triumphantly. My vision lined with red, the call for his blood something fierce within me.

Call it a mother's need to protect her child. Call it a self-defense mechanism. Whatever came over me in that moment destroyed any perceptions I had of myself as a peaceful person. I never wanted to hurt anyone. Never wanted to resort to violence.

Where had that gotten me?

I opened my mouth to speak, releasing a gasp when gunshots made the windows vibrate. He narrowed his eyes on me, looking at me like I'd betrayed him and given away our location. When the gunfire sounded closer to the front door, he moved. I bolted, going for the stairs and a place to hide safely.

The hand he dug into my hair prevented me from getting far, and I screamed as he used it to force me back to him. An arm wrapped around my throat, until finally he pulled a knife from his pocket and held it to my throat, making me still immediately.

Deep breaths. I centered myself, those breaths becoming everything I would need to keep a clear head in the next moments. Sadie was at the forefront of my mind, and I swore I would never stop going to the gym with her and even stop complaining about it if I walked away alive.

The door burst open, and Adrian spun with me still in his hold, and my head cocked back as far as I could to avoid the piercing of the tip of the blade against my skin. Adrian raised a pistol, aiming it at the door as Matteo stepped inside. His eyes narrowed on the knife against my throat. "Adrian, put down the gun," I said on a wheeze. "You know he'll never let you walk away after this."

Matteo leveled his own gun on Adrian, but I knew from the look in his eye that he would never fire. He'd never risk me like that. "I don't need to walk away to break him," Adrian whispered, and I moved.

I kept my hands close to my body, raising them slowly until I was a breath away from touching his arm. I grabbed his forearm just as he tensed to slit my throat, pulling down and to the left while I cocked my right shoulder. My head slipped under his armpit, and I used his own twisted arm to stab him in the side three times.

Still he fought, and I knew from Sadie's lessons that the adrenaline pumping through him meant he hadn't even *felt* the wounds yet. I focused on that wrist, twisting until he released the knife and turned to thrust it up under his chin.

The gun dropped from his hand instantly, and the gurgling sound he made would haunt me for the rest of my life. But it didn't stop me from speaking to him, the last sound he ever heard my voice. "You shouldn't have threatened my baby." I yanked the knife free, watching as he flopped face first to the floor and the puddle of blood surrounding him grew. His lifeless eyes stared up at me, like a little broken doll. Horror spread through my veins, unable to believe what I'd done.

Unable to believe that I didn't feel one bit of remorse for killing a man.

"Ivory," Matteo whispered, and I looked up at him. Blood

coated my hands and my dress. "You're bleeding." I nodded, glancing down to my left hand where the knife had cut into my palm in the struggle. "Let's get you cleaned up and have that stitched, okay Angel?"

"Take me home," I whispered, feeling everything return as the haze of adrenaline faded. The pain, the horror over what I'd done.

"After we go to Doc," Matteo answered, wrapping an arm around me and guiding me from the house.

I didn't know when I started trembling. All I knew was that it didn't stop for a long, long time.

34

IVORY

The trembling continued, accompanied by silent tears streaking down my cheeks. "Angel," Matteo murmured, wrapping me up in his arms in the back of the car while Simon raced along the streets. Matteo had torn his jacket and held it to the wound in my hand, while I shook in his arms. "You should have just gotten away. If you hadn't been in the shot, I could have killed him."

"Fuck you," I whispered through chattering teeth. "He took me from my home. He threatened to sell our baby. I'm going to be a mother, and I will do whatever it takes to protect this baby," I whispered, glaring at him.

His mouth molded into a smirk at my ire. "You were a badass, Angel."

I groaned. "Don't give me your shit right now. I just stabbed a man."

"Rather fantastically," he laughed. "Never would have thought you had that in you, my angel."

I glared at him mockingly. "Maybe I'll stab you next."

"What? Why?" he chuckled, and Simon made a noise while he tried to suppress his own laugh.

"Because you're pissing me off. Being all snuggly when I'm covered in blood. Fucking psychopath, that's what you are! I bet you're all turned on too, like a creep."

I could only describe the face he made as one of absolute glee as his body shook with his roar of laughter. "You wouldn't be entirely wrong."

"Gross!"

"Ivory?" he asked, and I turned to find him staring down at me. My breath caught from the emotion in those blue eyes as he pressed his forehead to mine. "I fucking love you. Whether you're my angel or a knife-wielding badass."

I rolled my eyes, "I love you too, Teo." His lips claimed mine in a slow caress that couldn't be described as anything other than making love to me with his mouth. I sighed into the contact, realizing just how much I'd missed it during our separation. As soon as the car stopped at the estate, Matteo tugged me out and into the house.

"How is he?" he barked at the two men gathered in the foyer.

"Stable," one said, nodding his head to the living room. I turned, my eyes landing on Scar's prone body laid out on the massage table where the doctor had put in my tracker.

"He's alive?" I whispered, and Matteo nodded, glancing at me uneasily.

"I didn't want to get your hopes up until I knew for sure." I slid out of Matteo's hold, moving to his body and staring down at his bare torso as I counted the bullet holes in his body.

Six.

He'd taken six bullets to protect me.

It was a miracle none of them aimed for his head. "When will he wake up?" I asked, turning wide eyes to the doctor who stood over him and looked exhausted.

"When he's ready," he breathed. His eyes examined me from head to toe. "Any of that blood yours?"

"Yes," I whispered.

"Go shower. Be quick about it. I'll look you over as soon as you're out." Matteo took my uninjured hand and started to guide me away, but I gave him pleading eyes.

"I don't want to leave him."

"We'll hurry back, Angel." Pressing a kiss to Scar's forehead briefly, I let Matteo take me upstairs to shower.

***

My eyes never left Scar's chest, watching the rhythmic rise and fall as the doctor stitched up my hand. "It will scar," he warned, and I shrugged. It wasn't the first time I'd cut my hand with a knife, and it wouldn't be the last. If I walked away from being taken by a crazed human trafficker who wanted me to be his wife with nothing but a scar, then I'd consider myself lucky. "Let me have a look at that head."

"It's nothing," I sighed.

"Doesn't look like nothing." I relented, turning in my seat so the doctor could poke and prod the wound. "Any loss of consciousness?"

"Yes. I don't know how long I was out, but I woke up in Adrian's bed." The room filled with Matteo's fury almost instantly, even from where he stood coordinating with his men regarding the cleanup at my house and Adrian's.

"Do we need to do an exam?" the doctor asked carefully.

"No." I shook my head. "He didn't touch me like that."

"You're certain? Maybe when you were unconscious?" I stilled, not having thought of the possibility.

"I don't—wouldn't I feel it? If he raped me?"

The doctor nodded. "Most likely, but there are no guarantees with these things. I'd like to do an exam—"

Matteo's bellow echoed through the room, and then he was punching numbers into his phone. "Ask the fucker if anybody touched Ivory while she was unconscious." He put the phone on speaker, and another man's screams of agony filled the room.

"Who is that?" I asked.

Matteo replied briskly. "Adrian's second in command. We took him alive."

Another man's cold, deadly quiet voice came over the phone as the screams died down. "Did anybody touch her? Was she raped or touched in any way when she was unconscious?" he asked, presumably to the man he tortured. I paled, and the doctor patted the back of my head to get my attention. Shining a light in my eyes, he sought to distract me while he checked for a concussion.

"No! We dropped her in the bedroom and left her to sleep it off! I swear! Normally, I'd have thought for sure Adrian would rape her, but he was different about this chick. Obsessed, man."

"You believe him?" Matteo asked the phone.

"Yeah, I do. He's singing like a canary, and so far everything checks out." I sighed in relief, and the doctor sat down next to me, patting my hand.

"You've got a nasty concussion, not surprising. I want you to take it easy for a few days, no cooking, nothing that strains your concentration like reading or long hours of television. Tylenol for the pain."

"Okay," I whispered.

As soon as he stepped away to deal with some other minor injuries, I turned back to Scar. Gripping his hand in mine, I finally allowed myself to break.

Everything hit me. My resounding relief over not being raped. My hope that Scar would wake up soon. The terror I'd felt when I first heard those gunshots. "Why isn't he in the hospital? Shouldn't he have a breathing tube or something?" I whispered when Matteo wrapped his arms around me. Tears fell steadily as I sobbed, leaning over Scar.

"Draws too much attention. Besides, it's not the first time he's been shot, Angel. He'll pull through just fine. Doc didn't even have to put him under."

He quieted, continuing to hold me through my breakdown.

Just held me.

Like he didn't have a million other things he needed to be doing, his hands slid under my shirt and caressed my stomach with nothing but relief in his touch.

We sat there for hours, despite Matteo trying to draw me away to bed. "I can't leave him. Not again," I said every time.

After the room emptied, everyone else finding their way to their beds, that was the moment when Scar's groan echoed in the silence. "Scar?" I whispered, hoping to God he'd open his eyes.

"Hey, man," Matteo smiled into my neck.

"Ivory," Scar groaned, jolting where he laid like he might sit up.

I touched his shoulder, applying just enough pressure to keep him lying down. "I'm here," I whispered. "I'm fine. Thanks to you." The sniffle I made sounded particularly pathetic in the quiet room.

"I'm going to go grab some guys to help him into a guest room, Angel," Matteo murmured, ducking out and leaving me to stare at Scar.

"Don't cry," Scar mumbled. "Hate it when you cry."

"I thought you were dead. Adrian dragged me through

the house, and you were just there. And there was so much blood."

"He got to you?" Scar's voice went taut.

"I'm fine, Matteo came quickly because of the tracker." I nodded, watching as his eyes went to the bruise on my face.

"Not quick enough. He make him suffer?"

"Ivory killed him," Matteo said, pride infused into his voice. "Bloodthirsty thing." I chuckled, completely appreciating the fact that Matteo seemed determined to turn my killer status into a joke. It somehow made it feel less real. Less like I'd stabbed a man four times like a vicious monster. "Come on. Let's get you to bed so the guys can help Scar to his bed. He needs to sleep."

I nodded, pressing a kiss to Scar's cheek as Matteo guided me away. "You're lucky I trust him. Otherwise I'd kill him for the way you're fawning over him," Matteo grunted, and I laughed all the way to bed where Matteo rolled me underneath him and held me for the whole two seconds it took for me to pass the fuck out.

EPILOGUE
IVORY

Not being able to drink at your own wedding was shit.

Like seriously.

I guess I should have just been glad that I wasn't sporting a huge baby bump, still in my first trimester. Matteo had been kind about it, agreeing not to drink with me.

Damn right I'd taken his offer. If momma couldn't get drunk then neither could he.

I smiled at the thought, staring up at my husband as he twirled me around on the rented stage on the estate property, the rose garden to our backs.

There had never been a discussion about where we would get married, we never even talked about whether the wedding was still on after everything that happened with Adrian Ricci.

I never once considered leaving Matteo. After all, I was a killer now too, regardless of the circumstances. I could have let Matteo kill him for me, I'd known that even at the moment. But something dark within me knew that I needed to do it myself.

Matteo had never once looked at me as anything but his equal since that day, and even though I often suffered from horrifying nightmares, I wouldn't have changed a thing.

Lino twirled Samara around the dance floor beside us, laughing despite the shadows under Samara's blue-grey eyes. I knew that her ex-husband was giving her trouble with the divorce, but Lino refused to talk about it much.

To be honest, I got the impression Samara didn't tell him much. He'd never done well with hearing the specifics of her relationships. I suspected he kept her as solely a friend for similar reasons to why Matteo had pushed me away.

That would change once the divorce was final. With every day that passed, something more and more possessive thrummed beneath Lino's skin. Like a beast hovering below the surface, just waiting for the right time to strike and claim Samara once and for all.

I couldn't wait. They'd always been perfect for each other, for as long as I'd known them both.

"How long do you think it will take Samara to realize what's going on?" I asked Matteo, making him vibrate with laughter.

"I think," he whispered, "that if she dances with one more man who isn't him tonight, he just might make sure she knows who owns her before the night is over."

Sadie caught my eye and grinned, tormenting Duke by making him dance with her. "I agree," she chuckled with emphasis. "If you don't want them to dirty up all your surfaces, you might need to get your shank hand ready."

"Sadie!" I hissed, throwing my head back on a laugh. Dad's eyes found mine, shining as he watched me. I looked away as my own tears threatened. He'd already turned me into a blubbering mess during our father daughter dance. There was no way I could let him do it again. Even Uncle Adam had given Matteo a pat on the back, the two of them reaching an easy friendship despite the differences in the way they approached the law. With me knowing the truth, Adam was the first to relent that I was a big girl, and only I could decide about what crossed boundaries for me. Sadie twirled Duke away, drawing eyes from our other guests. I didn't have the heart to tease Duke that he should be leading.

It would take a very strong man to lead Sadie anywhere.

I loved the girl to death, but she was terrifying.

And stubborn.

And both things had saved my life, all the relentless lessons she'd given me for self-defense, drilling me with the most dramatic and outlandish scenarios she could come up with. Without her, I could easily have died.

Without her, I wouldn't have a husband and a baby on the way.

We owed her everything.

"Has it been everything you wanted?" Matteo whispered, smiling down at me. The stars twinkled in the night sky, the lights hanging from the house and worked into the rose garden echoing the romantic feel.

"All that matters is you're my husband. But yes. You've given me everything I could ever dream of having."

"Well then, my wife," Matteo growled. "I think it's time that we went to bed." He swept me up into his arms as I giggled, hiding my face as our guests stared at us.

"Oh God," I cried, kicking my legs. He didn't care. Matteo's feet carried us to the house and inside, ignoring the hooting and cheering behind us.

"Go get him, girl!" Samara shouted, shrieking when Lino moved to grab her.

The house was empty, except for a few guests waiting in line to use the bathroom. "There's no one to save you now," he teased, taking the steps slowly.

"Who said I wanted saving?" I whispered, pressing my face into his neck and breathing him in.

If there was any one thing that comforted me above all else, it was the way Matteo smelled.

Like him. Like his soap.

Like me.

I'd never considered myself possessive aside from Matteo, but if he ever smelled like another woman or touched another woman, I just might need my shank hand.

He set me down in our bedroom, turning me to face away from him. Matteo's hands drew down the zipper at the back of my dress, oh so slowly.

Teasing me.

My own fingers released the clip that kept my hair pulled to one side, reveling in the way Matteo's lips skimmed the back of my neck. The A-line dress pooled at my feet in a puddle of white. I turned, facing Matteo so he could get the full experience of my lingerie. He'd been nothing but gentle since my concussion, making love to me every chance he got but never giving me the rougher parts of him I loved.

I wanted to test his control, feel it snap. The strapless corset hugged my growing breasts perfectly, and I backed onto the bed with a little smirk on my face. Rubbing my thighs together, I watched Matteo loosen his tie and strip off the jacket of his tux. His smirk matched mine. I should know, since I'd learned it from him.

Watching him strip off his tux was a thing of beauty,

revealing sculpted inch after sculpted inch until he wore nothing, and I had to fight the urge to pounce on him.

My pregnancy was a gift and a curse to Matteo, giving me a sex drive impossible to keep up with.

He gave it a good run for his money, but I worried that I'd distract him from his work. He climbed into the bed with me, sliding into the cradle of my thighs and taking my mouth in a passionate kiss. Those kisses melted any resolve I could have ever put up, any wall I could have ever built between us.

Those kisses were love.

Pure, untainted love.

No secrets, nothing standing in our way.

"I don't deserve you," he murmured, trailing lips down over my collarbone. "But I will spend the rest of my life proving that you're mine, anyway."

A smile graced my face, watching as his fingers worked the little closures at the front of my corset. "You don't have to prove anything, Teo," I whispered. "Because I choose you. Always." His eyes flashed to mine, relief and longing mixed in those pools of blue. I hadn't realized how much he needed those words. How much I'd hurt him by saying I needed to choose him, as if it wasn't a foregone conclusion.

To Matteo, it had been a condemnation, a denial of the love that vibrated between us like an electric current.

But I'd have loved him for the rest of my life, even if I couldn't be with him.

Always.

He was inside me, part of me in every moment.

And I knew that nothing would keep him from me. Not even a rival gang member. He tore the corset away, yanking the panties away until they tore beneath the force of his desperation as that control snapped.

I reached a hand between us, guiding him inside me so we moved in tandem. He surged inside, filling me to the brim and filling my ears with the sound of his pleasured groan. I wrapped my arms around his shoulders and drew him down to kiss me, lifting my hips to accept his thrusts. "I love you," I whispered against his lips, staring into his eyes like I might connect with the deepest parts of his soul.

"I love you too, Angel." One of his hands came up, cupping my nape as we shared the air between us, and his other palmed my ass in his hand. His chest touched mine, brushing against my breasts and stimulating the oversensitive flesh.

There was nothing but us, nothing but his skin on mine and the place where we connected. His lips touched mine, tongues tangling in an intimate embrace that sent me spiraling over the edge until I dragged Matteo with me. Heat filled me as he came, and it was in the moments after sex that I whispered the name of our child.

"Luna if it's a girl."

"Luca for a boy," he murmured, pressing his forehead to mine as we laughed.

"How did I get so lucky?" I teased him, thinking he'd scoff at me like he always did.

"Love finds a way," he whispered back, shocking me with the easy smile that took over his face.

That it did.

***

Thank you for reading Bloodied Hands! I hope you enjoyed Matteo and Ivory's story. Please consider taking the time to drop me a review. Hearing from my readers means the world to me.

ALSO BY ADELAIDE FORREST

Bellandi World Syndicate Universe
Bellandi Crime Syndicate Series
Bloodied Hands
Forgivable Sins
Grieved Loss
Shielded Wrongs
Scarred Regrets

Beauty in Lies Series
Until Tomorrow Comes
Until Forever Ends
Until Retribution Burns
Until Death Do Us Part

Other Dark Romance
An Initiation of Thorns - Cowritten with Tove Madigan
Pawn of Lies

Romantic Suspense Novellas
The Men of Mount Awe Series
Deliver Me from Evil

Kings of Conquest - Cowritten with Lyric Cox
Claiming His Princess
Stealing His Princess

Printed in Great Britain
by Amazon